+++WASYL NIMENKO

Wasyl Nimenko's father was from Dnipropetrovsk in eastern Ukraine and his mother was from Tubbercurry in the west of Ireland. Although he spent extensive periods of time in the west of Ireland he was educated in Suffolk at a school run by De La Salle Christian Brothers. He worked as a labourer, kitchen porter, doorman, store man, van driver, waiter, barman, tent erector and as a freezer man in a factory before studying medicine in London. He studied psychiatry at Oxford and in London but switched to train as a psychotherapist and general practitioner. He worked extensively with the Armed Forces and the homeless and was one of the first medical doctors and psychotherapists in the UK to work with survivors of torture as well as with the NYPD in New York after 9/11. He has written about Carl Jung and the East and researched the use of archaeology in the psychological decompression of wounded soldiers. Wasyl has lived in India, New Zealand and Australia but now lives in Gloucestershire in England.

Wasyl Nimenko 14.3 2013

+++WASYL NIMENKO

INVISIBLE BULLETS

INVISIBLE BULLETS

ISBN 978-1-908-142-10-8

Published in Great Britain 2013

To
All Protectors of the Defenceless

What's not resolved will be repeated

That's why invisible bullets go the deepest.

+++CHAPTER 1.

"Too cold."

"What?"

"The beans."

"The beans?"

"Can't eat them. They're not heated up. I don't mean to be so fussy. It's just that I love beans."

"Sorry Robby. I'll heat some up. Here's another tea." Tatyana filled a mug with tea and placed it on the counter. The counter was a yellow gloss painted four foot high table topped gate which separated the kitchen from the café. She looked up at him and waited for him to take the mug.

"Take a seat. I'll give you your breakfast in just a minute." She smiled at him.

"Ok," said Robby, nodding his head as he took the mug of tea back to the empty table.

Robby sat down with the tea. It was the greeting that had thrown her. Usually he was quiet or just said 'Hi.' Today he had actually said, "Hey Tatyana!"

Tatyana switched on the gas ring to heat the beans and smiled again. This was the kind of incident which reminded her that the job at Vinny's made her happy. The few words Robby just said made her smile. It also reminded her that she didn't actually like the cooking part of the work, because she knew she was a lousy cook. What she also didn't like was being on her own from seven until nine in the morning when the rest of the centre opened. Sometimes like today, when there had been a problem at the local prison the night before, Robby made her feel more secure. A prisoner was still at large after escaping by hiding above the axle of a delivery lorry.

As Tatyana warmed up the beans she smiled to herself. She welcomed the beans being sent back by Robby because she thought how in a commercial café, sending back food would probably have provoked a grumpy reaction from the proprietor of the café, but Vinny's was different.

In the kitchen, as she used a ladle to pour the hot beans on to Robby's breakfast plate, she pretended to cough and put her hand to her mouth so that she could turn her head around to look at Robby. This let her glimpse him sitting at his table looking out of the window down on to the high street. On the table there was a small pocket umbrella which she noticed Robby always had with him.

To Tatyana the baked beans incident was the first time Robby had shown her he still had dignity; that he had choices and standards. She wondered if he had been organising his thoughts to work his way out of being homeless. This made her feel uncomfortable about herself because she could see she would be stuck with herself in the early mornings. A sense of wanting to move on and go with him began with butterflies in her stomach. A flutter of her heartbeat briefly excited her but it was soon extinguished by thoughts of her responsibility to Vinny's and to her father.

As she looked at Robby's lean and large frame she thought he had probably lost weight and been a larger and a much more powerful man. She guessed that he was about six foot two or three and she thought he looked around twenty five. She liked his soft brown eyes and his thick black hair which now grew over his collar. Tatyana thought he was the smartest of the visitors to Vinny's in his clean black jeans and walking boots. She had always had an interest trying to place a person's accent with where they were from but she had been unable to place his as he said so little and she hadn't asked him. She just let him be. She often wondered if he might be from somewhere in the West Country like Bristol or Gloucester. Tatyana particularly noticed that he was very private and avoided other people because as soon as they started to arrive, he would leave.

Robby was the earliest as well as the quietest of the daily visitors to Vinny's throughout the late summer and early autumn. He was also a bit jumpy and Tatyana saw that people were instinctively a little worried by this, so they left him alone. She felt slightly worried that there was little she knew about this man. She had heard talk from other visitors that he was ex-forces but no one was sure. Whatever his story was, he was taking care not to give it away.

It was obvious that he didn't really speak much to anyone, so coming out and saying to her that the beans were cold was definitely a sign that things were different.

"Ok Robby. Hot beans," Tatyana said slightly loudly, as she could see he was just like her father, locked in a thousand yard stare out the window and not aware of her. Tatyana knew he was far away in an inner world.

"Beans," she said louder and she shook her head to get her long dark hair out of her eyes. She waved her hand in big circles right in front of his line of vision and put her other hand on his shoulder to shrug him out of his stare. "It's alright," she said after seeing that Robby was startled by her voice.

"Happiness and memories," Robby said as he turned up to look at her but he fell silent. After the silence he looked up at her again, his soft brown eyes staring right into her green eyes which looked straight back at him. "I think you know." This surprised her because he had said it emphatically.

"Yes," she said nodding her head and sweeping her very dark hair over her shoulder. "I know how old memories can take over the present," she answered honestly.

"Who is it?" asked Robby as he looked straight at her and handed Tatyana the empty plate together with money for the breakfast.

"My father." Tatyana said. She was relieved to tell Robby because she felt she could trust him.

"I see," Robby said, nodding his head.

"I've got nothing more to lose by telling you. He won't talk about the war, or can't talk about the war. So I don't know anything about what he did. He was an orphan whose parents were killed by the Communists before the Second World War. So I don't know if I've got any relatives in the Ukraine who survived."

"War's not something you want to talk about. You only want to forget it."

"Sometimes he just stares into space. Other times he's anxious. I don't understand. I just can't get through to him. I've thought maybe there's something wrong with me and I need therapy."

"Now that would be crazy?"

"How do you mean?"

"When a room's filling up with a hundred gallons of water a second, it's not the best time to start asking personal questions about your family history. You've just got to find a door or window and get out. You just need to be practical."

"You're right. I need to find out."

"My aunt used to say that the only thing in the way of happiness is the mind. She was right."

"What do you mean?"

"All I want is to find happiness inside myself. I want to get rid of the stuff in my head about Afghanistan." He looked away out of the window.

"You've been in a war. How does someone like me do that with my Father?"

"You can't make him talk... but there are other ways of finding things out about someone who's been in a war. Sometimes there are things you have to know... people... so you go and find them. Maybe you need to go to the Ukraine to look for relatives and maybe speak to people who were with your father during the war. If he's alive some of them will be too. We've both got wounds. Mine are a bit confusing... but information heals wounds like yours."

"I've been here for two years since I left Bristol. I'm twenty four and I've never thought of going to the Ukraine. Dad still speaks to an old friend in Scotland. Maybe you're right. What's going to heal your wound?"

"I'm working on it." Robby looked down at the floor.

"It looks like I need to find out what's going on in my father's head to get free and you need to find help to sort out the memories in your head to get free," Tatyana said as she walked back into the kitchen.

"You're probably right about us both."

Tatyana looked up from stirring some onions in a pan and was surprised by a man whom she had never seen before who came through the open door. She saw that the man was about the same size as Robby and that he didn't notice Robby as he came up to the counter. He pulled the counter top up, opened the gate and quickly walked straight through.

"Oh no!" Robby shouted as the man walked straight up to Tatyana. The man picked up one of Tatyana's carving knives and started to raise it, grabbing Tatyana's black t-shirt over her left shoulder. He had dyed short cropped blonde hair and his dark brown glaring eyes looked straight at her as if he was on drugs.

"Give me your money or I'll kill you. Where is it?" He waited for her to respond but Tatyana could only take a big breath, filling her lungs with air.

Tatyana noticed Robby behind the intruder and saw his hand around the intruder's hand with the knife as the man's feet left the ground. She heard a cracking which she knew was the sound of several of the lower ribs on the right side of his ribcage breaking as a result of two rapid punches from Robby. A couple of seconds later she heard more cracking sounds as Robby worked up the right side of the intruder's back, quickly jabbing him and breaking his ribs. Tatyana could see Robby was hitting him without restraint to make him drop the knife.

Tatyana found her t-shirt released from the intruder's grip so she immediately stepped backwards out of harm's way. She saw Robby drop the intruder back to his feet, but he hadn't dropped the knife. Robby jabbed the intruder's left side twice which produced three cracks, which made her shiver. Tatyana saw he didn't release the knife and she was confused.

"Drop it, ok?" Robby said quietly. But the man ignored him.

A second later Robby held the knife hand with both of his hands and suddenly spun the man around to face himself. Tatyana saw that the intruder was gasping but still gave Robby an angry fierce look which Robby returned with a smile.

"So you really do want to be in hospital for a very long time?" Robby said whilst standing quite still. "Last chance?" Even though

Robby held the hand with the knife, the man immediately tried to plunge it towards Robby's neck. Tatyana gasped at the scene but it was clear that Robby was in control. She saw Robby's right knee came up so hard and fast, catching the intruder's crotch so forcefully that both his feet left the ground.

The intruder took a gulp of air and Tatyana gasped as she saw that he was still clinging onto the knife, still desperate to get Robby. She noticed that Robby had only moved one of his feet in the struggle and she could tell he was very surprised that the man wouldn't let go of the knife. Robby threw a punch with his right hand which hit the man in the middle of his throat hitting his wind pipe. But he still didn't drop the knife. Robby hit him in the same spot again, and Tatyana could see it was a lot harder. Tatyana heard a throaty gurgle as his injured windpipe struggled to let air into his lungs. He slowly slid to the floor, releasing the knife as he had lost his strength. Tatyana reckoned that less than twenty seconds had passed since the intruder had picked up the knife to him dropping it.

As Tatyana began to recover from the pounding of her rapid heartbeat, she realised she was shaking. Trying to control herself she breathed out slowly, and then she took a slow breath in. She gave a huge sigh and whispered to herself, "He was going to kill me." Then she realised that Robby had dealt with the man like a professional. She was astonished not by his strength but by his masterly control of the whole problem.

Trying to calm herself down with slow breaths, Tatyana observed Robby kick the knife away and pick up the cell phone which had fallen out of the man's trousers. He dialled 999 and whilst it was ringing he gave the phone to her.

"Ask for the Police. Say you've got an escaped prisoner who is waiting for them in Vinny's. Tell them they'll need an ambulance with 'blues and twos' and a surgeon to meet it at A&E. He's probably got a punctured lung and a ruptured spleen."

"Ok," said Tatyana, immediately pressing the buttons on the phone.

The man was groaning and holding his scrotum but he was still struggling to get up and have a go at Robby. Robby saw the man's right hand searching for the knife, so he stamped on it twice. Tatyana heard several snaps of breaking bones coming from the floor where the intruder's hand was.

There were groans but then Tatyana saw the intruder's left hand grabbing at Robby's trousers as it searched for the knife. Robby's foot caught the wrist which he pinned to the ground whilst stamping the hand with his other foot. Tatyana heard the crunch of several bones break at the same time. She was astonished that the man would not give in to Robby and he still tried to hit Robby with his arm and kick him hard with both feet. Tatyana knew Robby had enough and she saw him stand with his full weight on the man's right hand. He stamped on his forearm as hard as he could. She heard the cracking sound of the two forearm bones as they snapped but the man still kept on kicking Robby.

"You're going to regret that for a long time," Robby said standing on the other hand. He stamped on the left forearm with full force and Tatyana heard the crack of the bones being broken. Robby stamped on the left forearm twice more with full force. The movement of the broken bones mashed up the soft tissue of his forearm producing overwhelming pain signals which arrived in his brain and made him wince. He stopped fighting.

"Can you wipe the mug and cutlery I used clean?" He asked Tatyana.

"Sure." Still in shock she quickly got the mug from his table, wiped it with a damp towel, knowing that she was removing all traces of him. Then she wiped the phone as finally it answered.

"I've got a prisoner you lost this morning," Tatyana said to the operator.

"Are you reporting a sighting from the radio description?" But Tatyana interrupted him.

"Over six foot, black suit, dark brown eyes, blue shirt with no tie and black boots. Right in front of me."

"Don't go near him. He's dangerous. I'll put you through to the police."

"No don't bother. He's here waiting for them in Vinny's café for the homeless. You need an ambulance with blues and two's and a surgeon to meet the ambulance at A&E. He's probably got a punctured lung and a ruptured spleen. Oh... and two broken arms." Then she hung up.

"Said he was dangerous and not to go near him."

"Yeah, I know. They could have said extremely dangerous. Met lots of them in the forces. Just want to fight. You never get used to it, just good at it. Not normal. I was close to breaking one of his legs to stop him. To have wanted to carry on with that much pain he must be a psychopath or have taken a load of gear to be able to stand that pain. "

Tatyana saw the intruder was still groaning and now struggling for breath as Robby removed the man's boot laces and used them to tie his wrists to each end of the large old wall mounted radiator. He deliberately tied each lace very tightly because he knew this man could still walk even though the paramedics would get there soon, so he wouldn't actually lose both hands.

Robby then undid the intruder's trouser's belt, buttons and zip. He grabbed the top of the man's trousers and underpants and in one movement he pulled them down beneath his knees to his ankles. Tatyana was half looking away but couldn't help asking Robby about him.

"What's happened to him? I mean his scrotum is all blown up like a rugby ball?"

"I was keeping the main aim the main aim. He's neutralised. Catastrophic damage to the testicles. They rupture, break up into pieces and bleed like a pig. More effective than that knife in his chest."

Robby pulled two chairs together back to back and lifted the man's legs carefully together, putting both feet on two chairs. He wrapped the man's inside out trousers around the top of the chairs and stood back as if very satisfied that he had done a good job.

"That'll keep more blood going to your heart and brain so you're alive until the medics get here." Tatyana could see the intruder look up at Robby in disbelief at what Robby had done to him because Robby had nearly killed him and was now helping him. "Aren't you going to thank me?" Robby waited for the reply he knew would never come. "It's quite funny really because it's the same in war. You shoot someone to bits, and then you help them," Robby said to him. "I was a medic once."

Tatyana noticed pain was starting to tell on the man's face and his hands were already blue. He was already starting to sweat and he tried to speak, but no sound came from his voice box apart from gurgling and gasps for air. But Robby could tell what he wanted to say.

"You're thinking I'm crazy?"

"Mm..." The man nodded.

"Well you're right. I am crazy. People in mental hospitals are either mad, sad or bad. You're bad. She's sad. I'm mad. I'm a serious danger to myself and to others. I need help. But you... you're bad." Robby could see the blue flashes and hear the bells from the distant ambulance and the sirens from several police cars coming closer.

"Down with me now. Can't leave you here with him," Robby said turning to Tatyana, grabbing her by the hand and leading her down the stairs. As the ambulance pulled around the corner at the far end of the street and waited for the police to arrive, Tatyana looked at Robby, who had let go of her hand and was already walking away from her.

"He would have killed both of us," Tatyana said as she held up her hand to wave.

"Yeah he would have done. Wanted to get on the run at any cost," said Robby as he looked over his shoulder, smiling and waving back.

"Thanks," Tatyana said realising Robby had already put the incident behind him.

"No trouble." Then he was silent for a moment. He looked straight at her and said, "You are a beautiful woman." He grabbed his bike. Then with his pocket umbrella in one hand he wheeled the bike around the first corner.

Tatyana left the police station at eleven o'clock after giving a statement which gave the police no clues as to who Robby was. She said she didn't know his name, the colour of his hair or his eyes. She said he was a stranger to Vinny's. They asked her if she was a nurse which she denied. Then they asked her how she knew precisely about the man's injuries and that a surgeon was needed in the A&E department to meet the ambulance. All she said was that it was what the stranger had told her to say.

At Vinny's, the homeless people they questioned said they had never seen the stranger, which for most was true, because Robby would only have passed them on his way out. Before they left, the police asked Tatyana not to mention the stranger who they thought might be a vigilante because it might seem like he had done their job for them.

+++CHAPTER 2.

"I'm on my way Sam," said Robby standing a few feet from the farmhouse door with his small rucksack on his back.

"Sorry to hear that. Thought we were going to have more time to talk about smartarse pilots and the crazy flights we did. But hey, let's leave that until next time. Know where you're going?"

"Somewhere warm for a while."

"I hope having some time out's helped you... you know." She said looking down at her feet, wanting to say more. She was a tall attractive woman only an inch shorter than Robby. Instead of the tough looking cropped hair she had when working with Robby in the RAF, she now had blonde hair cut just above her shoulders.

"Getting there," Robby said but he was shaking his head.

"When I left the RAF it took me a whole year to start to see myself as a normal person and not just part of an air crew team. I know I only did a year more than you, but it still took so long to get out of the conditioning they put me through. So take your time. And hey, I haven't been through what you went through. If you want to stay on or if you go and want to come back, just turn up any time. But hey, next time please stay in the farmhouse not in the woods. You're not a bear."

"You still make me laugh. I'm all camped out. You know I've got some work I've got to do. Thanks. It's been peaceful here. Thanks for being a true buddy and a straight talker."

"I know old friend. I'll never stop being honest with you. Of all the people I've seen become very strange Robby, you're the one I'd put my money on that you'd make it back again. But the truth is you haven't. I'm being honest."

"Going to get through this. I'm not giving up."

"You haven't turned to drink and drugs. But you look terrible, that stuff is still going around in your head and you're still homeless. You're going fight this to the death. Good luck. I've heard of strong people like you try and fight this and end up destitute, in jail or on heroin. You're clever and won't do that. But you could end up dead. Get some professional help. Go see someone who knows about this kind of stuff."

"Tried that. Now got to do it my own way. Got to go find that out."

Robby disengaged his eyes from hers and turned towards the trees. After Robby turned away from Sam, and for just a moment, he sensed he was up against some giant force which was going to slay him. A shiver made him arch his back and he felt cold.

As he walked away through the trees, although he was feeling nervous about his next step he gritted his teeth in determination to beat it and win. He turned and waved to Sam but she had already gone. He walked to the group of trees, mostly oaks where he had camped all summer, away from people and machinery. He took the handlebar of his push bike and pushed it to the lane. He looked back at his daily routine of a walk and then a cycle ride into Vinny's where he had a wash and a shave in the sink in the gents and breakfast cooked by Tatyana. Now as always, he felt he wanted to talk to her and ask her out. He could still feel the effects of her beaming smile from earlier when he gave her back the cold beans.

His thoughts were wandering as his bike took him along the lane to the village shop. He cycled faster knowing he had to deal with his own problems before he could ask anyone out. He slowed down as he felt his anxious thoughts were making him ride too fast. He was feeling unsure if he was doing the right thing by leaving Tatyana at Vinny's. He was feeling selfish about leaving Sam's farm to work on himself because he knew he had taken but not given. He thought fondly about Tatyana as he now slowly peddled. He knew she was unusual and beautiful and he wondered, as always, if she had a boyfriend. As he was about to park his bike against the wall of the village shop, he hesitated getting off the saddle. He thought he could go back and see her and thank her for putting up with his daily silence. He would promise her he would come back for her. But sitting on the bike, he no longer felt like a hero on a mission from which he could return. Remembering how he had dealt with the intruder confirmed there was no return to Vinny's which would be under police surveillance for some time. His heart sank knowing he would never see her again and so he got off the bike.

He bought some simple provisions for the rest of the day, but avoided the papers in the shop. He had a single rucksack which had a change of clothes, his small tent and a sleeping bag. Apart from Sam, no one ever saw him come and go in the mornings. Now no one saw him pedal his bike, out of the village which he now left unlocked outside the bus stop for anyone to claim.

It was early autumn and getting too cold to live in a tent in Norfolk. Robby was on the move to somewhere warmer on the coast. The bus took him to Lowestoft where he began his walk hugging the coast. Robby was particularly positive because this walk was an opportunity to take him somewhere to change one way or the other. It also gave his mind a rest as he saw walking as something neutral and simple. His aim was a caravan park just a few miles south of Lowestoft which he had noticed out of a window on a Hercules when he had been in the RAF. At the time he thought it looked remote and now he thought it would probably be a quiet place to be out of the tourist season and a peaceful place to watch the sun rise.

By mid afternoon he had rented a six birth caravan in a very quiet spot on the site, just a few yards in shore from Kessingland Beach. He decided it was safer and more flexible than staying at a bed and breakfast. It was spacious and was plugged into the local conveniences of running water and electricity. There were no neighbours and the only sound was the wind, the sea and a few birds. He got onto the bed and tried to rest for the afternoon. He thought the weather might be milder. It wasn't. He thought that a warm room and a more comfortable bed would give him more of a chance of getting some normal sleep. It didn't. After an hour he was plagued by his now increasingly fearful restlessness, knowing the images would soon be back.

He was only there to work through what had happened to him, wanting to free himself from the fear and the guilt and so he needed time. Robby also needed provisions to get by. He walked to the camp shop and bought himself one week's worth of provisions so he could start to work through his thoughts alone in the caravan.

Because the RAF doctors had failed to understand him he concluded that only he could sort out the problems he had and he was determined to work out how to get control of things and get back to being his old self. He sat down at the table and set to work writing down without interruption what had happened to him in on the road in Helmand. He believed that if he could write down what happened, then he could find out what was making his mind and body go so out of control. He thought he could identify it, but it wasn't that easy because the words came with difficulty.

There was a Land Rover and us. It was so hot. There had been a bang and we swerved…

He had to stop. He looked away from what he wrote; he decided to draw what he saw instead. He moved himself to the linoleum floor and sat on a cushion and set to work. First he drew a road under a blue sky. Then he added a light brown camouflaged Land Rover with two people in front of it in uniform. He drew three people beside a flat tyre at the rear. He tried to add another person but stopped.

He had got stuck with the drawing and couldn't draw any more of what happened. He felt he had to be in control of the images coming into his head or they would take over him so he switched back to writing down what he had seen. He wrote down one of the two memories which were the most intrusive of his flashbacks.

I was undoing the large wing nuts which held the spare wheel on the side of the Land Rover when this Afghan girl, a pretty dark haired girl, probably seven or eight years old, came walking towards me. She was smiling with something in her hand. The next moment I seemed to have moved and I was crouching on one knee in front of the Land Rover, smelling the smoke from the bullets. Looking down I saw the small pink socks on her feet. The pink sock…

He was on one knee kneeling on the linoleum of the caravan but right in front of him he could see her lifeless body, sense his profuse sweating, and he had a salty taste of something wet that hit him in the face and went straight in his mouth. He felt his face wet with her blood. The salty taste made him heave with nausea. Still on one knee he vomited on the linoleum in the caravan. Palpitations pounded in his chest and the numbing sense of shock as things slowed down completed the takeover of his mind. He was out of control in a vivid flashback. When he fell sideways and hit his shoulder and head on the floor of the caravan, he began to come back into the present moment.

At the end of his first day's attempt to help himself he walked the whole length of Kessingland Beach. That night he had his usual nightmare every half an hour. He woke every time feeling scared and sweating. In the morning the sheets and mattress were soaking.

After putting the mattress outside to dry, Robby tried to carry on with the writing but felt blocked. He switched back to doing another drawing. He drew the Land Rover but this time he was on both knees. Behind him were his pilot and co-pilot and in front was the young girl but he had to stop as he couldn't draw what he saw. Instead he switched back to words, which seemed to let him access the images easier.

The young girl walked towards me. She had a beautiful smile. The next time I saw her two pink shoes, she was…

Robby felt his face was wet but not with sweat and he was back in the fifty five degree heat of an afternoon in Helmand and not on the floor of the caravan. He was on both knees and put his hand to his face to feel if he was physically injured but he wasn't. His face was strangely wet and it was wet with her blood which he could feel was sticky. He could taste the salt from her blood and bits of her tissue on his lips. He fought the feeling of wanting to vomit. He focused on being back inside the caravan and managed to stand up, open the door and get some fresh air on his face. The nausea subsided. This did it. He could think a bit more now and see what had happened. So he wrote again.

This is the most terrifying. The colour pink, feeling wet on my face, feeling her sticky blood with my hands, tasting salt in my mouth. And small children are all triggers which set my mind into a state of complete loss of control. It is only an hour or so later when the smells, sounds and sights have gone that I can be sure it was a flashback. I only get back when I see I'm not actually in Helmand but in England. I know I avoid getting my face wet with the rain with my small pocket umbrella. It helps. I avoid children, children's clothes shops, and the colour pink. I can't stand salty food in my mouth. Having a brew settles me. Eating simple food like bacon or sausage sandwiches, where I don't have to interact with people makes me calmer.

By the fifth day he had done several drawings. The problem was that now he didn't sense the flashbacks were becoming longer and more frequent. They were getting stronger and he was getting weaker. His dreams were getting worse and he now tried to stay awake to avoid the really terrifying nightmare; the corridor dream. Robby felt that not sleeping was better than having the corridor dream, but he was functioning less normally every day because of the exhaustion.

After the tenth day in the caravan, Robby was beginning to have less and less time where he thought like a normal person. He was stretched beyond his limits and a different person from only a few days earlier. Feeling more irritable and sensing the danger of this, he avoided people. His mind was alight with imagery. The problem was that this fire had been lit for some time and now it didn't matter what he did to put it out; it was already out of his control. This fear forced him harder to put it out but only fuelled it to grow stronger and fiercer.

The doors of the corridor dream which took him along a white corridor would not open for him no matter how hard he tried. Robby noticed words written on the doors of the corridor becoming slightly less blurred and a little clearer each time he had the dream. It was a dream from deep in himself which he couldn't seem to escape. A new fear appeared which was the thought that he might have to live like this for the rest of his life.

Whilst only just coping with his tense hyper-aroused body and his hypervigilant mind, Robby desperately tried to think to find solutions to living with the uncontrollable flashbacks of the girl, the corridor dream and the crippling guilt. Robby wasn't one for losing control. But that was Robby before Afghanistan.

On the twelfth day Robby saw the solution which he knew would work. He took a train from Lowestoft via Ipswich to Liverpool Street Station where he got a tube to Waterloo Station. He then took the first train going to Brockenhurst in the New Forest. The only thing he did in the village was to go into a hardware shop and buy one thing.

For the entire train journey from the caravan to Brockenhurst he was trying to do everything to avoid any of the trigger factors which set off a flashback. Just as he had come into Brockenhurst he noticed a sign for the school. He crossed over the road at a bus stop because there were children waiting. He crossed over again at a shop with children's clothes in the window. But he was caught unawares by a rocking horse in an antique shop and instantly a memory of a child's smiling face appeared and almost took over his mind and his body. A car backfired three times which brought him to the brink of being very irritable, not with the driver but by the physical terror that appeared through his body's memories of the shot's he'd fired one after the other into the girl. Robby's body and his mind were no longer under his control but he managed to carry on walking. He felt if he could get into the open forest he would be safer from the intrusive images.

He carried on through Brockenhurst until he got to the water splash, where he turned left on the road out towards Ten Bends. He was relieved to leave Brockenhurst and get in to the country side of the New Forest as there were now very few buildings and no people. The images seem to have stopped and he sensed calmness in his pace. It was three in the afternoon when he got to Ten Bends, a series of almost right angle bends in the road. He knew this was the landmark which indicated that he had arrived at one of the most quiet and lonely places in the New Forest; Hincheslea Wood.

As Robby turned left and off the road towards the forest, for the first time in months, he was struck again by a special sense of calm. He started thinking about his days in the RAF as a loadmaster based at Lyneham in Wiltshire and later at Brize Norton in Oxfordshire. He remembered that he had started training as a paramedic but after an accident at RAF Lyneham, he discovered he couldn't stand the sight of blood. He applied for a transfer to aircrew as a loadmaster and got accepted.

As he walked through the New Forest, images of happy times flooded in to his mind. First he remembered his training as a loadmaster on the C130 Hercules at RAF Lyneham. Then he was posted to Brize Norton in Oxfordshire with the reformed 99 Squadron and trained on the C17 Globemaster. He thought about how much he used to like the Globemaster. Apart from the crew of pilot, co-pilot and loadmaster, the C17 was an entirely different aeroplane from a Hercules. Because its avionics were so advanced it didn't even need a navigator. Its wings were swept backwards and instead of four propellers it had four large jet engines. The RAF had eight of these planes which could each carry over 40 tons of cargo, which was double that of a Hercules. As he walked towards some trees, he felt proud of having worked with these machines. He stared straight ahead recalling the worst of times when their cargo's weight was in pounds and was particularly precious because it was in coffins.

Robby walked slowly as he was in no rush. He was relieved as he looked back for the very last time at what he had been through. Once or twice every week one of the Globemasters would be involved in a mission codenamed PABE to repatriate the dead service men and women from Afghanistan and Iraq. Robby's job was supervising loading the coffins onto the Globemaster and securing them with the movers until they arrived back at RAF Brize Norton. Everyone on the eight RAF C17 Globemasters disliked this work. It impacted on all the crew but mostly the loadmasters. Nobody spoke about it. It was the most solemn duty which came with an unspoken expectation to deal with it, keep quiet and move on. He lost count of the number of repatriations he had done after ten. One repatriation blurred into the next so sometimes it seemed like that was all he did. To Robby the C17 Globemaster he had admired and loved had turned into the ultimate hearse and he the loadmaster, its pallbearer.

As he walked his feet sunk into the soft bed of pine needles on the forest floor. Except for the occasional snapping sound of twigs giving way to his weight it was as if he was walking on a carpet. He was beginning to feel more relaxed. Robby remembered how his work suddenly became very involved with death. He remembered very clearly when it happened. In 2007 there were so many British armed forces personnel killed in Afghanistan and Iraq that the Oxfordshire coroner had such a large backlog of inquests waiting to be done, that the British government decided to transfer the inquests to coroners more local to the bereaved families. This resulted in the location of the landing site for all repatriations being switched from RAF Brize Norton to RAF Lyneham, where Robby had previously felt more at home.

In his new found calmness, the worst moments he recalled were before the unloading of the bodies at Lyneham. For every repatriation, before actually landing, the C17 Globemaster would ritually fly low and slow at 80 knots over RAF Lyneham, right over where the parents in grief waited with their hearses. To the bereaved families the C17 Globemaster's low and slow flight was symbolic of the 'last flight,' and this was the moment when the tears began. Everyone on the base also just felt deeply unnerved by the enormous presence of the C17 Globemaster's low and slow ritual of bringing back the dead. The low frequency sound of the huge engines shook everyone on the base to their core as they each knew that if someone was sick who was supposed to be deployed, then without notice, they could have to take their place and be deployed to theatre. They could easily be next on that final journey home.

It was very quiet in the forest as he walked and it reminded him that during those two or three hours on the base, everyone was usually quiet, just hoping they wouldn't get the nod to be deployed to replace someone. Few people went ill before an arranged deployment because of the massive impact on their replacement. Likewise, anyone injured or killed would have to be replaced immediately without any notice and anyone could suddenly find themselves in harm's way. Getting pregnant deliberately just before a deployment was seen as the ultimate cowardly behaviour, and particularly so by the woman who had to replace the pregnant woman. She would have no time to get ready or prepare her family, knowing her parents might suddenly be watching her return as cargo in the back of a C17 during its low and slow ritual over RAF Lyneham.

Robby stopped walking and stood still looking around the open forest and he remembered that before the cargo door was allowed to be opened, there was an inescapable forty minute wait whilst the defensive flares of the C17 Globemaster were inactivated. Everything was still, just like now in the forest. But it was over. There were no people around. It was bad enough for him, but he knew the de-flaring of the aircraft was an excruciating wait for the parents. He just had to wait inside the aircraft and sometimes the forty minutes to deflare felt like a very long time. When Robby got the ok that the aircraft was de-flared he double checked that the large curtain separating the coffins from the rest of the cargo bay was in place and then the massive cargo door was lowered until it touched the ground. Six service men from each person's regiment then carried each coffin onto a pair of simple wooden supports under a small awning on the runway. A chaplain would then say a few words before the parents collected their children for the very last time.

His clear view of the forest reminded him that it was only on these days that the base was silent because RAF Lyneham was closed to all movements of traffic whilst the bereaved families and relatives were on the base. Standing to attention he had a good view high up on the ramp of the C17 Globemaster looking across RAF Lyneham. He remembered he could clearly see the parents driving with their children past the Comet C2 XK699 'Sagittarius' which was the station gate guardian for RAF Lyneham. When he saw the cars following the last hearse clear 'Sagittarius,' he gave the all clear to the pilot and navigator. The captain and the tower then gave the all clear to all personnel on the base that the PABE was over and that movement could begin again on the base. He was clear. He had a sense of massive relief because he hadn't had to meet the parents. Now he was clear to move on through the forest.

The Globemasters did frequent UK hospital medical evacuations, bringing back the severely wounded who were confined to their beds and needed medical care. There were five Intensive Care beds and most of the casualties had limb injuries or missing limbs. This meant they would be in and out of the rehabilitation unit at Headley Court in Surrey for months. There were also the horrifying injuries involving the faces which always turned Robby's stomach.

But he knew the amputees with genital injuries from IUD's were the worst. They usually had such deeply penetrating wounds going up through the pelvis. The highest fragments got as high as their lungs, which made them die from their penetrating wounds weeks later in Selly Oak in Birmingham. Robby knew from medics at Selly Oak that this often took place there in front of divorced parents who now spoke for the first time in years, still blaming the other for not stopping their child joining up. He felt free of that now. No more repatriations. No more coffins. No more draped flags. No more blood. No more complications. Only the sight and smell of the green forest.

Robby remembered it starting ever so slowly. As the fighting carried on and the repatriations became more frequent, they never became routine for him. What Robby didn't notice was that each time he worked on a repatriation, he felt slightly more uncomfortable in himself. He had thoughts which he never imagined he would have. He wondered exactly what the body looked like. One time the crew were asked to meet the parents of the repatriated soldier but it was so painful he avoided it and from that one onwards, he dreaded the possibility of having to meet the parents. He was getting anxious. Each PABE made that day gloomy but also made him a great deal more serious about his own fate. What Robby also didn't realise was that this changed the way his brain would respond to any traumatic incident in the future. He was now in a preconditioned state where a traumatic incident stood a good chance of not getting processed properly and might render him very anxious with intrusive thoughts.

Robby inhaled the fresh pine air of the New Forest, and then he felt it on his cheeks. His focus changed from his cheeks as he remembered a female doctor's cheeks. Two months after his experience in Afghanistan Robby presented himself to the Medical Centre at RAF Lyneham to see one of the GPs. Robby told her he was having difficulty sleeping. He was surprised she didn't ask him anything about his dreams or about the nature of the thoughts which were intruding on his normal thinking. He could still remember her facial muscles being very well toned as if she trained every day, but she was overweight. He recalled how he was disappointed as he realised that her facial muscles looked well toned, but only because of her permanent sense of agitation. He remembered looking into her cold steely pale grey blue eyes which made contact with him twice, but each time only for a second, when she wasn't using her computer. He was surprised when she gave him two weeks' worth of sleeping pills and said his sleep would get better as time passed. It didn't. It got worse. He then went to see another GP on a stopover flight at RAF Kinloss hoping to get a different answer. But he got exactly the same answer and more sleeping pills. He was looking for understanding but instead Robby got a medal which to him marked the end of his career with the RAF.

Because he tried not to sleep so that he could avoid the corridor dream, Robby had become permanently exhausted and he therefore had very little energy. His concentration was only a fraction of what it had been and he became increasingly irritable, spending most of his time desperately trying to avoid the trigger factors which started off the flashbacks.

He sometimes had the corridor dream fifteen times when he slept. But now the corridor dream had changed. He noticed one detail this morning. In it he was walking down the white clinical corridor with several doors to each side which he couldn't open. Each door had a different name in black and white, which at first he couldn't read because the names were blurred. Until this morning Robby couldn't read the sign on the double doors.

The flashbacks and the corridor dream left him sick with guilt and anxiety. His memory had become more and more useless but one thing he could remember was that Hincheslea Wood was the quietest and loneliest part of the whole of the New Forest. He couldn't remember where he had heard it and it didn't matter now; he just knew it.

Robby walked towards the densest part of Hincheslea. He had kept the main aim the main aim and now felt relieved to leave the last house behind him, so he would see no more people.

He found an oak tree standing with several others but he picked this one because it looked easy to climb. He took off his coat, removed the pocket umbrella from the back pocket of his trousers and left his coat and umbrella neatly at the bottom of the tree. He wound a rope around his waist and around the trunk and used this to inch himself up to the lowest branch which was fifteen feet from the ground. Robby tied two knots in the rope. One went around the branch and he tied the other around his neck. As he jumped, he saw the look on the girl he had shot. Tears ran down across his cheeks. He no longer had to live with the crippling guilt. When the rope tightened, he felt his neck burn with the grip of the rope, and then stretch in pain as his neck took his full body weight.

+++CHAPTER 3.

"I'm Anita," said Dr Johnson. "Pull up a chair." They sat
six feet apart in two green easy chairs in her consulting room.
Anita was an attractive forty five year old therapist with shoulder
length dark hair who, although dressed casually in denim jeans
and a white shirt, looked very serious. Robby was in new black
denim jeans and a black shirt which he bought at the hospital.
He didn't feel like talking.

"I'm a psychologist. I work with people who've had
psychological trauma."

"I'm not really sure of where exactly I am."

"You've been discharged from the orthopaedic ward at
Southampton General Hospital to this place to see me. This
is a privately run psychiatric hospital which is used mainly
by the NHS. It's called 'The Refuge.' It used to be an old
country manor. We are near Hythe between Southampton and
Lymington. How's the leg?"

"Better. No pain killers."

"And the head without the sedation they were giving you?"

"Twitchy. Memories are creeping back in today. Since the
stuff they gave me, I haven't had a nightmare or anything. It
must have been heavy stuff because I'm pretty crazy." Both of
Robby's shoulders seemed twitchy as if he felt uncomfortable
in the room.

"From what I've been told about you, I think you've
responded normally to abnormal circumstances. I think you
could be helped by a modern treatment called EMDR. But
only if you use your brain."

"Can't. My brain's gone. Isn't doing what it's supposed to.
Not what I want. I've been edgy. I avoid people because of

my frustration and anger. Because I can't be normal makes me angry about them. I've had to live apart just in case when I'm with someone, I can't tell what's real. Can't tell what's real any more. That's why I don't want to be here." Robby was tapping his fingers on the arm rests."

"Have you heard about the Vietnam vets suicide rate?"

"No."

"It's kept hidden by the Americans; otherwise no one would ever go to war. Fifty eight thousand Americans were killed by physical injuries in the Vietnam War. Since then over sixty thousand Vietnam Veterans have committed suicide. The official suicide statistics are much lower because the suicides are hidden in the statistics by being reported as accidents."

"No that's not true. That's dumb."

"You don't want to hear this but I'm going to tell you because you need to hear this. The establishment is not really interested in you. You represent what war really does to people; how it messes their heads up. The establishment doesn't want the public to see more of people like you. They want you to naturally dumb down to a low level where you won't cause them trouble. They are content for people like you to be taken care of in other ways like getting in to fights and going to jail. They are content for you to be jobless and homeless. You can't relate to ordinary civilians because of the thoughts in your head. When you are homeless you are out of the public's eye." Robby's gaze was right through one of Anita's rugs on the floor. He was still and they were both silent.

"In America, male Vietnam Veterans who commit suicide by crashing their car or shooting themselves are officially reported as a single car drunk driving accident, or an accidental firearm discharge whilst cleaning their weapon. So both officially appear as accidents, not suicide. The British Veterans' suicides have now overtaken the deaths in the Falklands and the two Gulf Wars."

"Why are you telling me this?" Robby was looking over his left shoulder at a picture on the wall.

"I get paid to get someone like you more or less back to what they used to be without all this 'stuff' going around and around in your head. I'm here to work only on the part of your thinking that's been traumatised by the incident. I'm trying to show you what has happened to you is common in war."

"I'm very messed up. Hospital didn't help."

"They fixed your leg."

"That was all. They didn't bother with me."

"You were on an orthopaedic ward. It's like a carpentry workshop. They got a psychiatrist to see you. That's why you're here."

"I got treated like I was dangerous, crazy and the word spread to avoid me."

"What were you looking for there?"

"Help. But I got none. No sympathy."

"Did you tell anyone how you had come to be there?"

"No."

"Well how can you expect them to understand you, let alone help someone like you? They're not mind readers."

"I'm just angry that no one asked me how I was feeling. I was laying there after I just tried to kill myself. This wasn't an attempt. It should have happened. I lay there for a week not wanting to be alive. I couldn't move or walk. After the op the shrink said she would give me an injection which would wear off today. It worked because I've been calmer but right now worry is building up in me. Can't believe no-one asked me how I was feeling."

"Look Robby, the world has changed. People have to do the bare minimum these days. Even doctors and nurses on a medical ward. A lot of the time, the understanding, empathy, compassion that our families were brought up with has just gone. There isn't time for it anymore because it's too busy. It doesn't exist anymore in the public sector. You can buy someone's time for fake empathy in the private sector, but it isn't real."

"Ok... you're right. Sorry for ranting."

"Let's get on with this now. I've heard roughly about your Afghan incident which is like the wedge of the cake. I can only work on that part of the cake and not the rest of you with all of your childhood memories."

"So it's like having a part replaced in the engine? That's just great." Robby slapped his hand down on the arm of the easy chair. "I'm going to be treated like a machine." Robby was aware he was agitated as he was crossing and uncrossing his legs and touching his face, making sure it was dry. But he was trying to stay calm and not get any worse. He looked to his left and up at a picture of a horse hanging on the wall. "Are you into horses?"

"No, not at all. Never been on one."

"Why have you got one in your office then?"

"When I used to get worried, my father used to say to me, 'Leave the worrying to a horse...' Know why?"

"No." Robby was calmer.

"It's got a bigger head." She said with a grin.

"You're crazy. You're just like my aunt." Robby gave Anita prolonged direct eye contact. "You're actually human. You nearly made me smile."

"Maybe you can talk about her later. Don't look so worried, as if I'm going to treat you like an alien or a machine. I'm going to treat you as a normal person who, like a car, has been involved in a crash and has had a big dent. We have to make the dent perfect again. There are no miracles, only simple psychology here. It's just getting the balance restored. Then the rest of you will feel better again. It's the very best there is. I will get you to understand the way you are thinking completely. Do you trust me?"

"Well... my other choice failed." Robby sat back in his chair looking more relaxed.

"I'll take that as a yes then. You need to see me like a mechanic with lots of different tools in my psychological tool box. There're two things I'd like you to focus on throughout this treatment and also after you've left."

"Ok." Robby sat up straight in his chair again to show Anita that he was not only paying attention but that he was actually interested in getting help.

"After the damage is repaired and you're strong again, I want you to look for the gold not the darker stuff. Like glue, the gold is the positive stuff about you, about life; it holds you together. I'm not going to look at all the old negative childhood memories. We could all do that for a very long time. That's not my thing. I'm not into that. One of the problems about therapy is spending so much time looking back in the rear view mirror. The danger is you get so tangled up in the past that you can't see where you actually are, where you're going and you can end up in a crash. So we will end up only looking for gold."

"No shit?"

"Yeah. Exactly. With yourself you should aim to be a gold miner not a shit shoveller." She smiled.

"You're hard?" He smiled back and sat back in his chair.

"Next, at the end of this course of treatment your world view will probably seem changed. It will help you if you see yourself like a child. Children don't have complicated memories and so they have to imagine more. But they know they are imagining and are only looking for what is true. They are open to it. You will know what is real again but be like a child. Be open like a child. Remember your world view will be different at the end of this. You can remember both of these by imagining the world, or a globe which has gold rays coming out of it."

"Sounds weird but now you've said that image I won't forget it. Doesn't working with people like me mess your head up?"

"I'm human and sensitive and certain things do get to me. I have coping strategies. Simple things like light. What I mean is being in light places. Let me put it this way. A long time ago, and I'm talking about my own personal life; I stopped watching depressing movies and listening to sad music. Now I only watch comedy and things that make me laugh and smile. I also watch things that interest me but I totally ignore this whole negative depressing side of information like the news. I like having fire around; candles around... and also heat. I collect wood and food and I try growing some as well. What I mean is I'm trying to always be my best and to grow in to what I am supposed to be. I'm like a seed which is supposed to just be something like a tree. All I need to do is just be what I actually am. I like to gather things in and I like swapping things. Do you remember like you used to do at school? Then it was never a problem always keeping it simple. There's your answer. Do you see it?"

"You sound just like my aunt. I used to argue with her all the time when I was younger about her being very New Age and middle class. You've got yourself worked out and under control. But me. I'm a mess." He fell silent as he stared down through the rug beneath his feet whilst Anita sat back with an arm across the top of her armchair. She seemed to know the answers to the most difficult questions and Robby could see that that she was relaxed and happy in her room. This gave him confidence about her which made him feel more comfortable and he raised his head a little.

"Let me tell you about this tool EMDR. It's the newest form of therapy helping to deal with traumatic memories. It's a bit of a mouthful but the letters EMDR actually stand for Eye Movement Desensitisation and Reprogramming."

"Yeah." Robby seemed interested.

"If you work with traumatised people it's one of the best tools you can have in your psychological toolbox. It's exciting and totally supported by research. NICE, which stands for the National Institute of Clinical Excellence promote it as a first line therapy for people who have been traumatised. It works immediately and you can use it any time after a person has had a traumatic experience."

"Yeah but I've had this shit going on in my head for ages."

"In the UK they only tend to use it quite a long time after, but in America they use it much earlier. The British lag behind a bit with psychological crisis intervention. We wait for things to stew a bit too long, but things are changing. The results of recent research just need to be put into practice by the MOD. It works much quicker than other therapies such as CBT... that means Cognitive Behaviour Therapy. I usually finish up between the sixth and the twelfth session Maximum. CBT takes at least 30-40 sessions. Each EMDR session is an hour and a half long and we can do them every few days. Under 10-15 hours."

"I thought I was going to be here for months." Robby was on the edge of his chair with interest.

"When you've had a very traumatic experience, sometimes the brain can't cope with processing the images and they remain stuck as if frozen in time and are stored in the raw state they were first seen in. They just don't move on. These memories remain unprocessed and very unlike ordinary memories. They get stuck in the lower more primitive part of the brain, at the top of the spinal cord, instead of being processed like ordinary memories and going to the higher outer part of the brain. You know the curly bits you see in pictures of the brain."

"Yeah." Robby nodded.

"These memories which are stuck can make the way you see the world very negative. You're probably aware that your world view is very different from what it used to be?"

"Totally."

"EMDR helps you process the traumatic scenes so that they move on. As they get moved on, they lose their terrifying quality and this changes your view of the world to a more positive one."

"Everything's shit at the moment. Can't change the past."

"You are completely wrong about that. This treatment it like editing the past. Do you understand how much difference this could make to you? This can take away the intense emotions you are feeling, especially the anxiety that comes with the traumatic images. It neutralises and wipes out the reactions which the body has to past events. So the way your body feels changes as well."

"Yeah. But what do you do? What do I do?"

"I start with taking a history about you to find out about you and what exactly happened to you and what you experience now. We then find out how you used to cope with stress and how you do now. I then find out from you what is the most negative visual image you associate with the memories. We find out what your most negative thought about yourself is and how you would like that to change it to a positive belief. I ask you about your feelings and what you experience in your body. I ask you to focus on the most negative visual image of the trauma and I ask you to also be aware of your body whilst you follow my fingers with your eyes as I move them left and right about two feet away from your face.

What happens to you is that the movements of your eyes following my fingers results in each side of your brain being stimulated quite quickly. This rapid alternating stimulation of each side of the brain enables the traumatic visual imagery to move on, to finally get processed like a normal memory. We know that the memory is stuck or frozen and for some reason it can't move up to the top of the brain like a normal memory. Stimulating one side of the brain then the other opens up some kind of door and the memory goes through it and becomes a normal memory in the upper brain. That's how it works. I end up checking your negative and positive beliefs about yourself and see if they change."

"Yeah I get the finger wagging bit of it. But what about my actual memory of it?"

"What you remember loses the anxiety attached to it and although you can still recall the memory if you want to, it doesn't suddenly intrude on your thoughts when you are awake, like in your flashbacks or when you are asleep in your nightmares. Your body becomes less highly vigilant and your feelings about the world get better. I get your eyes to follow my fingers for about twenty to thirty seconds each time. Often another image will appear during the eye movements and we then do the eye movements to that image too. In a single session we might work with five, ten or even more images with eye movements."

"When could I start?"

"If you are up for it, I can begin the whole thing right now and we can do a whole session, but it will be about an hour and a half. Most sessions are at least an hour and a half so it's tiring. It's up to you."

"I've got nothing to lose."

"First you are going to have to tell me about your parents, your childhood and what happened to you."

"Well that'll be easy because it was all shit."

"Ok, but first I have to just run through how you are right now. You seemed very angry to start with and resentful about the hospital and how no one asked you how you were feeling. You seem a lot more relaxed and I wonder if you can tell me how you are feeling right now."

"I'm more relaxed than when I came in. I trust you because you seem to know what you're talking about. Don't know why but I feel safe in this place. I don't feel anything is going to happen to me here. I feel a bit chilled out, like it's over but this time I don't have to end it. It's going to be ended by what you do. What I do." Robby had stopped feeling his face and looked relaxed, taking the odd quick glance at the picture of the horse head and shaking his head and smiling. "I trust you because you've got a sense of humour. That horse head makes me smile." Robby looked up at the horse twice as if was out of place.

"You are as ready as you will ever be but first we must stop for a tea or coffee and use the toilet because the session can be long. What would you like?"

"Just a brew with sugar ta."

"The toilet's opposite the door to this room," Anita said as she got up and re-boiled a kettle on a table and handed Robby a mug of tea.

"Thanks for that. I'm fine."

"Feel free to look around; I've just got to go to the ladies room."

Although Anita's room was spacious Robby thought it was a bit cluttered. It had four small rugs covering the wooden floorboards. There was no main light on the ceiling as the room was mainly lit by daylight and three desk lamps. There were a few unlit candles in the room and two walls of the room couldn't be seen because the shelves from the floor to ceiling were covered in books. There were not hundreds but thousands of books. The shelves extended on both walls down a passageway leading to an exit. Robby felt comfortable enough to get up and look at them. Almost all the books were about psychology or trauma. There were some about the armed forces and piles of journals going back years. He came across some books about rock music and several about poetry. He picked one out which interested him and was about to put it back when he saw a large colour booklet. He picked it up because it had a familiar picture on the back cover. It was Anita. Robby was surprised to read the title and the biography. It was an academic paper presented at a conference only three months ago.

Special Forces and Infantry Soldiers Same Day 'Mission use' of EMDR compared with delayed use of EMDR after Deterioration in Mental Health. Professor Anita Baker. Psychology Department. University of Southampton. Visiting Harvard Professor...

Robby felt as if he was in special company because he understood that Anita was an expert in the UK and in America treating Special Forces and front line infantry soldiers. He sipped his tea and again looked around the room wondering what else might surprise him. It was like someone's own special room. Nothing about it resembled an office except a table with a small computer. It was as if he had been invited into the person's innermost room. He noticed how quiet it was and how he felt at peace until Anita came back.

"Too many books," Anita said with a grin.

"You read them all?"

"Yes, all of them," she said beckoning Robby to come and sit down.

"You wrote some of them?"

"Yes, just a few. I've written mostly articles given as lectures which appear in other people's books. They'll all have to go some day. Too many of them."

"And you are a Professor?"

"At the university only but not here. This is the clinical part of my work where I try and actually help people get better. At the university I get other people to do my research. Psychologists and psychiatrists working in field hospitals and here in military centres, they send me data I've asked them to collect. I process it. I see you found a book."

"Yeah was going to put it back when I got distracted."

"You can borrow it as long as you give it back."

"Yeah. I need something to do. As a kid I used to have lots of songs in my head. But they seem to have gone. This book shows you how to write verses. Sure I can borrow it for a bit?"

"Yes you take it. What sort of things did you used to write about?"

"I used to write songs every night. All crap. Was never taught how to link lines up and all that kind of stuff. But I got my feelings into them because Mum and Dad never really listened to me. Mum was from Scotland. She ran a frock shop in Bristol and Dad was a physiotherapist. Mum and Dad drank lots every night, so they weren't really there for me a lot of the time. And I had two older sisters who were... well just into their own thing. I was lonely."

"So how did you deal with being lonely and with difficult times, unhappiness or stress?"

"Evenings I would write songs. At weekends I used to go on long bike rides in the countryside around Bristol. Always had a calming effect on me. Sometimes I would have an aim like getting a cold drink at a shop in the county. Other times I would just ride."

"Were you a happy kid?"

"Pretty crappy really. I was the youngest so always got talked down to by my family. I suppose that's why I don't see them anymore. They made me feel smaller than I needed to feel. I felt they were simply trying to stunt my growth by their comments about me being junior. If I saw them today I would still be called the baby. Don't need that crap. I was always treated as though I knew less. I think they wanted me to know less, so they would seem bigger in their own way. I don't need to be treated like crap just to make someone else feel better."

"Any idea why they would do this?"

"I guess that was just them. I think it was simply that they never got over the pecking order thing. I was relating to people outside my family in a more honest way. Once I saw what I could be like, I couldn't be bothered to play their game of just believing what they said about me. I didn't really need being treated badly. I felt like my growth was being stunted. After I left home I contacted them several times but they treated me exactly the same on the phone so I stopped ringing them. Unlikely I'll see them again. Don't want the pain back. All I did was admit to myself I'd had enough pain. The good side was that I had a lot of time to myself and they had less impact on me. That let me see how I could break free from them. It was the main reason for joining the RAF. I could leave home and train in something without having to be with them."

"That sounds like a good reason. Anyone else?"

"I've got one aunt up in Scotland and I've got really good memories of her and her husband. I used to argue black was white with her. She was into healing a bit like you. My uncle died recently. I've realised that they were really good to me and that they are my true family. I kept meaning to get up to see her. But I'll get there. Like me she didn't get on with my family."

"And relationships?"

"I had girlfriends. You know, the RAF is full of young men and women who are sexually charged up. But I'm not sure if I've ever met the right person. There was one girl I thought was incredibly beautiful and I admired her but I was going through so much. She worked in a homeless centre in Norwich. But I can't remember her name... Sometimes I still see her face, her eyes and her long dark hair. I think she knew part of me really well and I knew part of her well but our paths crossed only for a while. When I think of her, I wonder if people like her are rare. I sometimes imagine seeing her here and there and some nights I dream about her. But she's a memory, just an image. Somebody will have snapped her up."

"Sounds more than a memory. Sounds like love." Anita calmly wrote this down.

"I'm not sure about that yet. It seems to have missed me for the moment."

"You seem to be your own person? But are you looking for something else?"

"Yes, Maybe. I don't know. Sometimes it's funny how you see yourself. I suppose they taught me that. Not wanting to be talked down to became my path of rebellion to becoming independent. Maybe I'm too independent now, but I'm happier this way."

"And school?"

"I did quite well at school and wanted to be a paramedic. I was going to join the ambulance service but I was eventually persuaded to join the RAF. I suppose looking back at it; I made the mistake of believing what they said. It would get me away from home and give me freedom."

"How did that happen?"

"My parents said the house would be better off financially with another income when I got a job with the ambulance service. Truth is it would give them more money for their booze. Got recruited at a promotional visit by the RAF to my school. They said they would train me as a medic after leaving school. Said being a civilian paramedic was boring with no lifestyle and the public you dealt with were often drunk and violent. Said I would get assaulted every shift. They promoted an RAF medic as a glamorous lifestyle with better pay, where you could do any sport you wanted. A great sense of camaraderie and support at all levels with the best free medical help. But the reality is that it was sold in an unbalanced way showing only a part of the job. I was given one sided information of what an adventurous lifestyle it was with lots of travelling."

"And the reality?"

"The first part of the sales pitch was right about travel and people. The real job was having to accept that I might be killed and as a medic I would have to carry a gun and kill people. You can't know the enormity of this until you're right in a real situation. I feel cheated by what they sold me as a very young person. Even the medical help wasn't there when I actually most needed it. They failed to recognise my problem. They didn't help me. I still feel resentful about that."

"Carry on and tell me more."

"The job came with a hidden invitation to Hell. The over promotion hid the real agenda of the job. It's a little like how cigarette companies don't tell you that what they are selling you will kill you. They don't take responsibility for what they are really selling you. It's just a money thing. At the end of the day, you're the one left with failing lungs or with no limbs. They walk away victorious with the money or titles."

"I hear you. Carry on."

"I don't think the Army, RAF or Navy should be allowed to lie to adolescents and only give them part of the picture. So many join up at sixteen. I was taken in by them because I had crap at home.

I was vulnerable and I needed something other than home. We were at war in two countries that hadn't attacked us. We travelled thousands of miles to invade people who had nothing against us in Iraq and Afghanistan. There may have been some terrorists there but it was none of our business invading their countries. Imagine if we had done that to Southern Ireland in the 1980's" Robby was on the edge of his seat thinking for himself. He was calm.

"How do you mean Robby?"

"Well imagine if we invaded Southern Ireland because they had a few terrorists, the world would have totally objected because they were white Christians. But Arab Muslims with a lot of oil and influential lands? The Americans and British couldn't resist the temptation to try and force them to think the way they do. It's only when you get there and you realise that the people there really do want to kill you. You start asking why that should be? What have we done? The answer is simple, because we had no right invading their country. We had no right to be there and kill their people. We're the real terrorists, shooting people and blowing them up with our bombs."

"But somehow they seemed to have lured you in?"

"I was seduced by the RAF's self promotion about being amongst the most elite of world powers. At that time I felt the RAF offered a young person like me all the things a young person would want; especially stability. Service is in exchange for the apparent security the uniform gives you. You get accommodation, food, travel and you can do any sport. I think for almost everyone joining at my age and at my level it's an escape from the life they lead. Most come from difficult family backgrounds, from abuse, violence or poverty. I know. I had to live with people like that and I was one of them. I used it to get away from being put down at home. And yes that was good for me. But what they're secretly really giving you is not real security because they are actually giving you the potential to be annihilated. They are handing you a loaded revolver to play in their Russian roulette game of who is not going to get killed. When I discovered I didn't like the sight of blood and I could see that there was a huge potential to see a lot of blood spilt, I started to feel a little insecure about the job."

"Really? I don't mean to sound funny but that must have been a surprise for a medic. How did you discover that?" Anita asked. Anita made an entry in her notes.

"Being a medic was always an idea and I hadn't really seen a lot of blood before or a big wound."

"What sparked it off?"

"An accident with a Land Rover at RAF Lyneham. The passenger was a young trainee cook. She was eighteen. The nearside tyre burst and the Land Rover careered off to the left and hit a lamp post. The cook hadn't used a seatbelt and she hit the windscreen."

"How were you involved?"

"I was one of two first responders from the medical centre. I was with another paramedic."

"Tell me what happened?"

"We got to the Land Rover and parked behind it. The driver who was about twenty was in tears. The Land Rover had a large dent in the nearside wing and it had bent the lamp post slightly. I was trying to open the passenger door when I saw... " Robby was staring straight ahead.

"Carry on in your own time Robby", Anita said encouragingly.

"At first I thought it was going to be a simple head injury, but then I saw blood had leaked out between the door and the sill... She was wearing her greens and her cap covered some of her dark hair. When I removed the cap I saw that her head was like a boiled egg after you had removed the top with a teaspoon because it had caved in. It was flat. Brain tissue had leaked out over her face and down the windscreen, over the dashboard. The blood had leaked along the floor, out the door and on to the small step under the door. She was lifeless but we had to get her back to the medical centre. When we got there it was too late. She had died instantly."

"What especially really got to you about this Robby?"

"It could have been me... I felt this shouldn't have happened. It was such a waste of a life. How ugly and obscene it all was. The wetness and the warmth of the blood and bits of this person's tissue on me too. It was her brain. It stuck to me and dried like it was my own. It was all over my hands, legs, in my hair and everywhere I washed I found blood and brain tissue. I had a holiday coming up and I applied for a transfer to train as a loadmaster and got it straight away." Robby sat back in his chair. He took a deep breath.

"Tell me about being a loadmaster. Did you enjoy it?"

"Yeah it was a great job. Lots and lots of travelling and I loved the aircraft. I was part of a team. I was in charge of loading and checking all of the cargo. I was responsible for its safety in flight and dropping it in theatre or unloading at various bases."

"And how did the war change your job?"

"It was alright to start with. But then it all became different when we started flying back bodies every week or so. I had to load and unload them. Sometimes it was two trips a week if there were more than five or six killed in a week."

"How did this affect you?"

"To be honest I didn't ever expect to be handling bodies in coffins. I didn't see it coming but it slowly made me... very slowly it unnerved me a bit. I realised that what we were doing in Afghanistan was not just enjoying our jobs with aeroplanes. It was lethal."

"Can you say more about that?"

"Sometimes I would go behind the curtain and see the coffins. I thought I could come back like that some day... with my belt and cap on top of my coffin. Sometimes this got to me more if I didn't go and see the coffin during the flight. I always wondered what the person, the body looked like. Were they in a body bag? How badly was the body mangled? How many limbs did they have? Was the face damaged? Was there a face? Were they blown to bits and were there only a few body parts? Part of me saluted the person. I used to stand outside the curtain and talk to them in my head and say, 'Goodbye friend. You'll be home soon. Home soon forever. I am here with you. I'm one of your last companions. Hope I've done a good job.'

"What was the worst thing about it for you?"

"The screamers... we."

"Yes."

"We... would be standing inside the back of the C17 waiting with the body. After the ramp was finally lowered the person's mates came in as pall bearers to walk the coffin down the ramp. That's when the screaming started and... you can't stop yourself crying. The screaming goes right into the middle of you... your heart. You can't stop it... no one could... we were all the same... the movers and everyone on the plane. The relative's distress is total, as if they've just realised it... it's awful... it changes you forever. Your heart goes out to them. Sometimes it was a mother, sometimes a wife or girlfriend. Once a seven year old girl ran screaming up to the plane to her dad's coffin. It was hell. I had no training in this. I can't describe it in words. They should use civilian planes to pick them up after the 'Goodbye Ceremony' in Camp Bastion and professional funeral directors to do all of it instead of us. They're used to it. It just wrecked us."

"Anything else Robby?"

"Sometimes the parents wanted to meet the boys who flew their child home. Did it once. The pilots and the engineer usually only did it once and we all did everything to avoid it again. I dreaded the parents asking me about myself. I was too frightened to say, 'I'm good,' while their child was in a coffin in front of us. I had no words. I could only bow my head and say 'Ok... I'm sorry about... ' But I did ok... well better than some. One of the loadies used to keep a scrap book with photographs of every one he repatriated. Bringing back a body was always worse than bringing back the injured... no matter how many injured. Repatriations were the worst part of the job for me... for everyone. I lost count after the first ten. I had changed. That was my world. I became more serious. The rest of the world of computers and televisions and the world of the media seemed asleep to this other world we had to be in. Wasn't what I thought I signed up for."

"Do you want to say more about that?"

"We were applying lethal force and receiving lethal force. That was the only kind of energy you experience out there. The C17 medical evacuations showed me just how bad it got out there. On average we used to bring back five intensive care patients at a time. Some of the Intensive care beds had people who had lost not only their eyes but their jaws as well as limbs by IEDs. Sometimes it was bad."

"How bad?"

"I was walking around between the doctors and medics before we took off one afternoon. I was checking everything was snapped down or tied down and nothing was going to shift around during the flight. The sun was shining through the open door of the C17 and a slight wind was gently wafting my face and also the hair of this lad. It was really hot and I could smell the fumes from the engines. His hair was just like mine... same colour... same style... wafting in the wind. He hadn't died when he was blown up. So he wasn't on the list of people killed in Afghanistan. He had lost both legs and his left arm. He was still breathing but now he was being ventilated on his way back to his parents who were waiting at Selly Oak Hospital in Birmingham. His parents would see him after the room was made nice and sit with him for a while, then give them permission for his life support to be switched off. I thought... I could be him... he could be me. It's a sense of deliberately not over identifying with that kind of stuff that toughens you up. You start to think... what kind of stuff could I get over then? How much do I have to accept is ok before I start to think I'm in the wrong place?

"Those were big questions Robby."

"The triple amputees were the worst. When I heard we had over forty people who were triple amputees, and some of them were blinded as well as losing all their genitals, I found it difficult to work out any reason to justify that. Everything is centred on avoiding IEDs. We were there to kill people and we were getting killed by them. Even when we were out there resting, lot of them spent it just shooting dogs with their hand guns for practice."

"How did you find shooting dogs?"

"It's obviously not officially encouraged. But they reckon it helps some people get used to shooting and killing live things. It's a kind of mild conditioning getting you used to using your weapon on things that move. They used to say it helps you get ready to kill someone if the need arises. I didn't get involved in that. Maybe if I did, I wouldn't have got into the mess I'm in now. I just couldn't think of a single reason to kill a dog that was just a dog. These dogs were never going to attack me because they were starving strays who were only hanging around for scraps of food. It was like a game for everyone. They were just having fun firing a gun at a living thing and seeing the reaction... the mess, the shaking of the limbs, the quivering of the body, the fear behind the dogs emptying of the bladder as it saw the final shot to the head was coming."

"Carry on."

"It was holding the weight of the gun, aiming, pulling the trigger and feeling the kick back, smelling the smoke and seeing the damage. Some people did it once and never again. Some people in the military out there who did it said they enjoyed it."

"How did that get to you?"

"They got off on it and that immediately made me realise two things about these people. First that I was with people whom I really had nothing in common with and second, I realised that I didn't like any of them. They were into power by force. They could only relate by being involved with applying force against someone else's wishes. Even their friendships were about relating competitively. I realised that I'm more of a loner and a listener. I began to see people as transmitters or receivers. I've always been a quiet person and listened to what's going on in my head. I ignore a lot of what other people say because they're so full of their own stuff."

"Can you tell me about the incident in Afghanistan?"

"Yes... yes. I used to practice with a piece of wood, a stone or an old tennis ball out there. I knew that I had to keep my eye in, so I fired a few rounds every week or so. People firing guns was totally normal and it was going on all the time during the day. God it was hot out there... over fifty five degrees centigrade in the summer. I was based at Brize Norton or BZN as it's known. I was with 99 squadron. Service number 31627914. It's like another name. You can never ever forget it." Robby was perspiring.

"Do carry on."

"It had been a routine flight to Camp Bastion. We landed on time after delivering a helicopter with its spares and had to turn the plane around quickly to collect the next one. But when it came to parking up, the computer showed a fault with one of the engines. This meant at least an extra day or two in Camp Bastion. It was a small setback and inconvenient so we just tried to work out how to pass the time. We were invited by some aircraft engineers to go and look at the site of a crashed Hercules, so we went." There was a pause as the images came alive and flickered inside Robby's head. He fell silent as if watching a movie and stared straight ahead.

"It's safe here. It's all in the past and it's alright to talk about it. What is said here stays here. Tell me more," Anita said calmly. But more little beads of sweat appeared on Robby's brow.

"Do you mind if I have a breather?"

"Let's stop for a while and when you feel ready to talk you carry on. Have a rest. Sit back in the chair and close your eyes." Robby lay back in his chair and closed his eyes for two minutes. Then he was wide awake again.

"I did some drawing of the incident a few weeks back. I was trying to work through this stuff. I wrote some things down as well. I've got them all here." He seemed calmer as he pulled out a large crinkled brown envelope from his small rucksack.

"Can I see them?"

"Yeah, I would rather show you some stuff than tell you." He knelt on the floor and spread all of pictures out. "I wrote some things down about it as well... when the memories got too vivid."

"These are the beginning of the work you started and the work we're going to do. We're going to work through this. The pictures, the words and the images inside you. We are not just going to bring them up. We are going to process them. Is that all alright?"

"Yeah. I just have to take it slow."

"We only work at your speed." Anita knelt down and looked at the pictures and moved them around on the floor. "These look like sentences or sequences in an ambush Robby. Is that what happened?" She said as she stayed kneeling on the floor and moving the drawings around. Robby could tell from Anita putting the pictures in the right order that she understood the series of drawings he had produced.

"Yes... that's basically what happened." He was breathing faster and sweating and now looked unnerved.

"These are very powerful images Robby. Can you talk me through each one of them please?"

"Yes." Robby picked one picture and pointed to the centre of it. "In the first one, we were on our way back to the base, when there was a large bang. At first I thought someone had taken a shot at us as we swerved and so we all automatically loosened our weapons. The two engineers joked as they always do and they bet us air crew two rounds of drinks that we couldn't change the tyre in five minutes. In the RAF you just have to rise to the challenge of being called wimps by these guys. They knew we didn't drink and would be even more miffed at having to buy them rounds of drinks so we were determined to win the bet." Robby gave a big gulp as if to swallow.

"Then what happened?"

"The driver pulled over more into the side of the road to get out of the way of any traffic. When we got out we saw we had a flat back tyre. It looked so easy even though it was baking hot and very dusty. That day it was summer and it was fifty five degrees. The other two crew members, Mike and Glen were at the rear of the Land Rover taking off the flat tyre whilst I was undoing the wing nuts which held one of the spares on the side. There were two other spares on the roof. We were excited because we wanted to win the bet. As I undid the wing nuts I saw a line of small two inch long bits of metal on the dusty road. It didn't click at first because it was so hot you could only just about think about very basic things... " Robby stopped to take a big breath.

"What was that silver line across the road Robby?"

"Seconds after I saw the line of nails, I realised that they had deliberately trapped us with a simple puncture, I realised we were all in a trap but there was no time to even say the word trap. I wanted to shout out 'Trap!' But I saw this pretty young girl coming towards me." Robby held his breath for several seconds then blurted out, "I sensed something was going to go really bad because everything slowed down."

"Take this very slowly."

"Then she looked at me and smiled... well it was more of a serene smile. She had a look of profound peace and happiness. What disarmed me for a moment was that she was so relaxed, happy, peaceful and... well smiling. I saw that she was trying to do something with her hands." Robby's breathing was speeding up. "She was pulling the pin out of a grenade in her left hand; just like it was a toy. There was no worry on her face or any sense of urgency for her. But for me... she was going to kill me." Robby's eyes were wide open with fear.

"Slow down Robby."

"Despite the heat I tried to work out what was happening because I hadn't come across children being used as suicide bombers. It was as if it wasn't real because it was never done. Women yes, but not children. Somehow we'd been spotted and we were now being ambushed by a suicide bomber who looked about seven or eight years old. She was only a child for heaven's sake, but she was going to kill us. I was taught that things like this are never an accident and so I knew there was a whole lot more I was fronting up against."

"What happened next?"

"I tried to think quickly. If that grenade came close to us it would take us out. But it all looked wrong. She was a kid. A kid in a bright pink child's dress. It was slowing me down. This wasn't unreal and it was fair because it was war. I'd always known in the Iran Iraq war that rows of children had been used to run through fields to clear them of mines, so I knew that what I was seeing was real. They had just altered their tactics. The fact that someone like me would have to think through the fact that this child was not just a child but something lethal was a new tactic designed to slow me down to give the child the edge, to give her more time and ensure her success. Being a child and wearing children's clothes was like the enemy having an extra layer or armour or a totally new devastating weapon."

"What did you do?"

"I acted according to my training which was to preserve my life but it was really hard. I really struggled with it because I knew the life of this child would be gone. I thought I should shout at her but I had no voice. Then I knew I could only stop her by shooting her... I shot her... but it didn't stop her. The bullet went through the upper part of the right side of her chest. I thought that would have done it. I thought as she was so small it would have killed her instantly. I can't remember hearing the bang but I felt the kickback and smelt the smoke."

"What were you thinking?"

"At first, I couldn't think straight because of what I saw. I expected her to wince and scream in pain after the bullet hit her, but she didn't seem to feel pain. I saw her move backwards with the impact but she didn't stop. She started coming towards me again. There was something very strange. It's a bit difficult to put into words but I can still see it."

"If it didn't seem like she was reacting like you expected, what did it seem like was going on?"

"I could sense that there was an air of perfection in what was happening. It was if it had been rehearsed by us for a very long time and now... in these few seconds this was our moment... our moment of perfection. Perfect action."

"What happened?"

"The second bullet got her in the middle of her abdomen. The damage to her spine by the bullet had made her buckle her knees. I thought she had totally given up trying to throw the grenade. I was wrong. She was still smiling when she raised her arm, her hand, with the grenade to lunge forward to me. The grenade was going to be coming my way. I had to shoot her a third time. The last bullet hit her in the middle of her chest and seemed like a punch which lifted off the ground upwards and backwards and then onto the gritty road, where she landed with a thud in a cloud of dust. I was waiting for the grenade to go off but I couldn't see it. After a couple of seconds there was a sudden noise muffled by her body as the grenade cut her in two, leaving a hole where her stomach used to be."

"What were you feeling?"

"My feelings were numb for a moment. Then I think I was in shock. I remember I could smell the smoke from the bullets. My hand felt the wetness of her blood all over my face and I remember the salty taste of bits of her body tissue in my mouth. It was the salty taste of her blood in my mouth." Robby paused as he put his head in his hands, then he looked Anita in the eye and continued. "I felt disgusted with myself. I couldn't believe what I'd just done. I was spitting out bits of her flesh. I was splattered in parts of her body. I felt I wanted to be sick but I was so dry. The whole thing was so disgusting and repulsive. That was until I saw her blink and her right arm moved. She wasn't dead. I instantly took two steps and knelt over her. This was against all my training because she could have had a second device or there could have been a sniper aimed at me."

"How did you feel?"

"I felt for her, because like me she wasn't just a soldier. We were two people but she was really only just a child. How could she know what a soldier is? Her abdomen was gone and her pelvis and legs lay there intact, looking strangely separated from her torso. I put my gun down. She was looking at me with exactly the same look she had before I shot her. I stroked her forehead. Her right hand took hold of my left wrist and she squeezed it hard. She kept on looking at me. Then her eyes seemed to stop focusing and I sensed she was going but I kept on holding her hand until her grip had gone. Her hand was curled around my wrist."

"So you held her hand for her and comforted her whilst she died."

"She was only a child."

"What else was happening? What about the other crew?"

"I was in a daze for a while. Mike and Glen looked at me and couldn't believe what had just happened. They couldn't understand what I did. They could see the girl but I was between them and the girl so they couldn't see the grenade. They had drawn their weapons but they saw I was in control. We all had bits of her body tissue on our clothes and in our hair. But me the most. We slowly picked them off and wiped the stained areas."

"And then?"

"We were all silent. No one said anything. We all knew why. When the smoke and dust settled Mike radioed in to the base to report the incident. We kept our eyes wide open and our guns cocked because we all thought this might be a large ambush and we might not get out of there alive. But there didn't seem to be anyone else around who seemed bothered by what had happened. However after Mike and Glenn got the tyre changed, they said it had nails in it and it had also been shot with a high velocity rifle bullet. We realised they had stopped us precisely where they'd wanted to. They were very thorough as they'd used nails and a bullet. But the main thing is they didn't get us. We won and they lost their child. We got out of there as soon as the tyre was changed. We didn't wait for a team to arrive, because we were sure the whole thing was being very carefully monitored."

"And is that the whole story?"

"Yes, everything."

"It's a mess but we can clear every single last piece of it up."

"I hope so because I wouldn't want to have to have any more flashbacks or nightmares."

"Right then. I believe you are ready so let's start to move on. What image represents the worst aspect of that incident Robby?"

"The pink socks, the pink dress, the pink and white trainers. Every time I see pink, anything pink, it brings her small feet back to me and the tiny size of her... and then the rest of the scene. The carnage... she was a young child. How could anyone send a child in to do that? Why would you send a child to throw a bomb against well trained soldiers when they're just going to get killed? Don't they love their children and want them to just be children before they grow up to be adults. But then I suppose we do the same."

"What else gets to you about the scene?"

"Just her coming towards me smiling. I was soaked in her blood; all over my face and my shirt. It was also very dusty and I could smell the smoke from the bullets I'd fired. Her blood was all over my face. I could taste the salt in her blood. I can't stand getting my face wet, especially the face. Then holding her hand as she went. And that look... there's something in that look." He was sweating again.

"Ok Robby, stay right here in this room. Often it's the physical things like smells, tastes, sounds and sensations on your body that can bring back flashbacks. Smell and taste are really basic senses which can be the most powerful triggers." Robby was shocked to hear this.

"That's me. Smelling the smoke, feeling a wet face and the taste of salt from her blood."

"Right, now come back here to this room. Tell me what else has happened to you since that day."

"Gradually I've slept less and less because of the dreams and the nightmares. I'm very jumpy with people, especially with noises. Cars backfiring take me back to Helmand. Rain on my face takes me back to Helmand. Seeing children takes me back to Helmand. Everything pink takes me back there. It's like being sucked in by a black hole. I had no choice but to end it to stop the guilt of killing that child. Even the rational thought she was going to kill us does nothing for my guilt. I could have, I should of, I would of." Robby clenched his fists on his knees in frustration.

"These are powerful expressions which all describe intense feeling of guilt... could'a, would'a should'a."

"I hadn't felt guilty before. It's the worst thing to end up feeling. I tried to avoid anything which would trigger these flashbacks. I tried to tell the doctor at Lyneham and I even saw another doctor when I was visiting Kinloss but I think they thought I was trying to get time off. I think they thought I was a bit soft and not tough enough. The tall overweight blond doctor at Lyneham told me to 'man up.' The short doctor at Kinloss asked me how much coffee I drank. She was already writing a prescription as she took a call about her car's MOT before I could even answer her. They both thought I just had a sleep problem due to bad dreams, but neither of them wanted to listen to me to hear what the dreams were about. I was out of there both times in less than ten minutes with some sleeping tablets called Zopiclone. I got out of the RAF but it didn't get any better. For me the world was now a very different place."

"How did you see the world as different?"

"It wasn't the place I'd left. Wanted to be alone. Needed to be quiet. I trusted nature but was frightened of things in the middle of a city. The world or the way I saw it was just a frightening place. I was dangerous... I knew because I was running on different fuel. I needed to be alone. I couldn't be with civilians."

"A change in your world view is common. In German there is a term for this, but there is no single English word which is equivalent. It's called 'Weltanschauung.' It means how you see the world, your world view. Some people who witness terrible things in war go in search of solitude. That's why after the Vietnam War, so many American ex-service men moved up to Alaska. Just to be alone, to be safe and not to be a danger to other people."

"Got it."

"Where did you go to?" Anita asked.

"I went to where I thought there'd be less people. I went to Norfolk to see an old friend from the RAF who'd been a loadie. She told me to get help. But I thought I had already tried.

When her dad died she left the RAF and moved into the family farm. I liked the peace of the Norfolk countryside. I wanted to be outside, in touch with nature and it was hot so I lived in a tent for six months. Most days I'd go into Norwich early to avoid people. I used to go to a centre for the homeless. The woman there understood and let me just be."

"And how were you inside?"

"Even alone, the guilt didn't go. It escalated and I started to enter the black hole before I went to this caravan site in Kessingland. I tried to work through what was happening by recording it on my own in the drawings and what I wrote down. I thought I'd get better but I hardly slept because of a night mare which I kept on having. During the day I was really jumpy in case I had a flashback. I was exhausted and out of energy so I ran on adrenaline from fear of having a flashback or that nightmare. Finally I realised I had no hope of getting rid of the guilt. The look from that girl was one of perfect peace. It was too powerful and it was a hopeless situation. I saw I could only help myself out of it by ending it. It was a relief to know that there was an end to it. I had some control back. It seems odd but the relief made me happier and gave me the energy to actually get on and do it. I felt so much better knowing it was going to be over soon."

"It often happens that feeling a little better actually gives you the energy to commit suicide."

"It was all I needed."

"What are your dreams like?"

"Just have the one. I call it the Corridor Dream. It draws me into it like a moth is drawn to a candle which is going to destroy it. It seduces me but it is lethal."

"What's it like?"

"It's like being sucked into a hole."

"Can you describe it?"

"I'm walking down a white clinical corridor with several doors to each side which I can't open. I've tried pulling them, pushing them and even kicking them but they don't move at all."

"Why?"

"I wasn't sure at first. These doors have signs on them. At first I couldn't read the writing."

"It is unusual to read writing in dreams unless they are very significant."

"Well I've been having this dream every twenty minutes or so and slowly the writing has become clearer on each door. For some time I could see blurred writing with no clear edges. Then the signs became clearer each time I have the dream. The writing is bold and each door is different as I walk down the corridor I can now see each one. FRIENDS, on the first door then FAMILY on the next. On the opposite side of the corridor there is WIFE on the first door then CHILDREN on the next. This is followed by HOLIDAYS then WORK and finally

PENSION. On the other side of the corridor are PROSPECTS then FUN and finally THE FUTURE. I slowly realise I can't go in any of these because of what I've done. I'm not allowed in. It's massive guilt. It's easier to carry on walking down the corridor. There are no more doors on the sides. I'm always drawn towards the much larger set of double doors which slowly creak open for me at the end of the corridor."

"What is it about this door?"

"The door at the end seems to lure me more. But I didn't know why until the morning I decided to go to the New Forest."

"Is there a sign on that door?"

"Yes. I avoided looking at it for so long. I looked at it the day I came to the New Forest. It says... SUICIDE. I tried to stay awake to avoid that dream for so long. Staying awake's got me so exhausted.

"I see... " said Anita. "This is a dream which is usually a prelude to a completed suicide or the failure of a really determined attempt where something went wrong." She was quiet for a few moments. It's lunch time and we both need a break Robby. I'll see you back here an hour."

Stealth notes: Entry 4107. Here I go again, getting out my own thoughts and feelings about a client. This never seems to end but it must. I mean all the damage done to the brains of these people. And vicariously to me. The damage from IEDs or seeing your mates getting blown up is always psychologically messy. But Robby is one of the most damaged people I've come across. He comes top of my 'A' classification of survivors. He not only had poor attachment to his family but he was primed to get PTSD by all those repatriations at Lyneham. I've got to get this out so here it is. I wouldn't like to be at a single one of those repatriations, let alone when there are three or four bodies. It would get at me too much. I wouldn't like to have the death of that girl on my hands. Not even when it was deliberate and absolutely necessary. I'm not sure how I could live with that and that is going to be a problem which Robby will have to look at.

Where has he got his strength from to keep on going for so long? He's been having all this stuff going around in his head for over a year.

He's got incredible psychological stamina. In twenty years of working in trauma, I've never come across anyone with so much stamina. Then he snapped with that one revelation in that dream. That dream is so rare. I've never come across anyone with it before, but I have heard it described by an American military psychologist in the old days before EMDR. He had come across two cases but they both ended up being completed suicides.

Robby's been through a huge fight with this dream. He kept it at bay for a long time by not reading the writing on the doors. It was showing him that what he had done was going to kill him if he didn't act by getting help. But he had sought help before which failed. This along with the pain from the flashbacks made him take the dream at face value and follow it through. He is so very lucky, I can hardly believe it.

He identified all the targets we have to work on. The easy ones are getting his face wet, the taste of salt from her blood and his sweat, the smell of smoke and children's clothing. The difficult one is going to be his guilt. That is the tough one which will take a lot of work from me. That area is where I have to give the most of myself because guilt is never the same. It is such a complex feeling to work on and most of the traumas he has been through are associated with some guilt. That is one area which takes the most out of me and always lets me know my time in this job is limited. Every time I see someone it always takes a little piece of me. I don't want to end up burnt out just because this is the only job I can do. I've got the opportunity at any time to leave. If I ever decide to quit, my long service entitles me to only have to give a months' notice.

Although he was angry for a while, it only reflected how damaged he is. The good thing is that because he is so damaged, he will see a colossal difference in himself very rapidly. His personality is intact and he writes songs and he can draw which will help him gather his own inner tools together to self heal. He repeatedly smiled at the horse and so he has humour and insight which will be hidden strengths later when he needs them.

His main problem when he leaves here is going to be forgiveness. I can't work on that, only he can. In terms of forgiveness, this is the most difficult case I have ever come across. It's not my job. It's a spiritual problem and he'll probably need some help. But not many religious people will be able to help him with this because this is a difficult set of circumstances.

Robby represents lots of things to me. First, I like him. He is a kind person and is he's not really like a soldier. Second, I'm very aware of my limited time in this work and on this planet and I don't want to waste any of it. I've been in such a negative environment with my research, my colleagues and by patients; I know my time is nearly done. Robby being one of the most severely damaged people I've worked with tells me I've got no more to do, no more to see. I've done it. So he represents a closing down for me. Will I be brave enough to put a date on and sign my letter of resignation, which I wrote six months ago? Just maybe working with Robby might make me do it. I've got to get him right first. Then maybe my self.

+++CHAPTER 4.

"I was disappointed and... well surprised the GPs at Kinloss and Lyneham didn't know what was going on with me."

"I'm not surprised that the RAF doctors simply gave you sleeping tablets for what was a serious psychological problem and didn't ask you to come back to be reviewed. It was ok to have been given those tablets in hospital so that you slept with all the noise but they were right to stop them a few days ago."

"How come you're not surprised about the RAF doctors?"

"Ok, let me explain some of the psychology behind military thinking and then you should understand what happened to you. I know that occasionally there are some of the forces GPs who aren't that concerned about their patient's welfare, only about their own welfare and the patient's commanding officer. But even the good ones are hampered by the condition you've got. You see one of the hallmark symptoms of traumatic stress, which is what you've got, is avoidance. If you've been traumatised, you do everything to try and avoid re-experiencing the memories which come in the form of flashbacks and nightmares. You especially avoid bringing up the memories and that involves avoiding talking about them with doctors and therapists. It is a difficult paradox even for doctors to understand. You want help with your psychological symptoms which are the anxiety symptoms, but you don't want to openly talk about the images behind them. So you are blocked by your anxiety and the doctor is disabled by not being given all the information. Do you follow that?"

"Yes."

"Then let me explain in more detail so you understand what exactly happened to you. There are of course the obvious changes in someone's behaviour after a traumatic incident, like shock and being tearful, but there are two classic presentations in the Forces. 'Crash and burn' and 'slow burn.' The crash and burners are usually less well educated, have a lower rank, have poorer coping skills and present rapidly with behaviour which is out of character, discipline problems, drinking, extreme violence and self harm. The slow burners are usually more educated, have a higher rank and have much better coping skills but eventually their coping skills are overcome. They present for help much later. It can be a year or even years before someone like you comes to see me for help. These are the ones who usually suffer the most because of the length of time they take to slowly burn up all their coping strategies. In the Army, they often present just before they are about to be deployed on another tour."

"It was slow and I did burn."

"Yes, I'm afraid so. The crash and burners are easy to spot because of their bad behaviour but not the slow burners. Some of the crash and burners get involved in fights with civilians and get discharged because of violence or drunk driving charges. Others get caught with drugs in their urine on compulsory drug testing days and they get discharged too. Lots of people with symptoms which are typical of traumatic stress get discharged because of them and don't receive the help that the military promised them when they joined. It's unfair, counter-productive and results in ten percent of homeless people being ex-Forces and ten percent of prison inmates being ex-Forces.

Some people take drugs to sedate their traumatic images and random drug testing of their urine shows this up and they are usually pretty much immediately dishonourably discharged. It's exactly these kinds of people who are taking drugs because of being traumatised who the military should be keeping on and treating.

Some day this will have to change. Their behaviour results from their experiences in the military and they should receive help from the military to get them fit to return to society. Instead they are just dumped back in society because the military has damaged them and their behaviour has changed. They should be repaired and restored to normal functioning first."

"What about the slow burners like me?"

"Many people in the Forces who have been traumatised are slow burners and discharge themselves like you did. Then they drift, many just getting worse until they can't cope with the intrusive memories any more. Most turn to alcohol and a few to alcohol and drugs. Some become homeless and others end up in jail. But there are also those who battle on like you."

"I thought they didn't understand me."

"GPs who join the military are frequently over-institutionalised. They are concerned with making sure as many people as possible are deployable to theatre. Some, but I'm not saying all, have the military and your Unit as their primary concern. The patient should always be their primary concern. In the NHS, targets and budgets have done the same thing and the patient's experiences are frequently not always the most important consideration and priority of the doctor."

"People like me. Have you seen other people like me ignored? What I mean is am I just a one off?"

"No you're not. And oh yes, I've had seen so many people who've been treated like you Robby where their GPs and Padres in the forces hadn't referred them with symptoms of traumatic stress. One reason is that people like you won't openly talk about what's going on in your head is because of the avoidance issue. You won't mention it to anyone because it might bring up the bad memories with the terrifying flashbacks and nightmares. That is called avoidance. You said it yourself when you said you only mentioned the bad sleep to the doctors. You didn't mention the nightmares."

"I see that now."

"But it is also the Forces fault. There is a very tough upper lip culture in the Forces. Think about the British military's expectations of you coping. They use the term 'soldier on' or as I said to you just a minute ago, you just 'battled on.' These terms 'soldier on' and 'battle on' describe the expectation of you to carry on no matter what because of your training. The military teaches you and highly conditions you to completely accept three things. These are that the spirit which inspires you to fight depends on a high degree of commitment, self sacrifice and mutual trust. The military believes these three maintain morale. You were heavily conditioned to believe that you might have to sacrifice your life for the overall military goal rather than your personal goal. The way you thought, behaved, lived and got on with everyone in the military every day was centred on these three beliefs."

"That's totally how you are trained."

"These beliefs are based on very tough psychological conditioning by the military and are not necessarily shared by people in civilian life, where they often don't trust each other and their aim can be to help themselves and be totally selfish. The people in Chain of Command in the military get you to do what they won't do because they use you in ways which you have agreed to be used. You know that."

"I know. You take the Queen's Shilling and all that."

"Things are changing Robby but the military moves very slowly. For example, there should be a much more hands on vigorous and continuous screening of all people coming back from deployment which should cover not just the 'crash and burners' but also the slow burners. But it's not happening."

"I know. I would have felt immediately stigmatised and labelled as being weak or having a fault if they knew what was going on with me."

"They have a way of practically enforcing that. Any of the three British Forces would have downgraded you which would have completely changed how they and everyone saw you. The Forces medical PULHHEEMS system grades you on a 2-7 for general operational fitness on the P which determines whether or not you are deployable. The U is upper limb grading. The L is lower limb grading. H is hearing grading. The two Es are the grading for your eyes. The M is mental capacity and indicates a person's ability to learn army skills and duties. S is emotional stability and grades a person's ability to withstand the psychological stress of military life, especially operations. Every military person hates the stigma of being downgraded because you are then numbered and labelled as if not fit for purpose; that is non-deployable. It's the same with the NYPD if you have any mental condition. They take your badge and weapon and every cop hates that."

"It's always there, right from basic training and entry medical exam. Our bodies and minds are measured up like a suit of armour. I always came out with the top score of P2 U2 L2 H1 H1 E1 E1 M2 S2. I did swimming, Tai Chi and running. I thought I should know how to fight with discipline and control but also needed to know how to run away and swim away if necessary, I was as fit as any athlete. I'm sure you know that everyone fights in the military as a rehearsal for deployment. That's what we did. And in all the fights I had, I always came out on top. They didn't pick anything up on my discharge medical but in reality I was probably P8 which means I was non deployable, mentally incapable and emotionally totally unstable and only fit for discharge."

"But then there is also the issue of the incident itself which you should know about. You may not want to hear this but I think you really do need to hear it because it might help you. The RAF would have seen you as a true hero for showing bravery in killing a suicide bomber. Under extreme stress, you calmly got out your weapon, loaded it, aimed it and repeatedly fired it, therefore removing the threat to the lives of other men. You managed fear perfectly in a high risk situation. You overcame fear despite the risk and that is true courage which is the highest level of behaviour possible in the military. They would usually have got a lot of promotion in the media for themselves by awarding the highest medals to you for your bravery because you demonstrated real courage. The big problem is that the public would have had a taboo about it being a small young girl, and British Forces couldn't be seen encouraging taboo behaviour. It would be as bad as admitting that Britain tortures people by getting other nations like America to torture people on their behalf. The military needs the public's support and their money."

"I totally understand that."

"The fact is that you were incredibly courageous in your management of fear, which is what bravery is. Bravery is overcoming the terrible thing that you see in front of you which you have to rationally decide on and act on. You have to choose it. It's never automatic. You were the bravest of the brave in shooting that small girl because there's nothing harder to do than that. For the same taboo reason that the military couldn't award you a medal, they were also reluctant to talk about the incident, amongst themselves and with you. You getting help was therefore made much more difficult just because it was a child. You are different because you faced it head on and you didn't turn to alcohol or drugs. You have trusted something of your inner self."

"Yeah and I'm still paying for it." Robby said despondently.

"I know you must feel that the military didn't help you. As I've said they are getting better at the caring side of their job. A military doctor always has a duty and obligation to the military which at some time can be at odds with their duty to you as a patient. The blunt truth is that with all authority you always have to believe that they don't have your personal interests at heart because they are always concerned with other bigger issues. Their issues. It's the same deal as your training. You were heavily conditioned to believe that you might have to sacrifice your life for the overall military goal rather than your personal goal. The same principle applies to whether you sacrifice and suffer in battle or sacrifice and suffer by being passed over. There is a saying in the military that loyalty is a one way street."

"I know. When I look back, I can see how the military are clever. It looks like they've got your welfare at heart."

"In civilian life large corporations do the same thing. The directors instruct mangers to make people redundant and pay them off, so it all looks as if they care, but there's no follow up with a long term care plan. So you're made to think and feel as if you are at fault as you endure the hardships of having no work whilst the directors retire to their yachts and winter holidays. Command and corporate directors want to retain their power and they often do it by inducing fear in others. The military use fear in the media to promote public support for fighting in wars and they promote respect for heroes. Corporate directors use fear to incentivise investors in persuading them they will not lose their money but will make money. They get their medals or their money as long as there's no taboo. So they are very selective about what they do and who they choose as public heroes. They are very secretive and are always backed up by lawyers."

"Ruling by fear is a childish way of controlling and bullying. I've seen it everywhere in the military. It's not ruling by real respect."

"Yes you are right. I need to make sure you understand what went on at other levels. I want to show you how it wasn't your fault. On the one hand the military want to ensure that everyone is fit to be deployed and so they encourage you to 'soldier on' and 'battle on' through tough times. But this message of 'soldiering on' which you're conditioned to follow can prevent you from presenting with psychological problems which you acquired during deployment. This together with the avoidant behaviour that comes with traumatic stress drastically reduced your chances of getting psychological help. Add in the military's taboo about killing the child with the grenade in your case and you had very little chance of getting help."

"I think I understand now just how I was passed over by the doctors at Lyneham and Kinloss. Is there anyone else from the military having treatment here?"

"I've got twenty one patients here right now in The Refuge. Two are currently serving with the military. Five civilians and the fourteen are ex-military. Two of the ex military had their symptoms ignored by both NHS GPs and GPs in the military until they'd become suicidal. Twelve were referred by their military doctors and saw a mental health practitioner."

"Yeah. So how come they landed up here seeing a mental health person like you?"

"I don't want to look like I'm repeating myself but remember, with all the criticism about military doctors that the military training is still to 'soldier on' and not to talk about it. With traumatic memories there is also massive avoidance because bringing up the memories causes a lot of anxiety, so people like you avoid treatment. There is another pressure that going to the doctor will result in you being downgraded which stops people like you getting help. You don't want to be downgraded and the doctor doesn't want to have to down grade you.

Another reason why soldiers avoid getting help is that they think they will look weak. This is a lethal combination which is frequently deadly. The combination of military training to 'man up' with the massive avoidance of traumatic memories has resulted in more suicides in soldiers returning after the Falklands and the first Gulf War than the number of actual deaths in both wars."

"I still don't get how they ended up here if they saw mental health workers whilst serving."

"Simple. The biggest problem is that the soldiers here who have already been seen by a mental health practitioner felt uncomfortable with the treatment. The avoidance of traumatic memories made them not turn up for appointments. When you miss two appointments in the military, you're sent a letter saying you're discharged. That's it. You can slip through the net and don't get seen again. They should be personally followed up if they miss that second appointment for a longer period of time. At the moment they're treated by the routine admin machinery which just discharges them. It's the same with all mental health appointments. Two strikes and you're out."

"I didn't know so many were in a place like this. I thought it was all NHS patients here." Robby sat back in his chair feeling completely relaxed in Anita's room.

"Except for the two still serving, the rest are all now NHS patients. You must know that you're a very lucky man Robby. I know you were unfortunate to be treated that way by the doctors at Lyneham and Kinloss but I think you can understand now why it's so common to ignore psychological symptoms in the military. It's part of their tough culture. There needs to be continual very long term monitoring of everyone who returns after being deployed who discharges themselves shortly after returning... like you Robby. Otherwise this problem will just carry on. The problem is that the British military has not got that far in practice yet, but it's slowly getting there."

"I must be lucky then?"

"For the branch on that tree to have broken, my only comment it that either luck was seriously on your side or you have a guardian angel looking after you."

"Yeah, I was lucky when that branch broke. I'm glad it did. But at the time I felt like I'd failed and cornered myself into a choiceless situation. When I came to, I was shocked by two things. The first thing I remember is that my face was wet. When I opened my eyes I could see why, because a dog was licking my face. A brown Springer Spaniel. The second thing was that I was in extreme pain but it wasn't just from the rope around my neck. It was my left leg. I remember raising my head and seeing the branch across my legs with the blue rope round it. I felt cheated. I passed out. When I came to again, the dog's owner was telling me to relax and said that he had called an ambulance to help get the branch off me and take me to hospital."

"Even the fact that the man was out there at that time of day was very lucky."

"I just feel so relieved about what you've told me about what's happened to me and just why the doctors and the military treated me the way they did. It all makes sense, whereas before I was just angry, and I see why."

"I'm going to summarise and explain what has happened to you so that in the long term you can understand how you got here."

"Ok." Robby sat back with one arm across the back of his chair, the other on his knee and he listened to Anita carefully.

"Early on you had attachment problems with your family which probably made you more vulnerable to traumatic incidents. Your fear of blood started after the death of the cook in the Land Rover. Somehow you associated her death with yourself, in that it could have been you. You avoided the anxiety that was set up by changing from being a paramedic to a loadmaster.

Unfortunately you were involved in bringing bodies back to the UK which also made you more anxious.

Repatriating the dead was the biggest contributor to your reaction to shooting the girl. If you hadn't done so many repatriations you might not have had the reaction. And you might not be here. I don't know for certain."

"It was very heavy work. Not sure how it got to me but it did."

"There is condition which a group of us has called Post Repatriation Stress Disorder, PRSD, which we describe as an invisible bullet."

"Never heard of it. What's the bullet thing?"

"An invisible bullet is something that happens in your mind after an incident but unlike a metal bullet you don't register at first what it does to you. You don't see what it's doing to you at first. It's an incident. Like doing a repatriation or shooting the girl. It can take a long time to show itself."

"Yeah... know what you mean."

"We know that Post Repatriation Stress Disorder results from an invisible bullet, but it's different to Post Traumatic Stress Disorder PTSD which is also caused by an invisible bullet. There's a relationship between them because PRSD contributes to PTSD. But we don't know enough about them yet."

"Still haven't heard of it but... did I get it?"

"Yes. That's another reason why you are here."

"What do you mean?"

"The Armed Forces are aware of PRSD. They know about it because several of us have told them about it. I presented some cases to them. I suggested they do a proper survey to show who it affects. I already knew from the cases I presented who gets it. There is the repatriation group which moved from RAF Brize Norton to Lyneham and then back to Brize, which is voluntary and they have their own rather unusual and strange problems but it's the non volunteers who are most likely to get PRSD.

"How come?"

"Well people like you and other loadies, pilots and engineers who fly with the plane aren't volunteers for repatriations. You get no special training in it, along with the others like the movers. You all have to do it as part of the job, and of course the bugler and some pall bearers on the ground have to do it as part of their job. The volunteer repatriation team get to meet after each repatriation and they go away together for an away day every six months, but guys like yourself just have to carry on doing their jobs. No one counts how many they do. So there's no telling how many one person has done."

"Yeah, that's right. We just had to get on with it. So it's changed now then?"

"No. It's the same. I have suggested they survey all the non volunteers involved in repatriations in the RAF, Army and Navy to see the extent of the problem."

"So are people like me who did lots of repatriations still getting no special help?"

"Yes, but help will become available. They know about it now so they have to do something."

"Do you know what it does? I mean you said you've seen a lot of non volunteers. What happens?"

"Five years ago I became curious about it. It's not normal to have your work colleagues killed and for you to have to physically deal with the funeral. I started asking everyone I saw who had been involved and every one of them had been affected. Then I remembered seeing the almost daily funerals on the television for the four hundred and twelve fire fighters, police and medics who were killed during the 9/11 attacks in New York and I wondered how it affected them... how it accumulated."

"Must have been the same with the Black Death and the plague pits. There must have been waves of deaths."

"Just one repatriation can get to you or the effects of them can be accumulative. The main thing seems to be over-identification with the person or some of their belongings, just like you said with their cap, their belt, the coffin or the flag draped over their coffin. There is usually an anxious avoidance of meeting the relatives and of future ones. As you said and as I mentioned before, your world view changes. I've already seen how this can prime you to react badly to trauma and get full blown PTSD. But there may be problems in later life for those who don't get PTSD. From what we've seen, we think these people suffer more with depression, anxiety, higher alcohol intake, relationship and family problems. We think some may get Complex PTSD which is more difficult type to treat than simple PTSD.

"I still don't get why they don't do something."

"The military are having to deal with it each time a coffin lands at RAF Brize Norton. The Royal Wooton Basset repatriations made them much more acceptable to the public but the military don't seem ready to take that one further step just yet."

"Shouldn't the soldiers at least know?"

"I think the solders really know how it affects every single one of them."

"And me?"

"You're one of the first to be treated for this so you won't suffer from any of the consequences I mentioned. As I said, it's really important to know how and why you got this to understand how you react to similar things in the future. But let's get back to summarising what happened to you so you can see the bigger picture as we move on.

Bringing back the wounded with their injuries contributed to this as well as you knew it could easily have been you. There was a build up of witnessing the aftermath of traumatic incidents which conditioned you or primed you to react the way you did to the incident with the child with the grenade.

These things, identification with the death of the cook and bringing back the bodies and the injured set your brain into a more stressed and anxious state than usual, which stopped you processing the images of the girl with the grenade. These images are still raw and unprocessed by your brain so they continue to affect you.

The death of the cook and bringing back the bodies and the injured put you in a psychological place where you were vulnerable to being hit by an invisible bullet; the girl with the grenade. The girl got you and you nearly died from your injuries."

"Yeah, but it doesn't stop the things I see in my head."

"The images of the girl are behind your intrusive thoughts like the flashbacks and the corridor dream. Your thinking is set in a very anxious way and your vision of things has become a lot more negative. Your body has been exhausted by the lack of sleep due to the hyper-vigilance and nightmares. The memories have got stuck, frozen in time. As I said earlier they're still in their raw state and they seem like they're still happening. You've tried your best to avoid triggering these memories, but they are powerful images which have become stuck; like pictures frozen in time. What we need to do is move these memories on, to get these images processed like any other memory. Are you with me Robby?"

"Yeah it makes sense."

"Ok, I want to tell you what you can expect from the eye movement treatments called EMDR. The EMDR will get these memories processed just like ordinary memories. You'll still have the memories but they'll be much more like ordinary memories. The important thing is that there won't be any stress or anxiety attached to them when you remember those things. The terrible anxiety attached to them will disappear with the treatments. Also the memories won't be triggered anymore like they have been."

"I've got that."

"Are you ready to begin?"

"Ok."

"What would you regard as a safe place for you to return to when you feel threatened by your thoughts Robby?"

"Looking out from up where my aunt lives in Scotland. From the guest cottage just twenty yards down from her house. It's high up and you get a really good view of the trees and houses in the distance. It's very special."

"I want you to close your eyes and imagine yourself there? So close your eyes." Robby closed his eyes. "Imagine you're standing there outside your aunt's guest house. It's a warm sunny day and you can see a long way. You can see the trees and all the houses. Stay with what you can see."

"Can you tell me what it's like?" Robby closed his eyes and after a full minute he spoke.

"The grass pollen gets up my nose but I like the smell. It's warm and quiet and I can feel a very slight breeze on my face. I'm just there."

"Stay there for another minute and then I'll ask you to come back to this room. I want you to try slowing your breathing down so you are breathing with your diaphragm, so that just your tummy moves slowly in and out. Drop your shoulders and sit back in the chair." Robby did this perfectly. Another full minute passed Anita spoke again. "Ok Robby, you can open your eyes now."

"I feel ok."

"Now I want you to go back there and see how easy it is to access that safe place." Another full minute passed. "Robby you can now return to this room and open your eyes."

"Ok."

"If you feel uneasy or uncomfortable at any time during this session, or subsequent sessions, I want you to go back to your safe place. Alright?"

"Yes I've got that."

"At the beginning of every session we'll go to your safe place twice so you know it's easily accessible. Is that alright?"

"That's fine."

"I'll be checking on what you are experiencing and so I need to know what's going on in with the images you have. The images might change and sometimes they won't change. I want you to imagine the image of the young girl whom you told me about earlier. Bring up the most negative image of the incident and tell me what words describe the worst thing the image makes you think about yourself?"

"I feel disgusted with myself. I killed a child. I deserve to die."

"Which of those statements most accurately describes how you feel about yourself?"

"I deserve to die."

"When you bring up the incident what would you like to believe about yourself?"

"I deserve to live."

"Ok."

"On a scale of one to seven, if seven is the true and zero is false how do you rate how valid that statement, I deserve to live?"

"Zero."

"When you bring up the incident what feelings do you have about yourself?"

"I feel so guilty it's almost unbearable."

"On a scale of one to ten, if zero is no guilt and ten is the worst guilt imaginable, how would you rate how you feel?"

"Ten."

"I want you to keep your eyes open, hold the most negative image and tell me where you feel it in your body."

"In my stomach."

"What does your stomach feel like?"

"It feels knotted and tight almost in pain."

"I want to try some eye movements with you now." Anita moved her chair so it was to the side of Robby's chair, but still facing him. She was now three feet away from him and raised her right hand with her palm facing Robby. She closed her thumb and fingers apart from her index finger and middle finger which she now held in front of Robby's face at the distance of his knees. "Keep your head still and follow my fingers." Anita moved her two fingers across in a straight line roughly from one shoulder to the other but still above his knees. After twenty movements of her fingers in twenty seconds she stopped. "How was that?"

"It was fine. I didn't notice anything."

"It didn't strain your eyes?"

"No."

"Good. Now I want to do the same movements but this time bring up the worst image."

"Ok."

"I'll stop and ask you if any other images come into your mind and we'll then do the eye movements to that image. Ok?"

"Fine."

"Bring the image to your mind and be aware of what you are feeling in your stomach." Robby found the image with no difficulty. "Right, now just follow my fingers," Anita said. Robby followed her fingers from side to side and after twenty seconds she stopped. "Is what you see the same?"

"No. It's moved on and I can see her hand pulling the pin out."

"Ok let's EMDR that." Anita did another twenty seconds of eye movements. During the next half an hour Anita did fifteen more sets of eye movements with each successive image and then stopped.

"On a scale of one to ten if zero is no guilt and ten is the worst guilt imaginable how would you rate how you feel?"

"Six or seven."

"I want you to consider that statement, I deserve to live."

"Ok."

"On a scale of one to seven, if seven is the true and zero is false how do you rate how valid that statement, I deserve to live?"

"Two or three."

"Ok. Close your eyes and scan your body and tell me if you feel anything."

"No nothing."

"Good. We've made some progress but that's the end of the EMDR for today. How are you feeling?"

"I feel alright. It wasn't what I thought it would be like."

"What were you expecting?"

"I was expecting it to be emotionally painful but it wasn't."

"The processing work we've done today will usually continue after the session and you may notice new thoughts, memories dreams. You may have new insights. If you notice any of these, take a snapshot of it in your mind and log it down on a notebook which I'll give you in a moment. We'll do another session tomorrow and just take it slowly."

+++CHAPTER 5.

"Well Robby, we are at week five. How are you?"

"I've worked on all the images from the death of the cook at Lyneham, the Afghan incident to me jumping off the tree. I've done it. After seven sessions my rating of deserving to live was seven out of seven and I rated my feelings of guilt at zero to one out of ten. The fear and anxiety are gone. I sleep right through the night. There are no flashbacks."

"We're going to change direction today and move things on even more."

"Are we going to do any more EMDR?"

"No we're done with that tool, but it's always there if we need it."

"Ok."

"This is our last formal session Robby and I know you were aware that you knew that getting better would result in this. It's time for us to close this down and for you to carry on from where you are now. You no longer need me as a therapist. You have your own self back. From now on you need to just see me as an ordinary person like yourself, with ordinary every day practical problems, like money, transport, work, relationships problems, with kids and relatives. All that kind of stuff. I've done all I can for you."

"I hear exactly what you say. It makes me feel more normal. Thanks."

"You're welcome. However I must conclude this final formal bit of this session by saying you never had any psychological problems which stemmed from your past or from you. The terrors you experienced only came from the trauma that you were put through during your time with the military. What you've done along the way is try to heal this wound. You're not crazy or mad. You were forced in to a physical and psychological state which had little to do with you, but which were only the result of the forces of the world of different nations at that time. You've been in an increasingly extreme state of hyper-arousal because of the stuck unprocessed memories. You've really been stretched to the limits of existence by war but you've never been at fault or made the wrong choice."

"I hear that... so very loud and clear."

"I thought you would. Now tell me Robby, what are your plans when you leave here?"

"I've begun wondering about that."

"Any ideas?"

"I think I'd like to work away from aircraft. I'd rather work with plants or animals. I'd like to meet someone and have children. It's never meant so much to me since that girl in Afghanistan. Have you got children Anita?"

"I've got a seven year old daughter and a six year old son who go to the local school."

"Are you in a happy relationship?"

"Yes but only recently again. I was married but it didn't work out. He was obsessed with work. I met Steve six months after my divorce. We were both ready to move on."

"I think I understand about ending pain. Being free of it. It's that word again; freedom. Tatyana... I've remembered... that's the name of the woman in the café in Norwich. We were both looking for freedom from pain." Robby laughed. "You seem just as vulnerable, just like anyone else." Robby said.

"It's good to see you thinking normally and remembering normally. Me... I haven't got any special armour plating. People like me are probably more vulnerable because we're usually not dealing with happy people. I deal with a small area of expertise which is psychological trauma because I like the challenge. We, I mean I, have to deal with people who've had the worst done to them that humanity can do to them. The only thing I refuse to do is to fix people so that they can go back and be re-traumatised by war. I never encourage anyone to remount once they've fallen in that business. It would be an abuse of what I do. But the rest of my life is just like anyone else's. I've got the same problems as anyone."

"How badly does it affect you?"

"It gets to me like it would to anyone and I know that it's time to stop very soon. I know I could do another fifteen years, but I don't want to. It wears you down just like the sea erodes rock. When I started working, I worked out how much armour plating I had and I know now that maybe in five or ten years I too will begin to wear. I want to leave with my full thickness of armour. Some therapists go on too long just to have a job."

"I can see that. People go on too long in the military too."

"You're right. You can't stay forever working at the front line. It's better to let another person do this work. Besides, I've got other things to do which compensates for the work I do here. I've got a small holding with some chickens, pigs and three calves this year. I've got two fields of grass."

"Is that what you're going to do when you get out of here?"

"No. I think we might move after I've got used to not working."

"Seems you're an inmate almost like me but you came here voluntarily to do a job."

"True. We both came here to do things. You came here to do a job and through your own choice. If someone met us in a few years time they wouldn't be able to tell who the therapist was and who the patient was. You're already that well. Now tell me what's your actual plan for when you leave?"

"I'm hoping to head up to my aunt's house in Scotland. I heard last year that she's not been well. I was going to see her after I got back from the Afghan trip. I did a lot of thinking there before I joined the RAF. I'm hoping she will let me stay for a few weeks so I can sort out what I'm going to do for work... what I'm going to do with my life. I know she will be fine about it."

"Is she close?"

"Yes. She's like a mother to me. I remember having happy summers up there when I was a kid. She moved there from

Bristol when she got married. Her husband was in the Forces and after he left he became a crofter. Last year she took over the croft when he died. I feel I should've been in touch since, but everything got to me more than I thought it would."

"I'm sure she'll understand."

"There's one thing I want to ask you?"

"Yes of course."

"Am I likely to get any recurrences of what happened to me?"

"No. You should be fine. Once processed, those traumatic memories can't go backwards and get re-frozen. They can't re-attach themselves."

"Am I more vulnerable than other people who haven't been through this? I mean if I get involved in something horrible will it get to me more."

"Yes sudden traumatic events might get to you more, but not like this one. You are more vulnerable but also more sensitive to these things, so don't go putting yourself in harm's way. Obviously don't do things like being a security guard or work in the emergency services as a medic. Otherwise you are robust and have a lot of strength and good qualities to deal with life and be happy. You have seen that none of us have minds which are bullet proof from sudden trauma in our life. But as you go on with your life, remember that we accumulate more negative and positive things. The negative events can tend to take us over things like ill health, people dying, other losses and things like being victims of accidents and crime. The negative things tend to accumulate like lead or mercury do in our bodies do until they reach such high levels that they give us symptoms of poisoning. It's really important to try and have as many positive experiences as possible to outweigh the negative ones. This will protect you even more. Remember go for the gold. Remember your world view has changed. There is a chance that you might need some help with understanding this. If that happens let me know and I should be able to put you in touch with someone who works with that. Remember be a gold digger."

"No shit!" They both laughed.

"You know that you're really ready to go."

"I was hoping I might be."

"I've got a small thing for you. It's a talisman." Anita handed Robby an ordinary looking stone, only the size of his thumb nail with a piece of nylon around it encapsulating it like a basket."

"Thank you for all your help through this."

"You're welcome. This talisman is to remind you to always keep grounded no matter what happens in your head. If you need its help, walk around outside barefoot. It's only a stone but also a reminder of what the world is you are on."

"I'll keep it with me. Thanks."

"It might be an idea to stay a few more days until you are a little stronger on your leg. Just so you can really gather your strength."

+++CHAPTER 6.

Three days later Anita waited quietly in her room whilst Robby called for a taxi.

"All ready to go?"

"Yep. Booked the taxi."

"Where to?"

"I thought about going to see the tree with the broken branch in Hincheslea Wood but then I thought of just where I am now. I thought of you and how you've influenced my thinking so I'm going direct to Southampton Parkway station. I want be a gold digger, not a shit shoveller and avoid the tree because it would be a negative experience. I want to leave the past and keep moving on in the present. I feel positive and even though I've got a limp, I feel as if I've got a spring in my step."

"You look like a completely different person. You smile. You've got great eye contact now and you are open to discuss things instead of having conditioned rigid views."

"I feel like after having a bad tooth pulled by a dentist. I feel so different, so good. I got to say I'm sorry I was so angry when I first got here. I'd just lost control." He offered Anita his hand to shake but she put her arms around him instead.

"You're quite different from most I see. You'll be very happy."

"This is for you." He gave her an envelope which contained one page from his notebook. "It's a song, a few words about the Forces. Thanks for the finger waggling and getting me out of the mess I was in. Here's the book back."

"Thanks." Anita said. "Here's my card with my details. Call me if you need to chat. Off you go." Robby looked at her and smiled. Then he pulled the door closed.

Anita leant against the inside of her office door with her back. She felt like she had done many times before when someone had got better but this time there was something different. There was a cheerfulness about Robby which she had not experienced with any other patients. She read Robby's song.

I was only thirteen when they came to my school
I had no idea they were just looking for fools
I tried to see with wide open eyes
But what they wanted from me was heavily disguised.

The RAF, Army, Navy said they would pay
For all kinds of travel far far away
They promised me money, excitement and fun
All I had to do was simply carry a gun.

They could have had criminals, bullies or thugs
Not vulnerable children more interested in hugs
They promised us that they'd always be there
And what ever happened they'd really care.

When your last freedom's taken from you
That's when they tell you just what to do
I took orders but couldn't make requests
And my bullied mind never got any rest
Again and again, again and again.

Now when I think of what they got me to do
These people would force your children too
I was hit by a bullet that I couldn't see
It was memory of killing that impacted on me
Again and again, again and again.

Flashbacks by day, then nightmares in bed
I couldn't tell if they were real or just in my head
My innocence has gone but not the memories or pain
Of scenes of a war which was truly insane
Again and again, again and again.

On the crusade of the economy driven war
I soon realised these wars had all happened before
The deaths, the losses, keep on happening again
So the victories the medals are all just in vain
Again and again, again and again
If you fight for peace war will happen again
Without negotiation and tolerance
It'll happen again, again and again.

Political bunkers protect leaders from war
While innocent children are blown to the core
They give the orders to kill everyone
But won't speak the truth to anyone
Again and again, again and again
If you fight for peace war will happen again
Without negotiation and tolerance
It'll happen again, again and again.

Let girls just be girls and boys be boys
Let children be children and just give them toys
Stop our children standing on the front line
Use words not children now is the time
Again and again, again and again
If you fight for peace war will happen again
Without negotiation and tolerance
It'll happen again, again and again.

The Crusades Vietnam the World and Gulf wars
Northern Ireland Afghanistan what are we fighting for?
It's time now to stop blowing others a part
Not be frightened to listen to their heads and their hearts
Again and again, again and again
If you fight for peace war will happen again
Without negotiation and tolerance
It'll happen again and again.

Anita slowly put the song back in the envelope and put it in a cupboard with other letters, cards, and poems she had received since she had been there. The one from Robby made the pile fall over. She picked up all the cards letters and poems and put them on the chair the patients sat on. She stepped back and looked at the pile and smiled. She walked over to her desk where she sat down and thought about her work and her life.

Stealth notes: Entry 4108. Halleluiah! Well this is it then. It's all over. No more research, no more finger waggling, no more trauma, no more draining my own self. Time for me… yippee! My last client's parting song on a single piece of paper was the one that tipped over the pile. When I picked up the letters, cards and poems, I had a sudden realisation. The weight of this field of work has become too much. It's over. The scales have tipped over and I need to leave. Halleluiah! The weight of other people's problems always takes something from me as it should in this job if you do it right. But now I'm leaving. Halleluiah! Halleluiah! The pile toppling over. Robby's song was a sign of things to come if I don't leave when I'm young and can still do something else. Halleluiah! Halleluiah! Halleluiah! Now I can date the letter of resignation I wrote six months ago. I've got one month's notice and I'm away for the next two weeks at a conference and then on holiday for the next two. Halleluiah! Halleluiah! Halleluiah! I wish I had a chance to say thank you Robby. I would jump up and hug you again. Robby you were someone special. Unlike almost everyone I treat, you're not just on the repair path but on the growth path. You've got a look in your eyes; one that sees things other people can't see because they are too busy. But you Robby, you are ahead. I almost can't believe I'm off. I'm stealing away. Thanks Robby. I'm free…Yippee! Yeeha! Halleluiah!

+++CHAPTER 7.

As the taxi drove through Southampton, Robby knew he didn't want to live in a city again. He found things so fast and competitive. He asked the cab driver to pull over so he could look at the city for a moment. Nothing seemed to come to a standstill so that he could just sit still and look at the world. Robby asked the taxi driver to drop him early, so he could walk for five minutes to the rail station as he wanted to stretch and exercise the leg he had fractured.

At Euston he rang his aunt to see if he should get the overnight sleeper from Euston to Pitlochry.

"Is that you Robby?" The faint voice on the telephone asked.

"Hey Eleanor." Robby closed his passport which had her number in the back.

"Where are you?

"Euston."

"I haven't seen you for so long. Are you ok?"

"I'm sorry I couldn't come to Ian's funeral but... "

"It sounded like you were in a lot of trouble. About a year ago you stopped sending post cards and we started getting our letters returned from the RAF. They eventually wrote saying you'd taken an early discharge."

"I'm better."

"Somehow I knew you'd make it."

"Yes. Just."

"Do you want to come up and stay?"

"Yes."

"Can you get on the sleeper tonight?"

"Yes. I'll get a ticket."

"That's great. I'm really looking forward to seeing you. I've got a bit of a problem with my stomach, so I'll get Fearghas to collect you."

"Fearghas then."

"Yes he'll be there."

"Nothing serious with the stomach?"

"It'll come right."

"Thanks. Anything I can bring up."

"Just yourself."

"Ok then."

"I'll see you for breakfast."

"I'll be there."

Robby hung up and felt so relieved Eleanor sounded alright. He was thinking about the view from her cottage; his safe place.

The sleeper train from Euston slowly thundered north through the moonlit night and the windy early morning towards Scotland. The sleeper rocked like a cradle sending Robby from side to side. He felt positive. He always felt happy when he was at his aunt's house. She helped him straighten out his thinking and he felt he needed her voice on what had happened to him and what he should do next.

As the train took him north, Robby reflected on flights he had made in the C17 Globemaster and then his train journey from Suffolk to the New Forest. For the first time in years he felt secure with the rocking of the train and relief at being transported without tremendous effort and responsibility. He saw he was out of harm's way and felt safe enough to look back at where he had been in the last year.

Robby: Pocket Notebook Entry 1. If I don't keep a record of where I've been and where I am now, I think I might get badly lost again and I can't afford that. I'm not going there again. I'm going to keep this journal as my friend. If I get lost then at least I can look back at what I've written, see where I've been and hopefully see where I went wrong. Then I can correct my error and get back on course.

Maybe my aunt can show me what I should do next. She and Ian were right about me not joining the RAF but I was in such a rebellious mood. I wanted to get away from home and I did the opposite of what they said. I remember heated arguments with them and I knew they were always right. I was only a kid and what did I know then? I feel so embarrassed about how I used to argue with them both. They must have cared a lot about me not to have thrown me out. I wish I believed when they said what I was letting myself in for. I've learnt two things the hard way. How to make my own decisions and how to listen to another person.

Changing from being a paramedic and training up to be a loadmaster on the C17 seemed like it was the best thing to do then. I was trying to avoid the sight of blood but the change to a loadie put me right in the line of fire and it was me who ended up pulling the trigger and killing someone.

It was just after that fateful flight into Camp Bastion. The crew of three of us from the C17, Glen the pilot, Mike the co-pilot and me were invited by some aircraft engineers to look at the site of a crashed Hercules and we had almost a day to do it in the Landover. If I hadn't shot the small girl with the grenade, we could all have been killed. When I look at the bigger picture now, it seems like a murky dreamy past but when I look at it in any detail, the naked fear and aggression don't surface. They are two things I feel a huge sense of respect for.

It's only been a few months since I left the Forces, but I feel during that time I've been in some far off country. Afghanistan feels more than ten years ago to me. But it wasn't. My job was being in charge of the precious cargo on the C17's. Now the only cargo I'm responsible for tonight on this train is myself."

As he lay down on his bunk with its clean sheet and coarse blanket he continued to write.

Robby. Pocket Notebook Entry 2. I've been to hell and have somehow escaped. I feel relief that what happened to me in the last few years is over. Relieved being transported; relieved to be going to my aunts; relieved to be going back to the only place I've ever been where I've had no baggage. Only there was I was able to be a boy and feel childhood naivety and innocence. I'm now always acutely conscious that being in the military nearly destroyed me. They had given me no warning when they welcomed me in and no help when I wanted to leave. But now I'm feeling positive about seeing my aunt.

She really did try to warn me about the military. I now know just how stupid I was to rebel against her and my uncle. They gave me every logical reason not to join but I just had to rebel against them. It was the worst thing I could do in their eyes and so I did it. Did it prove a point? Yes but a bloody minded one. And it proves another one which is that they were right. Why do we have to have an adolescent rebellion to break free? Maybe just as cubs grow bigger, their parents frighten them into leaving by some measured fighting with them, otherwise they would stay around forever.

I really am much better. The terrifying nightmares, flashbacks and other intrusive thoughts have gone. I'm no longer extremely jumpy and I don't avoid certain people and certain things. I've got it off my back and can function normally without breaking out into sweats at the sight of children or their clothes or shoes. I don't get powerful palpitations. I'm not overwhelmed. I'm in control. I'm together. I'm coping well. I have a future. I'm calm. I'm free... but I'm not free.

Robby lay back on his bunk and the rocking of the train sent him into a brief sleep when he woke he still had his notebook in his hands...

Robby: Pocket Notebook Entry 3. I was doing my job and I was following my training. I found myself in a situation where I had to react. The result left me with awful memories which only got worse with time. Yes I looked for help and self help but I was left with only one way to end the pain. I tried to kill myself. I failed because the branch of the tree broke. I was lucky. My leg's good now and the most modern therapy has got rid of the barrage of horrible images and fear. I'm calm. Yes I'm calm. But in this calmness something large seems to be rising up. Part of me senses something else is coming. It's what comes after the but. I'm not free of that.

The but and what comes after it seems to be about a sense of restoring balance. I've got my life back but my life's out of balance. The balance hasn't yet been restored and I need to find out how to do that. I need an ordinary life. I need my life, a life back. When I look at my life, I don't have much apart from my life. I need a life about something, someone. Maybe that's what I'll find.

He stopped writing, closed the notebook looked straight ahead because now he wasn't afraid to look inwards. He felt thankful to Anita at the Refuge for all the help she had given him. But then a moment later, it was as if there was something else which he had to look for, something else he had to find in himself. He sat back on the bed and started to write again.

Robby: Pocket Notebook Entry 4. Forgive me...forgive me...forgive me. I owe something first. This is what's making me uncomfortable about having a calm balanced life. It's not calm and balanced. My integrity has been broken. What I've got is nothing apart from a very serious debt. I owe that girl. I have to make it up to her. To myself. Having a calm balanced life after doing something like that is a lie. It's always going to be there. If I address it, it might stop getting bigger. I need to put this right. There's something unfinished about myself and that incident. I feel obliged to feel blame because I did it. I shot a young girl. Even though she came at me with a grenade and was going to kill me, I am responsible for taking her life in her country. I would never have chosen to be there. I couldn't have escaped the time I owed the RAF who trained me. I'm not sorry because I would do it again. I am not sorry. I can't say sorry to her but forgive me...forgive me Little One, forgive me Little One...forgive me Little One.

The first thing the Forces did was to get me into debt with them. Then I was totally stuck with them. Their power over me was to make me feel like I owed them a huge debt. From that moment on I was trapped. They owned the underpants I wore, the socks and the boots. I ate their food and slept in their bed. I didn't have the money to buy myself out. They saw an animal easy to trap and that was me then. The me now is not angry at them. I am more annoyed with myself for being lured in without asking for full information about the risks, the full details of the deal of being in debt to them and about being trapped. I just didn't see it because I was too naïve. This is the first time I really feel I can see very clearly. And I can see I was really stupid and that what I did was completely the wrong thing by joining the RAF.

They didn't tell me about the conditioning of my mind. They didn't tell me about the blind obedience. They didn't tell me about the institutional bullying from top to bottom. I was made to think all the time that I could lose my rank, my pension, and even my future references as a civilian. They had power over me. That was their job. That's how they operate. It was all about power over people. They could have removed my life. I'm just relieved to be out of it. And I've got my own life with nothing to do with them.

Even though I have my life, I was there and I did it. I have to carry the responsibility and somehow make it up to her. To her family, to her tribe, to her country. I did it because of all the reasons which are nothing more than excuses for doing it. They don't justify what I did. They are only excuses. What I did was wrong and I need to make it up to her and her country and I need to forgive myself for using the excuses I did for being there. I need to change. I need to get real about what I did and what I'm going to do to make up for it. It won't make it any more right but maybe I can find out how to forgive myself for believing in that crap they lured me in with. The so called 'glamour,' the fitness, good friends, exotic places, no worries about money or houses... the fast planes. Being angry at them is not the answer. Action is the answer but I don't know what. I can never go back to Afghanistan as a civilian. I feel blocked with everything that comes next. I'm stuck. Forgive me little one... forgive me little one... forgive me little one.

At six fifteen the train pulled to a halt at Pitlochry and Robby was the only person who got off. It was raining heavily and there was a strong wind which made it difficult to see. Then he noticed the lights on an old Land Cruiser flash once in his direction. Fearghas was Eleanor's oldest brother, a retired Black Watch sergeant. He'd always had a full head of black hair and Robby remembered him as always being lively and youthful in spirit, always willing to get down and do what was necessary. Robby also remembered a few times going with his Uncle Ian to get Fearghas out of the local pub. At Euston Robby had felt like he was going up to Scotland empty-handed so he bought a bottle of single Islay Malt whisky for Fearghas which he knew was his favourite. As he approached the Land Cruiser, Fearghas got out and Robby searched for his wise looking caring grey eyes.

"Hey Robby." His face smiled as he gave Robby a gentle hug. Then he gave Robby a strong farmer's hug. "You're a changed man. Nae a wee man nae more."

"Hey Fearghas," Robby said, smiling as he returned the strength of the hug. "It's been a while." Fearghas looked a healthy fifty four year old, still with the dark hair but with more lines on his face. "Thanks for coming for me. Here's a small drop for you." He handed the bottle to Fearghas which he put under the front seat.

"Ah there's no need to have done that Robby but thanks." Robby's calmness not only woke Fearghas up properly, dragging him into full consciousness in the cold light of the early morning wind and rain but he also made Fearghas more vigilant. Robby was different and Fearghas tried to wonder why as he carefully drove the Land Cruiser to Eleanor's house, which had been his own childhood house. Fearghas wondered what had happened to Robby during his RAF days but he didn't feel this was the right time to ask him. A small single track bridge took them over the River Tay to Strathtay where the Land Cruiser turned left at the village shop and wound around the Tay for a couple of miles. Fearghas slowed down and took a very sharp right turn which went back on itself into what was a rough windy track up into the hills.

"Are you alright Robby?"

"Let me just say I'm back from the menders."

"Your auntie's looking forward to seeing you. She's been unwell for a little while with her stomach, back and all sorts."

"Maybe it's the stress of Ian's death and having to do all the work around the house on her own. I was so sorry I couldn't come to the funeral but I was all messed up after being in Afghanistan."

"Don't worry; she guessed that there was something wrong."

"How is she?"

"She's accepted some help now to make it a bit easier. She's renting out most of the land but keeps sheep on 400 acres so there's still a lot to do there." Fearghas made a large effort in swerving the Land Cruiser to miss a red squirrel.

"See your driving's not changed then."

"Those bastards! Those crazy red squirrels! The grey ones just don't do that. They jump out of the way real fast. But these reds are kamikazes. I swear they seem to wait by the side until you've got to brake sharply to miss them. I think they're having a laugh. I remember when my great-grandfather used to do this run by horse and cart. But no point in making it hard work when you've got one of these." Fearghas laughed. "If we had walked directly from Pitlochry over the hill it would have taken less than a couple of hours and we'd have had good exercise."

"I haven't walked here for far too long." Robby said, as if he had an ache to get out of the Landcruiser right that instant and walk over the hills.

"Walking's probably the best exercise on your own for comfort or with company for pleasure. There's not much that beats it." There was a pause. "Let's do some walks while you're up here Robby."

"Whenever you want to." There was another pause as Fearghas sank into silence as he revved the engine to take the hill.

"Heavy on the gas?"

"I run it on LPG most of the time so it's only half price."

After a few minutes they had driven up through a farm and past several of its small outlying cottages and they were still heading into the hills. The road had turned into a rough track with lots of large potholes which slowed the Land Cruiser to walking pace. After five minutes, Fearghas slowed down as they went around a concave bend which ate into the hill side.

"I remember this corner. It used to almost fall off in heavy rains every few years."

"Still does," said Fearghas. They drove up another few hundred yards until a house appeared on the right.

"Fearghas, it's a really big thing for me missing Ian's funeral. I'm really sorry about Ian. I couldn't come because... well, I was crazy. I was really messed up by what happened to me in Afghanistan." But as Robby turned to look for Fearghas's answer, he sensed a silence and when he looked closer he saw a tear in Fearghas's eye. Fearghas cleared his eye, and then looked over briefly at Robby.

"We had some good times. Ian loved you like you were his son. He would be very pleased to know you made it back up here. We thought the worst had happened to you. We thought that something had happened to you and that you'd got seriously messed up in the head and had turned to drugs or alcohol."

"No I tried to fight it all the way."

As memories of the years since he last saw his aunt came and went in his mind, Robby wished he had never left his aunt's. He remembered how his parents said he had to move on and get a job and they told him that anything in the RAF was a good career. And when he said he was going to Scotland, they said he shouldn't stay too long with his aunt either. His parents told him he had to get a trade or a profession or he would be broke. Now as he thought about Eleanor and Ian, he could now see that his parents tried to motivate him by fear of being poor instead of motivating him by the sense of happiness.

Robby remembered just how Eleanor and Ian had a very different relationship with him. They left it all up to him. For the first time since he left, he now remembered the words they had both said to him about joining the RAF.

"The first thing is this Robby," said his Uncle Ian. "You don't have to do anything or go anywhere. There's no pressure and you are free, only you probably don't see you are. You don't have to join the RAF or get a job. You can just stay here and see how you feel about your life. Have some space and time. I only wish I'd thought harder about joining the military. I wouldn't have joined."

"You must have the time and space to make your own choice." said Eleanor. "The RAF's not as brutish as the army. But they're just as dangerous. They always seem a bit more educated than the army but they're not. They don't talk like elderly army colonels with false haughty accents but they are as snobbish. They are not trained just to go out there and fight hand to hand and bayonet someone, like the army, but they sometimes do. They seem a bit more sophisticated but they still bomb people. Don't forget. They're a force that controls people and they are armed. You must not forget that because you'll be part of that if you decide to join."

For the first time he really regretted his decision to leave and wished so much he had just stayed there with them. Robby had spent six weeks with Eleanor and Ian before joining the RAF. They offered to take him on and train him up to look after the property and its livestock. Looking back Robby would have loved to have stayed there and become one of the ordinary people living in Strathtay. He realised now that at that time he hadn't really understand the subtle underlying pressure from his parents to get a job instead of carving his own way in life and he hadn't understood his need in the past to rebel to find his own way.

He still remembered the day he left. Eleanor and Ian dropped him at the station in Pitlochry. They hugged him as if they might never see him again and they gave him a solar powered Casio watch which was also a compass, barometer, altimeter and thermometer. With it was a postcard of the River Tay. On the back was one Ian's favourite sayings about relationships.

"If you love someone let them go free-if they come back it was meant to be." Robby. You are like a son to us. Come back soon.

Love Ian and Elle x

Robby was thinking about how right they'd been and about what warm and loving people they were when suddenly Fearghas tapped him on his knee pointing at the house. The Land Cruiser stopped dead.

"You'll have to go round the back of the house. Use the back door. The front one's insulated to keep out the draughts. Big winds up here sometimes and she feels the cold."

"Ok." Robby slipped his seat belt off, pulled the door handle and stepped out of the Land Cruiser. "Thanks for the lift Fearghas. What about that walk over the hill?"

"Maybe in a day or two after you've spent some time with Eleanor. Let me know when you're up to it."

+++CHAPTER 8.

Robby walked past the path down to the guest cottage, where he had always stayed and up the gentle steps by the side of the stone house. He realised that his leg was heavy and he was still walking with a slight limp. He looked back as Fearghas slowly manoeuvred the Land Cruiser down the rough road. The cloud had lifted and Robby gazed back over all of Strathtay. He could see about twenty five houses and farms under the blue sky. He tried to take in the fact that Ian wasn't there but at the same time he felt open now to a new beginning and looked forward to staying a few days and discussing things over with his aunt. He could see his aunt's sheep looking smaller and smaller in the more distant fields where she kept them. Robby could almost see his aunt's face as it was four years ago. He felt a sense of fun and warmth for her, which he didn't feel for his own mother or his older sisters. She was forty eight when he last saw her. She never wore make up because she was attractive enough without it.

"Eleanor," he shouted as he knocked on the back door. He waited. "Eleanor?" But there was no answer. He twisted the bare metal ring shaped door handle, pushed the door and peered in. "Eleanor," he said more softly. There was still no answer so he slowly walked through the small rear door into what he remembered of her scullery. It was unchanged. The same large flagstones were on the floor. On the left there was a large enamel sink with a single central overhanging brass tap which delivered fresh spring water. It looked no different from a few years ago and from many years ago. Even the crockery was the same.

But he couldn't see his aunt. He wondered through the scullery into the kitchen where in the centre was the same long pine table stood surrounded by four chairs on either side and one at each end. On it were two trays, each with a bowl, a mug and a spoon. Beside the wood burning stove was a saucepan with boiling water, next to a bag of porridge and a coffee pot. He could see that she was probably preparing breakfast for them both.

"Eleanor," he called again, but there was no answer. He was still unsure of where his aunt was so he walked through the kitchen and into the hallway where he could see the front door, which as Fearghas had said, had been heavily insulated against the wind. Across the hall he pushed open the door and felt the heat from the logs burning on the open fire in the sitting room.

Eleanor was stretched out, asleep and snoring lightly in her large armchair which seemed to make her look smaller and at the same time embrace her. He was about to call her when he noticed she looked very different. He looked at her and Robby suddenly realised what he was seeing. The shock made him look again as if he had seen the wrong scene in front of him. Instead of his youthful aunt he saw a skeletal like figure whose knuckles stood out as if her hands were very large.

"She's dying; this is what I have to accept," he said under his breath several times; as if to get used to it. He didn't want to accept this and awkwardly looked at her as if she was just asleep. After a minute standing right in front of her, the shock turned to feeling uneasy about standing there, so he decided to wake her.

"Eleanor," he said. She had been writing in a note book or school book and still held the ball point in her hand. He could see her writing had changed from her once right slanting letters to uneven and weak marks with the ball point. She didn't stir and Robby could see she was breathing slowly and she was fast asleep. He walked over to her taking half a step, bent down and gently squeezed her left ear lobe. "Eleanor," he said again and she began to stir her head and hands.

"Robby," she said before her eyes opened. Her head slowly rose up and her arms came forward to reach out to hold him. Her voice was so weak, it confirmed exactly to Robby what he didn't want to hear or accept. Robby took in that she was very ill and that she clearly couldn't get up without help because she was so weak. Straight away he saw that she had lost a lot of weight and that the whites of her light blue eyes were yellow. Her hair was cropped short and white. He was still overcome by the shock of seeing her so transformed. Tears ran down his cheeks.

"Eleanor." He bent downwards knelt on the floor, putting his left cheek against hers and his arms around her shoulders. "What's happened to you?"

"I'm so glad you're here Robby." She put her left hand on the armchair and put her right hand out for him to take so that he could help her. "Help me out of this chair and we'll go and have breakfast. Fearghas came over and got it ready before he went to collect you." Robby gave her his left hand and used his right arm to support her right shoulder and prevent her falling backwards. As he steadied her he could feel the skin running over her ribs and her profound weight loss made him realise that she was just skin and bones. He walked with her very slowly to the kitchen and he took her to her chair and gently helping her to sit down. He felt there was hardly any more life left in her. There were more tears in his eyes but he held them back so as not to distress her.

"You can switch the coffee on and cook the porridge."

"Still want to cook it without milk?" He said, struggling to talk but also noticing that there was water in the saucepan and not milk, which was how he remembered how she had her porridge.

"I'll add it when it's done."

"I remember that." said Robby as he put the coffee pot and the saucepan of water on the wood burning stove.

"So you've been in the wars Robby."

"Not as bad as you Eleanor."

"Are you better?" She asked as her blue eyes gave a small sparkle.

"A lot."

"What happened?"

"I'll tell you if you tell me."

"You first."

+++CHAPTER 9.

"A young Afghan girl maybe seven or eight was trying to throw a grenade at me. I shot and killed her but the memory drove me crazy. So bad I tried to hang myself. I seriously thought that was it. I made sure I jumped so hard that I wouldn't hit the ground and the rope would tighten around my neck. But the branch just gave way. Then I got some new therapy. I'm better."

"It sounds like you must have an angel looking after you." Eleanor had always seemed very 'New Age' to Robby before, but this sounded normal to him now. "You know I'm not religious but you didn't get blown up by the grenade. No one shot at you after that. I think it was an angel looking after you. What made that branch break and not your neck? Maybe your determination to end your old life, to change things was so strong. Maybe you jumped so hard, with so much determination to change that it gave way to your journey and broke. Were you surprised?"

"Yeah, I was really surprised when I came to. I was shocked that my life wasn't over. I so wanted it to be. Something else had taken control of me. I had put all the effort into thinking how to make sure that I would be dead and that no one stopped me. I told no-one. I bought a blue nylon tow rope so as not to alert the shopkeeper. But the branch broke."

"You really did end that old life you had."

"I had to finish with it. I wrote you a note. It's still in my wallet where I left it for you."

"You still got it?"

"It's here." Robby reached into his back pocket and pulled out a green nylon wallet. He opened it and took out a piece of paper which he now realised was from the same note book he had only last night started using to record his thoughts in. He handed it to Eleanor. "It was meant for you. So you can read it." Eleanor unfolded and read the note, her soft tears dripping on to the lines on the paper.

Dear Eleanor,

Shot a young girl in Afghanistan. Tried everything to get rid of the images of her in my head. No use. Can't go on like this. Too painful. Had enough pain. Understand there is no other way for me. Forgive me. Until we meet again...

Love, Robby

"I knew it had to be bad."

"There's not much worse. But the therapy worked and I'm back." She handed him the note back which he folded and placed back in his wallet.

"You're certainly on a journey, which someone wants you to complete. In a way you're blessed. Surviving what you did is rare. It's as if you're marked. Maybe you have something to bring out of all of this to show others."

"I'm just trying to get some kind of life back. That's all I want. I can't help anyone else apart from myself and I'm still finding out how to do that."

"Maybe you've got a new way of perceiving and sensing the world."

"It's as if there's no urgency in the world any more except for me to be the right thing for myself."

"I'll try and tell you what I know about just being yourself. But later."

"But Eleanor, tell me... what's happened to you?"

"Yes of course. Well a few weeks before Ian died, I went to see the doctor because I had a pain in my side. It had been there a few weeks and I'd been moaning about my back. I was beginning to get just a little short of breath. He said my blood pressure was up and he also said the thought he could feel a lump in my tummy. He tested my urine and there was blood in it so he got a chest X-Ray and a scan of my tummy a few days later." Robby noticed she stopped feeling uncomfortable about exactly how to tell him.

"The GP in Aberfeldy was straight with me. Said, 'You've got cancer of your left kidney. It's called a Grawitz tumour and it's already spread locally and a lot farther to your liver and lung. It may be operable but only a surgeon can tell you that.' He was kind. I saw the surgeon the next day in Perth. He was brief but kind and said it was inoperable and that I'd probably get six to twelve months. I had weekly injections of a drug called Temsirolimus. It's for people with kidney cancer who've got a very poor prognosis. It probably helped to keep me going so that I could get a bit of extra time to see you. I've recently been on steroids for a while to shrink the cancer but they're not working so well now."

"I'm so sorry. I can't believe that's just it. I've just escaped two near misses with death and now I find you dying. Isn't there something the surgeon could do?" Then Robby realised the futility of what he had just said. "I'm really sorry to hear you've been through so much and I'm sorry I was ill and out of touch." He squeezed her hand. "Why does this have to happen to you now? It's not fair."

"But I'm at just over a year and that's where I am right now with my life. In the last year I've had three shocks. Losing Ian was the worst, even though finding out I had cancer had been bad. And thinking I may not see you again was painful."

"I thought you were going to be around forever. I thought I'd be old when you were old." Robby said.

"No Robby. An angel of death has visited me and asked me to go with them on that long journey. In a dream last night they've said it'll be soon. I'm not in pain, just haven't got a lot of strength to do much. You don't know what a great final gift it is to have you here. To know that you'll be alright. That you've broken out of all that conditioned thinking about having to be this or that."

"Just let me know what I can do to help?"

"Just stay. I'm so glad you're here. It's like you were sent. Will you stay?"

"Of course. No question. I've given up trying to answer all other questions apart from ones which concern the present."

"You're so much more switched on Robby. I'm not being funny." They both laughed as much as they were able to. They were smiling despite all of their troubles.

"I think you can understand why I couldn't get my head around anything and especially to come up for Ian's funeral."

"I knew something like that was happening to you. I'm just glad you survived."

"Do you mind me asking what happened to Ian?"

"Rotten luck."

"Rotten luck? How do you mean?"

"Ian was unlucky. He was coming back from a shopping trip from Aberdeen when he was in an accident. I was totally shocked to hear that because he was a careful driver. It was the Aberdeen police who had to come out with the truth. Two witnesses in a car behind Ian's saw what happened. Everyone in Scotland knows the A9 is a death trap of a road but this crash was something very different. Apparently they saw a car swerve from the other side of the road in front of Ian's car. They said it looked like there was going to be a head on collision but Ian swerved to the other side of the road to avoid the car. The car passed Ian on the wrong side of the road, and then it changed back to its own side of the road. The couple in the car behind Ian said it looked like the driver had become distracted, crossed the road and crossed back again. He didn't stop. Ian's car went straight into a wall. He was killed instantly with a broken neck. He wouldn't have felt anything."

"It was almost like a 'hit and run?"

"It was the worst shock of my life but I'm not so bad now, knowing you are here."

"Selfish bastard. It's like Ian died for nothing."

"I've been through it all and Ian wouldn't have wanted me to have died first. He knew I had cancer and he knew it would kill me. He would have been in too much pain alone. I knew him so well. In a way, Ian's death has left me relieved that I can die not having to worry about him being left behind."

"I'm sorry I wasn't there for you to give you support."

"I can't tell you how extremely lonely I've been without Ian. His birthday and Christmas were so painful and awful without him. But I've moved on to try to deal with my own closing down. But now you're here it's a lot easier."

"How do you mean?"

"Robby you need a life. Your own family are as good as gone forever for you. You have family up here who are much more like your real family. There is this place right here which needs looking after until you give it to someone else. I'm asking you if you want to stay on here and take over the croft. It's yours if you want it."

"I would love to but it's so thoughtful and generous of you Eleanor. It's a lot more than a croft. It's where my heart is. It's home to me. It's a very large piece of land."

"Well that's a yes then. It's a huge relief for me that I can go to sleep tonight without worrying about who's going to look after it. I can finally let go."

"But Eleanor, what about Fearghas. Wouldn't he want it?"

"No. He's been helping me around the house almost full time for the last six months but he's had to take on an extra hand at his own croft just so he can help me out. He was so glad to hear that you were coming up. He jumped for joy. He was hoping you weren't badly injured or in a mess so that you could take over from him straight away. I think he knew your heart is here. He needs to get back to his sheep. I told him not to say I was sick."

"I'm not sure I know enough to do everything. I haven't helped around for a few years. But yes. I've always loved being here. It's really been like my home."

"If you spend a few days walking with Fearghas he'll be able to tell you everything. What he can't tell you, you can learn as you go along."

"I can't thank you enough. But how can I help you."

"Just by you taking over... I can start to let go."

"What do you mean?"

"I've been hanging in just to hear from you. Until I knew you were coming."

"But I've only just got here."

"Now I can relax and embrace what's coming rather than struggling, keeping it at a distance. At last I can move on because I was stuck." Tears flowed down Robby's cheeks.

"I'm sorry."

"Now Robby, we must not get sentimental about what we've had. We must keep on with what we've got now. I must tell you a few practical things. There is a will which was made years ago by Ian and me bequeathing everything to you in a trust when you were a child. It's not the material things that will make you happy in the will but the legacy of learning the art of being. You don't understand the 'art of being' now but you might later."

"I don't understand?" Robby said softly.

"There are no debts on the properties or any complicated arrangements. It's probably wise to keep everything as it is and keep on renting it for a year or so until you've sorted yourself out. Maybe you might want to keep on leasing the land to the local farmers. Maybe you'll want to lease it all out. It's less effort than looking after a load of sheep."

"But you... what about you?"

"It won't be long now. I'm seizing up a bit more each day. Dr Jones in Aberfeldy has offered me painkillers but I've not had any pain. He said if I want, he'll be here at the end to make it more comfortable for me. He said if I'm in pain or if I lose consciousness, and if he doesn't know if I'm in pain, he'll help me out with Diamorphine. I've had a long chat with him and signed a living will saying if I'm in pain or unconscious, that I want him to give me Diamorphine. It'll end it more quickly but that's what I've had to do to all the two dogs we had. It's not right to let an animal's death drag on."

"I won't leave you," Robby said reaching out and holding her hand. Streams of tears poured down his face.

"I've given Fearghas written instructions for after my death. I've made special arrangements for me to have a church service in Kenmore. But I don't want to be buried. I'm going to be cremated like Ian."

"Anything you want." Robby was uneasy about her talking about her death as if it was very close.

"But back to now and the next few days. Whatever you feel, don't worry. The plans for the wake and funeral are all in my will. Forbes the solicitors will give you all the details. His number is on the notice board over there" She pointed to a list of numbers on a cork board beside the window. Stopped going to the surgery four months ago. Can't really do any journeys. Dr Jones, he comes up once a week but he comes up if anything new happens to me. You'll meet him in the next day or two."

"Haven't heard of him before."

"No he's only been here a few months. Can you give me a hand back to my armchair Robby?"

"No trouble," he said as he went and stood beside her to lift her by her waist and arm.

"I just need a small sleep."

Robby set her down in her armchair by the fire and pulled out a small stool on which he placed her feet. She was nearly asleep before he covered her with a thick multicoloured woollen blanket she had bought in Morocco years before. When he tucked her up she was peacefully asleep.

+++CHAPTER 10.

Robby walked back into the kitchen and looked out of the window. He could see how easy it was for the view to keep someone living here for years. He thought that wherever he had been he had never found such a beautiful place.

He thought he had better find his old bedroom so he walked up the wooden staircase to the upper floor. There was one bedroom to either side. Eleanor's room looked like it hadn't been used for a long time. He could also see that his old room had a towel and some bed linen on top of a duvet. Fearghas must have come in and prepared his room the night before as Robby knew Eleanor couldn't have got up the stairs. The room was half of the upstairs with simple whitewashed walls, a beamed ceiling and a pine floor. He looked out through the window and could see further across Strathtay's beautiful area of hills with the mighty River Tay running through it. He had an uncomfortable sense of certainty, a moment of needing to check everything, so he sat down at the table and got his notebook from his trouser pocket.

Robby: Pocket Notebook Entry 5. I've not only lost my uncle Ian, but I'm also about to lose the only person who I consider family, Eleanor. I can't believe that soon she will be a memory. She'll be gone. She's left me everything she has of her life, but I can't bear to see her leave. All I can do is be here for her. I'll speak to Fearghas soon.

I can't really ask Eleanor what she thinks I should do. Fearghas can't advise me either. I don't think I can help where I'm going because my life seems to be like a path unfolding in front of me. It's as if I'm just following the events someone else has written about me in a book or a film. I feel powerless, but not as powerless as I did when I jumped from that tree. Writing about where I am gives me some sense of control of myself. I feel as if it gives me more insight into my own psychological processes. It's probably time for me to start really looking at what I'm going to do.

Even though Eleanor's clearly dying she seems to have come to terms with everything. She's done everything she's needs to do so she can let go. She's not anxious or panicky. She's not fretting or concerned with anything. She's been through so much but that seems to have ended with me arriving. I only hope that doesn't mean that she'll die very soon. She seems at perfect peace with everything. I've never seen anyone so calm. She seems to have let go of the world and seems in another world already. She seems more there than here. The strange thing is that she's waited for me to come.

Robby was woken by a tapping on the back door. He put his notebook in his back pocket and went down stairs to open the door. There stood a man a little older than him. He had old green wellies, jeans and a warm jacket with a corduroy collar which his slightly long hair almost covered.

"Jack Jones. Eleanor's GP in Aberfeldy." He held out his hand. "You must be Robby." Jack was forty but was skinny and looked younger because of his slightly long dark hair and his casual way of dressing.

"Yes Robby." They gave each other firm handshakes. "Come in out of the wind." Jack walked in and saw the unwashed dishes in the sink. He sensed Robby was probably shocked at how he had found Eleanor.

"How is she?" Asked Jack. Robby's head dropped.

"You know more than me but I'd say she probably only has a short while left."

"Now you've arrived. She'll let go."

"Why's that? Why does it have to be?"

"She's been ready for you to come for some time. She wasn't ready until she had done all of her psychological housekeeping. She got everything in order. She's already said goodbye to everyone, written to others and phoned a few people. She just wants to be. It's really already over and she is really at peace with herself and the world."

"I didn't really want to believe her or you," Robby sighed.

"Sorry about that but that's how it is. Come on let's go and see if there's anything she needs." She was asleep and Robby gently tried to wake her by squeezing her earlobe.

"Only ever seen doctors and nurses do that," said Jack.

"Used to be a medic in the Forces."

Eleanor woke suddenly.

"How are you Eleanor?" Jack said very gently taking her hand.

"Robby's here. I'm happy."

"I'm so glad for you Eleanor." Eleanor smiled at him.

"Are you in any pain?" Jack asked.

"No. I want to stay conscious if I can. So I'd rather not have anything."

"If you need something to help any pain just call me."

"I'm fine. It's so good to see you Robby. Can you hold my hand?" She held out her hand which Robby clasped. She had small hands and her left hand griped his firmly and then she laid back her head and rested before her eyes closed with sleep. The doctor went back to the kitchen. Robby let go of Eleanor's hand and followed him.

"If you need me just call." Jack said to Robby.

"I will."

"It won't be long." Jack softly added with a nod of his head showing compassion.

"I know. Thanks for being open and frank." Robby felt sad but still wanted to make sure Eleanor was comfortable. He went to the fridge and took out some cold chicken which he reheated in the oven with some gravy. He cut the chicken up into small pieces and took this with some small pieces of dark chocolate to Eleanor. He knew these were her favourite things and if she was going to die then she would want to have had her favourite things as her last meal.

"Robby it's like an angel has sent you just in time." Eleanor started eating the small pieces of chicken with a fork.

"Can I get you anything?"

"No just stay with me."

"There's nowhere I could go."

"I know." Eleanor was sitting in her favourite chair which Robby knew had been Ian's father's. It was made of old oak and the sturdy frame was interspersed with different cloths, almost as if it was some patchwork quilt. It was so deep; it was almost like a small sofa for one person.

"I'll sit with you," said Robby pulling over a stool to sit and hold her hand.

"Robby. What has become the most important thing for you?"

"Just having peace from all the memories that haunted me from Afghanistan. The only thing I want is to feel happy in myself. I now know there's nothing more important in life."

"Yes those memories have gone. So what's replaced them?"

"Just being here. It's peaceful to be back here."

"It's been peaceful for me here too. You being back here has let me not worry about any last things. My body's been failing slowly for some time now and it's beginning to fade away from me now. Will you be alright staying here?"

"Yes. If you want me to."

"What bothers you about her?"

"Who?"

"The child. The Afghan."

"It's not over. Me having gone to her country, killed her and then just leaving. I need to restore the balance. It's wrong. I don't feel free of it yet."

"Do you know how to do that Robby?"

"No. Not yet"

"Soon you'll be ready for your long journey Robby." She re-gripped his hand so the grip was palpable. "It's so good to hold your hand."

"Your hand feels like the sister I never had."

"Yours feels like my brother's, my father's and a son's. But now it's the last bit of the long journey for you."

"What do you mean the long journey for me? It sounds like the last journey before I die." Robby was confused.

"The long journey was always referred to as the last part of someone's life while they were dying, but that's not what I mean."

"That's a relief."

"It's more serious."

"What can be more serious than dying?"

"Seeing where you are now, you are almost ready to die. To let go of all your previous ways of seeing the world. Only when you let go of your old self, your mind, can you truly be your real self. You have to unlearn to learn because learning is only learned ignorance."

"I don't really understand, but I hear you."

"There's an arrangement you have to make first to tie up things. There's something you need to tidy up before you can be yourself."

"What do I need to tidy up?"

"As I said you are truly almost ready to let your old mind die and become yourself. You don't know it yet but this is the inescapable journey which you've already begun. But as I said, there is an arrangement you need to make to tidy up what has gone on in your life. Hold my hand. I'll show you. Remember let your mind die and you will just be your real self."

"I don't understand," he said and she held his hand firmly.

"If there's anything you feel uncomfortable about, you have to try and correct it to make you ready to move on. The little Afghan girl first."

"What exactly do you mean?"

"Your old life will soon be over and you'll become something else, just like a caterpillar becomes a butterfly. After you've found her and brought her here, you'll be free. You'll be able to move on from what's happened to you and enjoy a life of bliss here. It's only ones such as you who have suffered a great deal who can see the way to your own self. It's only inside you that you find happiness. Remember it's only the ones who suffer who are able to see the self. Others have no need to find happiness. They find it in the outer world in pleasure through the senses, but they are the unlucky. I'll show you. But not now. I'll show you soon. Remember let your mind die and you will just be your real self."

Robby realised both his eyes were closed so he opened them quickly and sat up more straight on the stool still hold

Eleanor's hand. He was looking at Eleanor. He wasn't sure how long he had been sitting there or if he had been asleep. Eleanor was smiling. Then he noticed she was quite still. Had he been dreaming? Or had she just been speaking to him for some time whilst he had been holding her hand. Had he dreamt her speaking? Robby now noticed her hand was warm, she hadn't breathed since his eyes had opened. As he looked at her eyes he saw that they were now open without blinking.

Robby looked at the watch that Eleanor and Ian had given him. It said it was five thirty in the evening. Had she just finished talking then died. Had he just blinked? Or, had he woken from a long dream about her in which she had spoken to him and after which he found she had died holding his hand? He couldn't work out which was real. Perhaps they both happened. Perhaps they were both real. Perhaps they were both unreal. He wasn't sure whether being awake or dreaming was reality. It was his first experience that it might not matter which was real.

He sat holding her hand for an hour before calling Fearghas, whose phone went on to messaging. Then he called Jack the doctor who said he would be two or three hours as he had to finish his surgery. During this time Robby sat on the stool beside Eleanor and reflected deeply on what had just happened. He wrote in his notebook.

Robby: Pocket Notebook Entry 6. Eleanor has gone. I'm not sure whether it was a dream or the last thing she said to me. In both she said that I had to find the Afghan girl and bring her here. She said that then I would be free; I would find happiness in myself and live a life of bliss. I don't understand. The girl is dead. I don't know any girls, any Afghans and I'm always happier on my own. I'd better write down exactly what she said.

She said 'Your old life will soon be over and you'll become something else, just like a caterpillar becomes a butterfly. After you've found her and brought her here, you will be free. You'll be able to move on from what has happened to you and enjoy a life of bliss here. It's only ones such as you who have suffered a great deal who can see the way to your own self. It's only inside you that you find happiness. Remember it's only the ones who suffer who are able to see the self. Others have no need to find happiness. They find it in the outer world in pleasure through the senses, but they are the unlucky. I'll show you. But not now. I'll show you soon. Remember let your mind die and you will just be your real self.' Then she was gone.

Three hours later there was a tapping on the heavy back door. Robby walked through the hall, into the kitchen and let Jack in.

"Hi Robby. Sorry to hear she's gone." said Jack holding out his hand again.

"Thanks for coming." He shook Jack's cold hand.

"What time?"

"Five thirty, when I looked at my watch."

"Sorry you only had a little time with her."

"I spent more time with her today than I've done in a long time. Somehow it was just right."

"I'll just take a look and see that she passed away in peace." Jack walked through the kitchen and hallway, into the front room where Eleanor's body remained reclining in the armchair with her feet on a footstool, just as Jack had seen her a few hours before. He looked at her for a few moments out of respect for what he remembered of her. He took in the situation. He observed her dilated pupils and gently with his middle fingers lowered the skin of the upper lids to meet the lower lids. He pulled a stethoscope out of his pocket and listened to her chest and as expected, it was silent. There were no heart sounds and no sounds of her breath. He felt her hand which was now already colder than it was earlier. Then there was a knock at the door.

"Hey Robby." said Fearghas putting his arm around Robby.

"Fearghas. She was peaceful. She wasn't in pain. Just went to sleep."

"Thank you." Fearghas looked sad but at the same time his face showed a sign of relief that it was over and she didn't suffer any more.

"Eleanor died happy Fearghas." Robby said softly. Fearghas nodded and smiled at Robby as he stood for a few moments looking at his sister.

"Right, well... I'll call Bank Street."

"What's Bank Street?"

"It's where all the undertakers are in Aberfeldy. I'll see who answers first."

"Did she have a preference?" Robby asked.

"No. Said she didn't mind which ones dealt with her. Oh she wanted me to give you a copy of the will before the solicitor arrives so you know what to expect." Fearghas handed Robby a long brown envelope. "Have a look. It's all very straightforward. Apart from one odd thing. There's also a letter from her to you which she wrote recently. Here it is."

"Ok." said Robby. Fearghas left Robby with the envelope as he went off to phone the Bank Street undertakers. Robby pulled the will out from the envelope with a letter which he read.

My Dear Robby,

This is for you after I've gone. You were always special to Ian and me. Like you, I never got on with my older sisters, only with Fearghas.

Ian and I talked about you a lot and how you seemed on a very difficult journey with the RAF. We always saw that you were probably going to go farther than the rest of us in terms of becoming your true self. We believed this to be true. It was something we could see. Since Ian died, (I know I might not see you again) I've never lost faith in what Ian and I saw in you. I believe you'll come back here to pick up where you were. I may be gone. That's why I've written things down for you. I've enclosed my will. You will understand later.

Until we meet again

Love, Eleanor

Robby was very touched by this straightforward and simple loving letter. He folded the letter and he put it in his back trouser pocket with his notebook. Then he read the will.

This is the last will and testament of Eleanor Brown.

I hereby bequeath all my assets, namely the house and contents, Ian's Notebook, his father's diaries, all my property, including all vehicles and the contents to Robby in accordance with a trust which was set up on his 18th birthday.

Robby, I have a favour to ask of you. It's simply this. Take my ashes and scatter them on the sacred hill. The hill has an inner path, an outer path and a direct path to the top. It was with a great deal of effort that I managed to get to India three months after Ian died. It took me that long before I wanted to leave the croft. But I had to fulfil our agreement. We agreed that whoever died first would take the others ashes to the hill and scatter them there. I scattered his ashes all the way along the inner path. Please scatter mine along the same inner path. It's the most important place of inner silence.

The trust document is enclosed, the trustees being Fearghas McCormick Thomas Stor and Robert Forbes. The executor of the will is Robert Forbes.

Eleanor Brown

"The undertaker will be here in about an hour with Thomas," said Fearghas. "Is it all ok?"

"Yes of course. It all looks straightforward to me apart from the bit about Ian's Notebook and his father's diaries. What's all that about?"

"I don't know but maybe Thomas will. Probably tell you when he gets here as he's officiating at the funeral and he'll give her the last rights."

"Right," Robby said.

"She wanted to be in the house overnight, then the church overnight and then cremated the next morning after the small service."

Two hours later, Thomas Stor the local priest who had a slight limp, led the undertakers in through the back door. Thomas had done a weekly visit to Eleanor since Ian died. Robby could see he looked like a straight forward padre just over fifty with salt and pepper hair which was cut short almost in army fashion. He put a hand on Robby's shoulder and offered him his hand to shake.

"Sorry for your loss Robby." Are you alright?"

"Yes. Getting there," Robby replied.

Thomas walked over to Eleanor and looked at her and stroked her hair. "You and Ian were like brother and sister to me. I'll miss you Elle." Then he turned to Robby and the two undertakers. "Robby this is Angie and Mike from Daltons in Bank Street." Thomas then looked at them and nodded his head, which was a very clear signal to the undertakers to begin their work...

"Sorry for your loss Robby and Fearghas." Mike said.

"Yes, we're sorry she was a lovely girl... We are going to move her now?" Angie asked.

"No trouble," said Robby.

"Aye... She's ready for you now." said Fearghas.

Eleanor was carefully lifted from her armchair where she had lain more or less horizontally with her feet on the cushion. Robby was surprised at first how they lifted her as she didn't bend at all. Rigor mortis had already begun to set in and she was so rigid she was lifted simply by her head and feet. The two undertakers slowly lowered her down straight into her coffin which rested on two trestles in the lounge. They adjusted the lace of the coffin so that it covered most of her.

"We'll be here early to pick her up Robby," Mike said. "See you tomorrow Thomas. Bye Fearghas.

Thomas said the last rites with only Robby and Fearghas present. Then there was a silence whilst all three stood looking at her for the last time.

"I'll stop by in the morning about ten Robby." Thomas said quietly to Robby.

"Ok." And with that Robby again looked what down at what was left of Eleanor. White frilly lace surrounded her and covered her lower body. Only her face, arms and hands which rested on one another on her stomach could be seen.

"Do you want me to stay Robby?" Asked Fearghas."

"No. That's kind. I'll see you in the morning."

+++CHAPTER 11.

Robby woke at seven and at first he wasn't sure if he had dreamt that Eleanor had died. Then he was surprised to find that he had slept all night in her armchair. The open topped coffin with Eleanor's visible remains silently confirmed he hadn't dreamt it. The only difference was that now in the cold light of day, she looked more yellow than the night before. But she also looked more distant. He felt she was further away than the night before. But although he sensed she had already moved on, he also felt part of her was still with him in the room. So he spoke to her.

"Hey Eleanor...Thanks for waiting for me... It was good to see you...Thank you. I will never forget what you said." Then he stood by her coffin in silence for what seemed like a couple of hours. At first he felt numb for some time. But then Eleanor came alive in him. He remembered the annual summer, Christmas and Easter trips he did up there where they would both meet him off the sleeper train first thing in the morning. He suddenly felt extremely sad and low. Robby realised that it was as if he had been a border in a Bristol school and every holiday he went up to Scotland to see his aunt and uncle. It dawned on him that although his biological parents lived in Bristol, his psychological and emotional parents were his aunt and his uncle. He realised that his main parents were gone now and he was an orphan. He felt alone.

When Thomas the priest came up to the back of the house to see Robby he noticed Robby was chopping up a large log with an axe. The priest saw what Robby was doing was more working out his feelings than just chopping up the log.

"Hi. Robby," and he held out his hand which Robby took and shook. Robby was quiet as he caught his breath and brought the axe down heavily in a log.

"Thanks for coming over last night," Robby said as he thought the priest must be the same age as Eleanor, only he looked sprightly, apart from his limp. "Cup of tea?"

"Yes. Sorry for your loss."

"Thank you."

"You were her favourite."

"Appreciate that." Robby said filling the kettle with water.

"Any special readings you want to read?" Thomas leant against the kitchen table.

"Can't think of any. Do you know any she liked?" Robby asked.

"No I can't say I do. Do you want someone to do a eulogy?"

"Don't know anyone very well who knew her. I mean apart from Fearghas and yourself. Do you? What I mean is do you think she should have a eulogy?"

"Yes. I can say a few words. One or two others might like to say a few words. I hope you don't mind me asking but I know you are her nephew but I've never seen any of her other family, other than Fearghas. Does she have any other family?"

"Yes mine. I mean her sister is my mother. But she hadn't spoken to them for years. She always said that they just didn't get on and always argued. And she didn't like the breaking up of her peace. So she never bothered with any of them." How do you like your tea?"

"Milk no sugar. And you how do you get on with them?"

"It was the same for me with them. I agreed with her so I didn't bother with them either. She wouldn't want me contacting any of them now, so I need to respect that. Her and me always got on really well. My family talked down to me and to her because she was the youngest sibling like me. I also disowned my family. It's better this way. Do you mind if I ask you something?" Robby handed Thomas a mug of tea and Thomas sat at the table cradling it.

"No, go ahead." Robby sat opposite as Thomas sipped his tea.

"In her will, she mentioned Ian's Notebook and his father's diaries. Fearghas didn't know anything about them but he said you might. Do you?"

"No. I didn't know he kept a notebook and I've not heard anything about his father's diaries. But if you come across them, let me know. He was my friend. He promised me he would let me into the secrets of his inner world one day but then he just died in the car accident. Maybe his inner world is described in his notebook, so yes please let me know. So the two of you had a sense of camaraderie?"

"Yes, but not just the pecking order thing. Yes we both had a similar way of being independent but I think it's because Ian was in the first Gulf War and suffered as a result. Years ago she told me not to join the RAF but I did. Eventually I left and now I'm here."

"What happened to you?"

"Oh you know. Just war. It's living in Hell. Wars are wrong," said Robby.

"Seems like you're still thinking about it. Some wounds hurt more after a long time."

"It was very true for me. What made you say that?" Robby turned and asked.

"Experience." Thomas lifted up his baggy khaki trouser leg to reveal a very badly scarred upper leg and a highly polished aluminium lower leg. "Just one bullet. But not a very nice sight I'm afraid."

"How'd you get it?"

"The First Gulf War. Same mission as your uncle Ian. He was a medic. I was a chaplain and was helping to evacuate someone on a stretcher. I got hit in the leg then Ian got hit trying to help me."

"I didn't know that he was rescuing you. He never said that. All I knew was that he had a false leg from a sniper's bullet."

"We got hit by a sniper who had some gun. It was a high velocity bullet so it made a classic shock wave in his calf. You know everything in the area about the size of a melon just disintegrates. It took most of it away with nearly all the bone. We were never sure if the bullet that got Ian got me or if it was a second bullet. I had fallen over and I thought someone had hit me with a hammer until I tried to move my leg, but nothing happened. I looked again because I wasn't moving and it was because my leg and foot weren't working. That sniper had blown a hole in my ankle. Had two operations, but the pain was terrible. Then had it fused and the limp was worse. Surgeon said I'd be better off like my mate Ian. Said I'd be able to run again. And that's why we each ended up with the classic Italian operation."

"Which was what?"

"Named after the Italian surgeon Belloni. The Belloni operation. Below knee amputation." Thomas laughed and Robby joined in. "You have to laugh. When I woke I was with a medic telling me I was ok, when my leg was in bits and Ian's had just been blown off."

"You're laughing at it but it must have made you angry that you lost your leg fighting for a war which wasn't our making. What really happened to the two of you afterwards?"

"It seemed pretty straight forward. We each had a new leg and we both wanted out. We both just came back, glad to be alive. I carried on as a priest and Ian carried on with Eleanor at the croft. Being hit once was enough for both of us. We were so lucky we weren't killed and he only got our legs, not our lives."

"How did it affect you?"

"The truth is that being there affected both of us pretty bad. We were at college together and together during all our time out there and got injured in the same incident."

"Was it the incident that got to you?"

"No, we'd changed long before that. We had seen a lot of injured people and some dead ones too. Faces, limbs, genitals all missing. Guts out of their stomachs. We knew some of these lads but we also saw hundreds and hundreds of dead Iraqis and we both started asking just what for. We were disillusioned but were still doing this job. It had taken its toll on us already. We didn't want to be there, but that's what you get when you've signed up and take the Queens Shilling. Then we became one of them with a limb missing too. Losing our legs was just our ticket home on a Herc. We knew we could never be the same after what we saw out there. It wasn't losing the limbs that got us at all; it was all the things we saw that got to us."

"And how did you adjust coming back?"

"Everything was different... but the same. What I mean is we had changed. Everything we looked at was the same but how we saw it was different. How we saw the world had changed. It was really hard talking to ordinary non-military people for a while. The doctors said we would just get better with time. What they could have said was, 'you'll never be what you were before ever again. It's changed you for good. We're done with you.' If we'd known that, if they'd said that to us before we joined up, Ian and I would never have joined. It didn't change us in a positive way. We were battle hardened and now we saw men differently. We were both in trouble and we knew it. Ian didn't have a belief or faith in any religion. I was the one in more trouble... I didn't believe in God anymore. He found something in himself. But I lost what I had."

"That must have been like hell."

"I didn't see it coming but the insanity of where we were, the madness of what we were doing and what was happening crept up on me. I became irritable and started swearing at God for inventing flies. Then I started questioning why any God would invent such negative things like flies or wasps. Out there in battle, survival of the fittest is so important... and then the whole Darwin thing started to make sense to me. That was what actually happened over millions of years. It's all the genetic mutations... nature trying to survive by being the best, the toughest, the cruellest. We are all wild animals and certainly not the most civilised. God didn't create flies or wasps... they survived because there was no creation, no God. It is the survival of the fittest."

"Don't understand how you manage to carry on as a priest?"

"I never got back into it. Bernard is the priest in Aberfeldy now. I'm there only in name. I don't wear my collar anymore. I help him out with people's problems and the congregations at weekends and occasionally during the week. But that's getting less because the congregation is dwindling year by year. And you know what, I'm glad. It took going to war for me to see that you can't know about God. Challenging and rejecting blind beliefs is a giant step of freedom away from people who are desperate to have power over other people. Religious people are actually arrogant saying that they know. I had a huge struggle. I really had to break down all my beliefs and thoughts. I now know that trying to uncover truth requires motivation and courage. Challenging our own and our ancestor's beliefs which held together families and society is like a catastrophic loss. But like a death, after the grief, it can bring something new which is positive and hungry for expression. I feel like I've got a young and clean mind again. I can see that when minorities with challenging beliefs oppose majorities with fiercely held traditional beliefs, cracks can start to show. I didn't just see cracks, I saw chasms. I now see the more traditionally held beliefs should be regarded as opponents of the liberation and development of mankind. When darkness is removed light flows in and this is what seems to be beginning. It's not just me; it is other people who are fed up with being conned by establishments. There have not only been movements against Communism but there are also movements against blind beliefs in religious gods, America, Russia, China, nationalism, tribalism, hedonism and egoism. What I am saying is that we are all trying to be true to our own self."

"But what I don't understand is how do you carry on doing it if you don't believe?"

"I've got nothing to do with matters of faith. I deal with people's problems like a psychologist. In reality every priest or padre is usually working as a psychologist. After what I've seen, I think all of the problems I've seen and I still see, are psychological ones. They are about how people think. Most people come to padres or priests with problems which appear religious or spiritual but are actually psychological problems, which need psychology applied to them."

"I still don't understand."

"Let me give you an example of someone I saw recently."

"Right."

"A woman came to see me a last week because her son had committed suicide by jumping off the top of a car park in Glasgow. She was very anxious about him because she believed he was in Hell because he killed himself. Her main concern was her belief that he was in Hell. She was thinking he was in Hell because that is what Christianity taught her. If you deliberately kill yourself, you go to Hell. She was in agony over it. She felt his whole life had been a failure."

"It sounds like a matter of faith."

"Not necessarily."

"I don't understand that. What did you say to her?"

"I said that when he was falling that maybe he changed his mind and didn't want to die."

"Did she accept that?"

"Yes totally. Because it meant that maybe had he changed his mind in the last few moments and died not wanting to kill himself, so he would be in heaven. She was now able to accept that he might have changed his mind on the way down. She could now see him in Heaven and she's now no longer anxious about him. So her problem was resolved by giving her a different way of seeing how he thought. Her thinking had changed. This isn't really anything to do with any religion or anything spiritual. It is simply a matter of a person wanting to have more positive thoughts than more negative thoughts. It is to do with happiness, which is always within. It's simple psychology. It is acceptance. Every chaplain knows this. Any type of God has nothing to do with this. It's just simply working with the psychology of mankind, nothing more."

"It's interesting. But why are you doing this?"

"One, it's because it's what I know. Two, it's because as much as I don't believe in God, the God I was brought up with, my time here since the first Gulf War has shown me that there is a spirit in us. I've given up on a God, but I've seen the spirit we have which is not our upbringing or our outer lives."

"But Ian... how did he cope?"

"He went off to India with Eleanor. They went there every year to some sacred mountain in the south. He had some photographs of the mountain. Ian's father went there after the Second World War. He had been tortured by the Japanese. I think he really found himself there somehow. Like his father

Ian was still not religious. But somehow, he became detached from what had happened, as if he was really happy in this world. He became happy with himself after the first trip. But I don't understand how he did it. He found something in himself and I always knew he was eventually going to show me. The night before the crash, he phoned me to say we should hook up for supper the next night because he wanted to explain everything he had learnt from his father and what he had found about himself in India, but it was not to be. Still miss him... my best friend. He was like my brother. The crash not only took him away but also what he knew and what he was going to tell me. I never felt I could ask your aunt what he was going to tell me because she had to suffer with his loss on top of her illness. The notebook and diaries. If you find them please let me know. I would really like to know what he was going to tell me. I'm sure you know what I mean. And you?"

"I didn't get shot. I'm ok."

"Did you get hit?"

"No..." There was a silence. "That would have been easier for me. I don't mean any disrespect. I don't mean easier for me than it was for you."

"Hey, I'm lucky to be here at all and I've still got one whole leg to power me around. So what happened to you?"

"I was called a hero for saving some of my mate's lives. They were the pilots on a C17 Globemaster and a couple of engineers."

"I know those huge American transport jets."

"Yeah, I was the loadie. We were out on a trip in a Land Rover in Afghanistan."

"On a trip?"

"Yes, I know it's not the place you would usually take a day off in but the plane was bust. We had a two day wait, so as you do, we went to have a look around at the site of a crashed Hercules. We suddenly got a flat in the Land Rover. While I was trying to get the spare wheel off, I saw a child coming at me and she was taking the pin out of a grenade. I shot her and she fell on her grenade. That was it. It was only later... well... "

"So you did get hit. The old invisible bullet. They tend to leave the worst mess. Worse than my leg. They leave bigger scars and they can make you go crazy."

"Yeah, you got it in one. I kind a went a bit crazy. A branch broke and so I failed at hanging myself. The branch broke my leg but then that got me a load of really good therapy. It got me though all the images in my head."

"And now how's the head?"

"It's not my head. It's gone from my head to whatever else is there."

"Do you know what that's about?"

"Yeah. I've half figured it out with Eleanor since I've been up here. She was in the middle of telling me when she died. I've gone through it all but the therapy doesn't touch that bit of me. All the intrusive imagery has gone and hasn't bothered me since the therapy. No flashbacks or nightmares. I'm not seeing the Afghan girl all the time or being reminded of her by things. And the best thing is I can sleep. I'm pretty well back to normal."

"What is it then?"

"I'm not happy and I'm just left with the feeling it's not finished. I can rationalise what I did and reason it all out until the cows come home. I've even worked through my anger about me and I've worked through my anger with her for doing this. There are no more images to work through. But I'm still left with having killed that child. Could her parents or her brothers and sisters ever forgive me for taking her life? Could they ever forgive the man who murdered their little child, their sister in their country, a place where I had no right to be, let alone no right to be carrying a gun?"

"No. The answer to your question is no. I hear what you say but you could never be more wrong. Don't ever think that. Her family will have been long gone. That's why she took up arms as a child. Her parents would have been killed. So there's no one to do any forgiving."

"Yeah, I hear that. I think that's what Eleanor was trying to say to me yesterday. She said she thought I was on the last journey before I died. But I wasn't going to actually physically die. She said I was on an inescapable journey which I had already begun."

"Did she say anything else?"

"Yes, she said there is an arrangement I need to make to tidy up what has gone on in my life. She said I had to find the Afghan girl I killed and bring her here to live. But that's impossible. She's dead. But the thing is... well Eleanor wasn't one for saying crazy things. She had insight like most people think is uncanny, but not crazy."

"Anything else?"

"Yes. She said after that I'd be free and enjoy a life of bliss and find happiness in myself. I don't see how. I thought I would forget what she said so I wrote it down in a notebook. What she said keeps on coming to the front of my mind all the time, like she is reminding me how important it is."

"Can I see it?"

"Come inside, I'll read it to you."

"I'm all ears. I wonder if it is what Ian was going to tell me." They both sat around the kitchen table as Robby read aloud.

"She said, 'Your old life will soon be over and you will become something else, just like a caterpillar becomes a butterfly. After you've found her and brought her here, you will be free. You'll be able to move on from what has happened to you and enjoy a life of bliss here. It's only ones such as you who have suffered a great deal who can see the way to your own self. It's only inside you that you find happiness. Remember it's only the ones who suffer who are able to see the self. Others have no need to find happiness. They find it in the outer world in pleasure through the senses, but they are the unlucky. I'll show you. But not now. I'll show you soon. Remember let your mind die and you will just be your real self.' Then she died."

"Yes," Thomas said. "I hear what you say." There was then a long silence whilst neither man said a word.

"What do you reckon?" said Robby. Then there was a continuation of Thomas's pause. Robby waited for a while in case Thomas hadn't heard him, but Thomas was deep in thought. Robby asked again. "What do you reckon?"

"Maybe that's it... maybe the only way is the way she said"

"I don't see."

"It has truth in it for me too. For you maybe you wouldn't like it."

"Why?"

"Well first you have to see that you have to forgive yourself. No one else's forgiveness can help you. It can only come from inside you. That's what's lost its balance."

"I think I've tried to do that for a while. I tried to think through it. I even thought of contacting her parents or relatives. As you said to me, I think I must have asked myself; do I really imagine she would have any left? I must have intuitively known the answer because I didn't go looking for any relatives. I know now what you said is true. Sometimes you have to hear it from someone else to hammer it home. She probably had no one and nothing left to live for. That's what must have made her so determined."

"That's the only reason an innocent child decides to be a fighter. Now you're getting nearer to what you can do."

"What can I do? I've tried to think. But I'm dammed if I can work out what I can do."

"You've already said it yourself. There's no one left to forgive you and you can't think your way into forgiving yourself. This has to come from your heart not your head."

"So what is it?"

"Eleanor's already told you. The answer is the Afghan girl. You might not like it when I tell you but it's probably the one thing you can do so that you're forgiven. What Eleanor meant is this. You should go and find a child, perhaps an orphan, who has nothing to live for, who has nothing left. Just like your Afghan girl, she could be an Afghan, an Iraqi or an Iranian. She might have family; she might not. You bring her here and you raise her and if necessary her family, your family. You become her provider. That's the payback that will let you be free."

"I couldn't do that. I'm not a religious person. I think religion is a great thing, just not for me. That's why we are at war. But not for me anymore. I'm out of that. I'm not getting messed up in any one else's religious crusade. Just look what it did to me. I've died once. Eleanor said I had to die again but I think it's more about dying in the mind and getting rid of it the mind, not taking in a Muslim refugee. That would be against everything I believe in, everything I've experienced. I would never do that. That's just the wrong interpretation. I appreciate your help but no. I'll find the real reason behind what Eleanor said to me."

"Just remember that what's not resolved will be repeated."

That evening when Eleanor was taken to the church in Kenmore. Thomas welcomed her and said a few prayers. The next morning, the only family at Eleanor's funeral were Robby, Fearghas, his wife Fiona and their two children, Fearghas the third and their daughter Eileen.

+++CHAPTER 12.

When Robby got back to Eleanor's house after the funeral lunch at the Kenmore Hotel, the house felt totally empty as if the wind had blown anything of value out the windows and doors. He felt dreadful and couldn't put it into words. He went and sat in her chair. He remembered that his true parents Ian and Eleanor were gone forever. He was a true orphan and felt totally alone. He felt utter despair. His hands came to his face as he howled loudly with tears of grief. There were tears for Eleanor, tears for Ian, tears for the Afghan girl. But mostly they were tears for himself. He asked himself what he had done to deserve such a desolate life. Emotionally he felt at was at his lowest. He got out his notebook so as not to lose track of where he was.

Robby: Pocket Notebook Entry 7. If Karma exists then I must be a world champion carrier. Nothing worse could of happened to me. I didn't ask for it. I didn't do anything before that Afghan girl appeared. I came up here to see my aunt to seek some refuge but she's gone and now and I'm on my own with a messed up past and no future. I'm weak physically. I'm not sure if my brain's actually working properly at all. And I feel I owe that girl I killed so much that it's impossible to even look at. Maybe Eleanor meant bringing the girl up here is bringing her into my head. I hate this. I'm so angry with that girl.

What did you mean Eleanor? What did you mean when you said my life would be free after I brought her up here? She is dead Eleanor, dead, dead, dead. I killed her. She's never coming back. Never, never, never. But she won't go away will she? My problem is not being able to forgive myself. How can I forgive myself?

And Thomas, you are so wrong. How could I bring up a Muslim girl here in Strathtay? The locals would hound her and me. Think of all the Scottish lads fighting out there in Afghanistan. That would be like putting the young Afghan girl in the lion's den. She would be devoured and so would I. And the ridiculous thing is that there probably isn't a single Afghan in Scotland. So it's stupid. Not an option. Total madness. Crap. I have to find another way. There has to be a way of finding forgiveness in myself.

Robby went to bed at four in the afternoon. He wanted to escape from the world. He tried to doze off to sleep but sleep wouldn't come. He felt so low, as if he had nothing to live for. The leg he had broken was uncomfortable if he didn't sleep well and now it ached. He got out his notebook again as he was confused.

Robby: Pocket Notebook Entry 8. I'm no use to anyone. I give nothing to a single person and I don't have any purpose. My purposelessness could be over if I got up, went down stairs outside and cut a bit of garden hose. I could put it into the exhaust and lead it through to the window of Eleanor's car, sit inside and start the engine. Could put on some relaxing music, put the seat back and I would probably lose consciousness in ten to fifteen minutes. After I died that would be it… no more misery. No more pain. No more struggle. Just peace. Just happiness. No mind. But she said, 'Remember let your mind die and you will just be your real self.'

Robby found sleep but he slept badly. He had a bad headache and he thought he must be having anxiety dreams about his future. When he woke he was unable to get back to sleep. His appetite was gone and all he wanted to do was stay in bed. He was feeling very low. He couldn't find any place to go in his head that would make him happy. He got his notebook out, sat on the edge of the bed and wrote.

Robby: Pocket Notebook Entry 9. I know where I should be. I need to be back on the street. I was free there. I've no longer got the flashbacks hanging over me. I can be at home being homeless easier than I can being here in this house of my dreams. My dreams have all been smashed. That is the answer. There is no point in staying on. I'll get my rucksack and pack. I'll go now whilst it's light. I'll drive to the station and see the woman with the dark hair, the woman who used to make me breakfast with the beans.

I'm stupid. I'm just reacting to Eleanor's funeral. I need to see a doctor to get a physiotherapist to look at my leg. I think if I sleep with my good leg on top of the bad leg it somehow irritates it.

+++CHAPTER 13.

A week later, after having told Jack Jones that he had broken his leg he turned up at a physiotherapist appointment with his referral letter.

"You managed to drive here then?"

"Yes. The physio in Southampton said if I had an automatic I should be alright to drive."

"I suppose so," Gina remarked. Robby didn't think she sounded very enthusiastic. "What sort of automatic?" Robby noticed that she was focused on the letter from Jack Jones and didn't make any eye contact with him.

"A Land Cruiser."

"That's an expensive car for someone like you," she said still looking up at him from the letter.

"What do you mean?"

"Most ex service men don't drive around in big four wheel drives."

"If it makes you feel better it's an old one."

"I've got the letter which says you need your leg strengthening. Doesn't really say very much."

"Seems pretty straight forward."

"He could say what for."

"How do you mean what for?" Robby was confused by her.

"It doesn't say why you need the input."

"Doesn't it say it hurts me if I sleep on it with my other leg at night?"

"Ok, but why do you want it?"

"To get back properly on my two legs without the pain a couple of times a week and I've still got a bit of a limp."

"Ok, but it doesn't say that."

"I've just told you what I want because you said it didn't state it on the referral letter. What else would you like me to tell you?"

"As long as I can see you're prepared to do the work."

"This is a voluntary scheme. Do you think I would have bothered showing up if I didn't want to do the work?"

"Some people only turn up once."

"The GP said I would need two sessions a week to start with."

"Blimey, he's got a cheek. What does he think this is the private sector? This is the NHS."

"I'm a veteran and the GP said I would get priority service."

"You are at the top of the waiting list because I don't have a waiting list. But I'm not doing two sessions a week with a fit ex-service man when I've got a waiting list of fifteen people who've injured their backs and legs trying to work and raise money to pay their tax to keep that war going in Afghanistan, when we shouldn't even be there."

"With the greatest respect. I'm not fit. I've got problems with one of my limbs. Do you want to help me?"

"I'll see you once a week but not if you're late."

"So what you're really saying is that you're not willing to help me?"

"No I didn't say that. I said you can't be seen twice a week because there are other priorities."

"I've been referred as a priority."

"This is my department. After you've been referred to me. I prioritise you."

Robby quietly got up off the chair and looked at her then smiled. He limped to the door then drove home to the Eleanor's house where he got out his notebook.

Robby: Pocket Notebook Entry 10. I was so mad at her at first. She was irritating and could easily grind someone down. I've thought about this carefully and I think I understand the physiotherapist I saw earlier. I was friendly, reasonable and I answered each of her questions. I put forward my needs which are basic but I was met with illogical hostility. At first I thought she was being rude and inflated about herself and her job. But actually it's quite the opposite. I feel sorry for her because her sense of self importance is not big enough. She needs to feel more important than she is. That's embarrassing because she has a problem with how small she feels and she is going around broadcasting it. It's unfortunate because it means her sense of self importance is more important than her work so she's not a helpful person. In that kind of work she's not going to get any repeat business. In a military setting, she would have been spotted and the situation addressed before it led to any harm. Anyway, working her out is better and more calming than getting angry about her.

I still need a physio. The physio in the hospital taught me the basic exercises but I know that's not enough. They know all sort of tricks and all on sorts of clever things that can help me improve. I'll find someone through Fearghas tonight.

I feel my mind is working alright but the events in my life are saying something to me. I had obviously lost my mind when I tried to hang myself. Perhaps I am supposed to lose my mind. Eleanor said 'Remember let your mind die and you will just be your real self.' I've been through various accidental forms of mind destruction lately but none of those were the kind she meant. I don't really understand how you can let your mind stop working. Using my mind to work that out doesn't really seem the best way to see it. I thought I understood what she said but actually I don't see it. I just don't understand how to see it.

If I let my mind die I would have to give up some of the things I feel strong about, like what is right and wrong. What's easy and what is hard. What is happiness and what is pain. For example, I disagree with Thomas's interpretation of what Eleanor said about the Afghan girl. If I were to go along with what Thomas said and bring up a Muslim girl and support her, that would be going against what I think is right, what the community here thinks is right and the Muslim girl. Dam, she would be proud to be a Muslim in a community like this and I would protect her from any abuse or harassment. Dam! Dam! Dam! Eleanor was right. I've just been resisting it. I have to go against my thinking. Dam. Why didn't I see what they both said?

This is insane and I must be losing my mind now. I'm actually thinking of taking what Eleanor said on face value. What she said turns my head on its side. It stops my ordinary thinking. I can't think like I've been thinking if I am to actually look after a Muslim girl with or without a family. I have this house here and there is the one just down from here which hasn't been used since I last used it. I could find a Muslim family who would run the farm. They could live in that house and I could pay them like a tenant farmer and they could look after some sheep for me too. The big problem is I wouldn't think that there are many Muslims in Scotland. Come to think about I don't think there would be any Muslims sheep farmers in Scotland. I'm going to sort this out and put it to rest. I'm going to check it out on the computer. Ok so there may not be but Eleanor didn't say Muslim, she said Afghan. If there are no Afghans in Scotland what about an Iraqi or an Iranian...

Well I'm completely shocked by what I've found, I looked up Iranians, Afghans, Muslims and Scottish and I found an Iranian Scottish Society and an Afghan Scottish Association. There are two huge Mosques, the Glasgow Central Mosque and the Edinburgh Central Mosque. So there are a lot of Muslims in Scotland and there is an actual Afghan Scottish Association. Eleanor must have known that. I'm going to call one of them and see what they say.

"Hello. Is that the Iranian Scottish Association?"
"Yes."
"Do you have any refugee families who need housing?"

He hung up I think he thought I was making a hoax phone call. I've got nothing to lose, so I'll try them all.

"Is that the Scottish Afghan Society?"
"Yes what?"
"Do you have any refugee families who need work and housing?"
"Are you crazy?"

Obviously a direct approach is not the way. I'm going to try making an appointment to see an Imam.

"Hello is that the Glasgow Central Mosque"

"Yes sir."

"I would like to make an appointment to see the Imam if that is possible?"

"When?"

"Whenever he is free."

"And the nature of your request?"

"I'm a farmer in the highlands and I have a house which I want to offer in exchange for looking after a farm, perhaps to a refugee family."

"Very unusual... but give me your number and name sir. I will call you back.

No one called back but the thought of possibly having a refugee family who are very needy being able to take something from this land and help improve themselves and their position makes me feel there is a possibility. I'll wait and see if he calls back.

Robby Notebook Entry 11. It is two days since I phoned the Mosque and today I got a phone call. He will see me tomorrow in what they call his surgery. They warned me I might get one minute as there is usually a long queue to see him. I said 'Yes I'll be there.'

So Eleanor and Thomas you were right. I can only move on after I go against my conditioning, my expected thinking and ways of doing things. If that gives me any forgiveness at all, I would be forever grateful. It's odd that it's not about guilt. It is about balance. I have to forgive her and I have to forgive myself. What a strange thing to come out of that whole episode. To get through that nightmare to find that I'm left with having to balance it now.

The next morning after an early start Fearghas drove Robby to the Imam's office at the Glasgow Central Mosque. Robby was nervous until he got to the front of the queue to see the Imam. It was a simple room at the side of the mosque. After three quarters of an hour the queue whittled down as the Imam seemed to see everyone very quickly. Most people seemed to want a blessing or permission to marry or advice about a relationship or money. As Robby's turn in the queue got nearer to the front he observed that the Imam was about forty years old and seemed very relaxed and not at all serious how Robby had imagined him.

"My name is Robby. I've come here to get forgiveness not from you but from myself. I am a farmer now but before I was a soldier. I have a position on my farm for a family who would like to look after my sheep and maybe work up to having their own flock."

"Yes." the Imam said nodding his head towards a door on the right. "I heard of this."

"You will come back this afternoon at one," said one of four of the Imam's aids.

Robby walked as upright and as straight as he could as he thought the Imam might notice his slight limp.

In the afternoon Robby was more relaxed as he answered more intimate questions from the Imam.

"Why do you want to forgive yourself?"

"I have recovered mentally being in the war but I've been unable to move on."

"Who is the man with you?"

"This is Fearghas. He is my uncle and a farmer."

"Why is he here?"

"He drove me here."

"You said you are looking for a family. Why?"

"I can give some security to them. Maybe a family with nothing left. They may have come here as refugees, or maybe seeking asylum. It is some security to start with, and then later the opportunity to maybe build up a flock of sheep and be independent."

"And you... his uncle. What do you say of some Muslim family suddenly appearing in your area working on your farm? Would they not be hated and ridiculed as having failed in their own country?"

"No they would not. Our own people are not interested in the land anymore. They're off in the cities and doing other work. Robby will be stronger soon, but even then he will not be able to look after the farm without help."

"What sort of farm?"

"Sheep and some of the farm is rented out."

"So why do you come to a Mosque and not a Hindu temple or a Synagogue?"

"When I was a soldier I killed a Muslim girl, maybe seven or eight years old who had a grenade. I am trying to forgive myself by making a big effort to help a family."

"She will always be with you. She was special."

"I now understand that."

"I am not a man of war. You speak as if you know war is wrong. I had to look after my father's sheep as a child. I will put your request into the community to see if there is anyone. Many Iranian and Iraqis Muslims were sheep farmers. Now they want to be doctors and lawyers. I doubt that anyone will want to take your offer up because who wants to go backwards? Also there is the issue of trust. You are a white European who has fought in our holy lands. There will be people who will not trust you and maybe even hate you because of that. However I understand what you are, your offer and it is honourable. I don't want to disappoint you but it is very unlikely that any Muslim in this advanced country would consider going backwards and becoming a shepherd."

Robby Notebook Entry 12. I got a disappointing response from the Imam today. He doesn't think anyone will take up the offer because they won't want to think they are going backwards looking after sheep. It was a good idea of Eleanor's but it's just not going to happen in this modern world where everyone wants to compete. The Imam should know. I accept that and I have to think of another way of coming to terms with forgiveness.

I've been looking back at these notes I've made and they are helpful. It looks like I'm at a rather big changing stage in my life because of everything that's happened to my mind. I don't feel as confident as I would like to be about myself and what I'm going to do with my life. There's no one around who I feel I can ask because I don't know if anyone would understand my story.

Robby sat at the kitchen table and decided to put his notebook away. He found some loose sheets of his aunt's plain white paper and he began to write.

Dear Anita,

I am writing to you because I have realised three things. First I never thanked you enough for the help you gave me so thank you! The other thing is that I promised to let you know how I was doing. I also need your advice.

But first. I hope you're well. I hope you are still thinking of moving on from being a therapist. You told me that you wanted to grow vegetables and work with wood. It sounds odd but wood is probably softer and more flexible than a lot of people you had to work with from the military; me included. I don't know how you deal with people all day, every month, with such dark problems as I had. I remember you saying that it's important to try and realise what the next step is long before you have to take it. I hope it's all worked and out and you're happy.

I'm doing alright. When I left working with you, I came up to Scotland to see my aunt. She died from cancer almost as soon as I got here. I didn't know that my Aunt and my Uncle, who died a year ago, left me their croft which is really a farm which is mostly rented out. But I'm going to have to take over when I am well enough.

Before she died my Aunt said that I should find an Afghan girl and bring her up. Moments before she died my Aunt said 'Your old life will soon be over and you will become something else, just like a caterpillar becomes a butterfly. After you've found her and brought her here, you will be free. You'll be able to move on from what has happened to you and enjoy a life of bliss here. It's only ones such as you who have suffered a great deal who can see the way to your own self. It's only inside you that you find happiness. Remember it's only the ones who suffer who are able to see the self. Others have no need to find happiness. They find it in the outer world in pleasure through the senses, but they are the unlucky. I'll show you. But not now. I'll show you soon. Remember let your mind die and you will just be your real self.' Then she died."

The last time I ignored what she said I joined the Armed Forces so I actually went to see the Imam in Glasgow Central Mosque. He was helpful but he said it was unlikely anyone would take up my offer because who wants to go backwards and be a sheep farmer? But he said he would put the word out.

I'm at a point where I'm stuck. I can't think of anything to help me move through the forgiveness which I must find for myself. If you have any ideas please let me know.
With fondest regards and thanks.

Robby.

P.S. If you're ever up this way don't pass by without saying hello.

Two weeks later Robby received a reply.

Dear Robby,

Thanks for your very welcome letter. I was so pleased to hear that you've got your life back.

You sound so happy and positive and lots of things seen to have fallen in place for you. I was sorry to hear about your aunt's death, so close after your uncle's. But I'm sure the farm will be a great help working through the pain of grief.

Thanks for asking about me. As you will see from the post mark we have moved. Steve and I got fed up with the south coast and how busy it was. We made a bold decision to steal away and leave our old lives behind. We each have children and we could see they would cope well with change. Steve had just been offered a redundancy deal and I wanted to finish working in trauma, finish working in therapy. I could see another five years ahead but I thought I could leave stronger and less worn out if I left now. There are so many things which we want to do.

We are renting a house just outside Kirkwall in the Orkney, where we spent a summer holiday last year. It's very quiet. We're still exploring the island and Isles. The children are really happy at school. There is a very low crime rate and the weather is unusual. The people are quite different in that they are quite serious and interesting.

I am still psychologically decompressing after all my years in trauma and I am finding parts of me that have remained hidden which is mostly a joy.

Now back to you. I don't know about the forgiveness aspect of what you are going through. It used to be something that a priest dealt with, but I'm not so sure these days. Some priests only survive because they are good psychologists and some psychologists survive because they are good at helping with spiritual problems. This area is blurred by its nature and by the fact that psychologists and priests work in the same area but have radically different training. Your problem may be both and that's why it may seem so hard.

But what a strange thing for your aunt to suggest. Apart from her possibly being delirious, as it seems from what you said that she was moments away from dying, there are really only two interpretations of what she said to you.

The first is taking what she said at face value and as the priest said, actually finding, adopting and bringing up an Afghan girl is unlikely. I have a problem with this way of seeing it though. It's a bit like King Solomon's wisdom in the Bible when two women claim to be the mother of a baby. King Solomon orders the baby to be cut in two and each mother be given a half. In ordering the baby to be cut in two, the true mother reveals herself by pleading with King Solomon to spare the baby's life and give the infant to the other woman. It is a realisation followed a painful sacrifice. Although it gets the result it is through extreme pain. I agree with what you said about bringing up an Afghan girl in Scotland. It may sound like a noble thing to do which no doubt might bring some measure of forgiveness.

But there could be something inherently wrong with doing it. But I am not saying it is necessarily the case. It could be like being punished and having to feel guilty. Feeling guilty is a negative thing and it does not make you feel better. It makes you feel bad.

I am being the devil's advocate to help you be careful. I think you can understand this if you see that it was the priest who said this, and making people feel guilt is a typically Christian technique. It enslaves you. It doesn't set you free. You need to be freed up not chained down by the circumstances of what happened. But I have to be honest; it could still be a good thing to do.

Also, what if the expectancy of forgiveness failed? You could be left feeling resentful too. So maybe you should have that in mind in making your decision.

The other interpretation which your aunt put so eloquently is on a much deeper level. What your aunt said was about you changing so that you can understand and be free of the mind, which is where your suffering is. Perhaps the look you saw on your aunt and also on the girl was one of someone who has stopped suffering. It is rare and when seen it can change us so we want to attain it in this life.

From what you have said about your aunt you must find your own path. This is beyond my realm of understanding because psychology is limited to understanding the mind. What she has told you to do is find out how to find to your sense of the inner self. That is not the mind so it is beyond my expertise. However there is something. Maybe just one thing.

There is a form of psychology called Transpersonal Psychology. Some psychotherapists are trained in it. It's more modern than the old fashioned behavioural psychology, classical psychoanalysis and humanist psychology but it acknowledges them. It's also known as the fourth force in psychology. It's all to do with the journey of the soul. I know they are not so much into doing typical therapy sessions. They are more like a guide. Transpersonal Psychology field is more an umbrella term including a spectrum of approaches to the self. It includes approaches to the self like various types of meditation, yoga, and the contemplation. They use aspects of Buddhism, Hinduism, Sufi and Christian mysticism.

There's a network of them around the world and there are some up near you. I think that might be your next port of call. You certainly don't need any more 'therapy.' I know transpersonal therapists work from the inside out. That might be what you need, so I've enclosed a list of them in your area.

Thank you for the invite and we will be happy to take you up on that when we are passing by. Meanwhile, likewise, if you ever come up here you are most welcome. We would be offended if you didn't stay with us.

Take care of yourself Robby.

With love and compassion

Your friend

Anita and family.

+++CHAPTER 14.

Robby parked the Land Cruiser outside Vicky's cottage. The detached cottage was smaller than he had thought it would be. It looked newly painted and had lots of flowers in the garden. As he walked up the path he caught a glimpse of runner beans growing on an A frame of long canes at the side of the cottage. He lifted the brass knocker and let it go. It made a double thumb on the heavy brass plate which it rested against. A few seconds later Vicky appeared as the door opened and beckoned him in.

"Robby?"

"Yes, thanks for seeing me so soon."

"The person I was due to see has got a really bad cold and didn't want to give it to me. Come and take a seat." All of Robby's senses were assessing Vicky who looked around forty five with dark hair which had just the occasional silver strand. She had a long skirt and a white blouse. She seemed straight to the point. Robby also picked up that she was warm and completely focused on him. The room had two old comfortable looking armchairs and an old extendable Victorian dining room table covered with boxes of crayons, colouring pencils and large sheets of white paper. On the floor were some scattered cushions on four old rugs which had all seen better days.

"Looks like a classroom." Robby smiled.

"Yes... for some." Vicky looked down at the floor in silence for a few seconds. Her gaze changed and she looked Robby straight in the eye. "You said on the phone why you wanted to be seen. You were involved in an incident which left you suicidal with traumatic stress which you cleared up with some sessions of EMDR. You now want to explore how this has left you as you feel as if your view of the world has changed?"

"Yes. When I was in Afghanistan I had to shoot a girl who came at me with a grenade. It was in self defence and trying to protect some mates. I killed her which saved me and the others I was with. I've worked through all the anxiety which this caused me. My attempt at suicide failed and I ended up having EMDR which has worked. Where I am now is knowing it's not over."

"What do you see?"

"I must make amends to balance what is inside me. I have to pay something back. I need to forgive myself. I've tried applying to adopt a Muslim family but got nowhere."

"What do you see?"

"I see her look."

"You seem to be ready so let's begin and go straight in. We are going to do a guided daydream using active imagination. I want you to do this on the floor lying down. So first of all lie on the floor and get yourself comfortable." Robby trusted her and slid out of the armchair and gathered two soft cushions to his sides. "I am going to ask you to try and see the things I suggest to you. It is better if you close your eyes to begin, then later you might want to draw some of the images. I will ask you if you want to write and draw what you see. Is that ok?"

"It sounds fine."

"Get yourself comfortable as you will be lying on the floor for some time." Robby put the two cushions one on top of the other under his head, and then he lay down with his arms by his side. Vicky pulled the curtains closed and dimmed the lights so the room was comfortable and relaxing. She began speaking calmly and clearly.

"Don't think about what you see. Just stick with seeing the images. Now you can close your eyes. I am now inviting you to look deep and explore what is beneath the surface appearance of your life." Vicky waited a minute then said. "You might like to write it down or tell me about what you see that has made you come to the place in yourself you now find yourself."

"I'm in a place of uncertainty. It's like it's all strange and yet everything seems right that is happening. I need to be sure I am doing the right thing."

"Yes is the answer."

"I suppose I'm not sure about myself and that's why I'm here. So much has changed. I'm just a bit bewildered by it all."

"In that case, what might help the most is to look at your image, the one you have of yourself. Years ago we used to use astrology to map out what sort of people we are. But these days one way of looking at our image of ourselves is to see ourselves as being composed of sub-personalities. These are seen as images, often people just beneath the surface. They can also be objects or even an animal. Each one is like a segment of a cake that makes us. These sub-personalities can talk with each other and they are always at play. Let's find them.

But before we do, first we need to find an inner sanctuary in you, your safe place you can return to at any time should anything get too uncomfortable. Second you must find a talisman to go with you. First I want you to find an inner sanctuary. Look inside and find an inner place which is just for you. A place where you feel safe but also nourished. It is a place where you can go for shelter or where you gather your sense of your world and earth yourself back to, should you feel adrift."

Robby could see his aunt's house. He was sitting. He was looking out from the guest cottage just twenty yards down from her house. He felt high up and had a really good view of the trees and houses in the distance.

"Now come back to the room for a minute... now return to the shelter but after a short while return back to this room. Do this twice more over the next few minutes so that you can access the sanctuary easily should you feel the need to go there for a while during the exercise."

Robby came back to Vicky's room, then saw the view from high up at his aunt's guest cottage. He stayed for a few seconds, then came back to Vicky's room. Again he saw his aunt's guest cottage then he returned to Vicky's room.

"I want you now to find a talisman. It can be a stone, a jewel or even something metal. It is a mentor and wise person who is your guide who will help you get through any obstacle you encounter. Find it and hold it in your hand. If you find yourself not able to understand any of the sub-personalities ask your talisman."

Robby felt vacant when trying to find a talisman then he saw a lump of half metal and half rock the size of stone.

"I want you to find yourself in a meadow or a field. I want you to explore this meadow. It is summer and everything is green. Take a few minutes to look around... "

At first the meadow seemed vast to Robby but then he noticed it seemed to have an edge to it. He observed that the grass was not long or mowed and there were wild flowers growing in places.

"Now, looking all around you, you see a building which you know is the home of your sub-personalities. Slowly move towards the house and when you reach it walk around it and see what kind of house it is. As you walk around the house you can hear voices inside and you know these are the voices of your sub-personalities..."

Robby saw that the house was T shaped as if it had three different parts. He walked around and saw the windows at the front seemed high off the ground almost as if to stop anyone getting in or seeing in. When he got around the back of the house it was the opposite. There were three sets of French windows which opened into a walled garden where fruit and vegetables were growing. There were lots of sunflowers. Each of the three parts of the house had a set of French windows. He didn't hear any voices as he explored the house but he had a strong sense that there were several people inside and that they were being quiet.

"When you come to the entrance you walk in and start to explore the house. You get a sense of what kind of house it is. You get a sense of the atmosphere in the house. Take a few minutes to walk around… "

When he came around to the front of the house he opened the door and went into the small hallway. He sensed that there was something going on here. It seemed like a homely place where people were happy to be. Then he saw some toys so he knew there was a child or children. There was a room with cushions on the floor for people to sit on. There were seven cushions. This was a very quiet room. It was silent and empty of objects, so he wasn't sure what it was for. In the second part of the house was a library with sofas and a table. There were books on shelves and on the table. It was a serious sort of study. In the third part of the house there was a large room with a hot tub, a small steam room in one corner and a small plunge pool. There were weights to lift and a rowing machine. To the side of this was a door leading to a simple old fashioned kitchen with nothing modern at all. There were herbs and chilli peppers hanging by a window and an old fashioned oven.

Robby went upstairs where he found there were bedrooms which all looked similar. They were all quite spartan. There was one room which he didn't go into because the people who lived there were all in there keeping quiet. He felt odd but he respected that and went back down the stairs.

"When you are ready, come out of the house and walk some distance from it. You then face the house and invite the sub-personalities you know best to come out one at a time to join you. As each one comes out of the house, give each a name or a symbol and take your time slowly to greet them and see what they are like… "

Robby walked out into the meadow and then invited the occupants to come out. First of all this young man came out dressed in white karate kit. He looked about eighteen and he was careful, walking barefoot. He looked naive and had a serious look. He walked like he was doing the doing Tai Chi which Robby had done. He seemed anxious to protect himself and others. Robby thought he was like a warrior or some kind of hero.

Then there was a very quiet girl of about eight or nine. Robby could tell that she really wanted to talk about all the things she had done that day but somehow she wasn't allowed to. She seemed to brighten up when she saw Robby and really trusted him and felt that she was able to be herself. She had a book in one hand and a tennis ball in the other and she really wanted Robby to play with her. She was in a yellow bathing costume and wanted to go swimming in the river.

Then out came an older woman. She looked like a wise woman. She was also beautiful and had lavender in her hands. Robby thought she was some kind of guide, but wasn't sure what kind. She had a long skirt and sandals. She had flour on her clothes from baking.

Next came a woman about twenty five years old with a book who seemed to be very distracted by it. She seemed to be studying something and was very serious about it. She was too occupied with it. She had a uniform like a lecturer at a university.

Then came a young woman who was in a white coat. She was a doctor who was some kind of psychologist. She had a small book in her pocket which also had pens and a notepad. She was preoccupied with helping other people. She was very knowledgeable, but she didn't smile.

The last person who came out was a very quiet man. He didn't speak because for some reason he didn't have to. Robby could see straight away that he looked the happiest of all of them. He was dressed in some kind of simple white robe, thrown over his shoulder.

"When they have all come out of the house, take the two that get on the least and take them some distance away from the others. Listen to them and find out from them what they disagree about and what can help them most to understand each other and live together more harmoniously. Find an image or symbol which represents this resolution."

Robby looked at them for a while and tried to decide which two got on the least. Eventually he decided that the female doctor didn't like the quiet man. He didn't have a problem with her at all but he seemed to annoy her. Robby walked away from the six people standing next to him and then called the quiet man and the female doctor over.

"What is it that you two disagree about that stops you getting on?"
He asked them.

"He's lazy and doesn't contribute to society. He does nothing all day apart from cook and eat. He needs to get something to do other than go on long walks."

"And you?" He asked the man. There was a long pause before he looked at her and spoke.

"Sometimes the less you do, the less damage you do. I admire you for working hard, being disciplined and helping less fortunate people than yourself. You know a great deal. You are a library of knowledge. However you are too stuck in thinking and you hold knowledge above all else."

"How can you understand each other so you can help each other?" Robby asked.

"He could tell me how he is so content with so little and with doing nothing. I wouldn't mind being a bit like that."

"What can you tell her?" Asked Robby.

"You could feel more relaxed, more happy and content with yourself and your field of knowledge if you took some deliberate time out to just be yourself away from thinking. Take yourself less seriously. Be a bit more spontaneous and just be yourself. You could try staying in the moment, the present here and now and not always be trying to work out the future. Just be still. You are not just your mind in that body."

"What do you make of that?" Robby asked.

"It's so true. So desperately and sadly right." She started crying and wiping her eyes at the same time. "I've always felt pushed to achieve. I envy you because you are happy just doing nothing. I wish so much that I could just do a bit of that but I don't know how."

"If you really want to you will find a way by just being still. Just be," the quiet man said.

"When they have helped each other take them back to the others and then bring them back into the house..." Vicky quietly said.

"Ok you two, thank you for that. Let's go back and join the others and go back into the house," Robby said to them.

"When you are ready open your eyes. Lay where you are for a few moments and then return to this room. Take your time."

"Now I want you to draw a circle and divide it up into segments like a cake. Put one sub-personality in each segment. Spend about fifteen minutes drawing and writing."

Robby opened his eyes, sat up and picked out the yellow, green and blue crayons and drew a large circle just as Vicky had suggested. He then put one of his sub-personalities into a segment of the circle. When he had finished he gave a sigh and sat back up in the armchair. There was a cup of tea sitting on the coffee table beside him. As he took a sip he nodded to say thank you to Vicky who was sitting in the armchair opposite to him.

"How do you feel?" Vicky asked.

"I'm not sure anymore now... what's real. Is that my whole life, I mean my real life... and is all of what's going on just a play? Is that reality and is being here the dream? The dream world seems more real to me now. How do I feel? It's like being privileged to see something."

"Tell me who is next to whom in the circle."

"Well, it was all a bit strange. I know you told me to put each of them in their own segment of the circle. But I didn't feel they wanted that. The earthy mother was in a segment with the boy dressed in karate clothes. The clever university lecturer was with the psychologist who was a doctor and the quiet man was with the little girl."

"Do these three segments mean anything or represent anything to you Robby?"

"Yes, but I'm not sure what. The mother is earthy but that's it."

"Well perhaps the one with the karate kid in and the earthy type mother... they're both earthy and physical."

"Maybe they are the physical body thing because she is a mothering woman and he is concerned with the physical body and using it to protect others."

"And the other two?"

"The two women are both very clever. They seem into knowledge so that segment might represent knowledge or thinking."

"Ok. Let's call that segment the mind then. And the last two?"

"The other segment with the quiet man and the girl who wants fun. I'm not sure. Maybe it's about peace, happiness."

"What aspect of you is about peace?"

"It's not religious but for me it is about being conscious of something else, something bigger than just me."

"The sense of a consciousness... the 'Self' with a big S."

"I understand now. My sub-personalities are concerned with the body the mind and the soul or self."

"Yes. You are doing really well. But now I want you to return to lying on the floor". Robby slipped out of the armchair and onto the floor once again and made himself comfortable.

"Now you return to the meadow some distance away from the house. You are in a special area of the meadow which is much lighter. You are in the centre of this bright circle and you now invite each one of your sub-personalities one at a time to come and join you. Some may have changed, some may have gone and there might be new ones. Ask each one what they want from you and also ask each one what you want from them. This is about finding out about each of the sub-personalities. Take your time... "

Robby returned to the meadow but it was so different. Things had changed. The first person to emerge from the house was the university lecturer, the woman who had been so stuck in books. But she was jogging on the spot in a tracksuit. Robby asked her what she wanted from him and she said that she wanted permission to relax her body twice a week in a hot tub and to swim. When he asked himself what he wanted from her he realised that she had already shown him that it's important not to lose his sense of balance. He realised he haven't kept as fit since he left the RAF. He used to run every day for half an hour, but he knew it had dropped to once in a while.

Next came the psychologist who was a doctor. Her white coat had gone and she was wearing a yellow sari. Robby asked her what she wanted from him and she said she wanted to know about discipline, so that she could have time every day to reflect on herself. He asked her how she had become so calm and serene looking and she said that she had taken the old man's advice and decided to just be still.

The earth mother then came out exactly the same as before, still covered in flour. He asked her what she wanted from him and she said she wanted a less busy life. Robby said that he wanted to be able to cook and to prepare good food but that he had never been given any instructions. She said with that patience if he bought a cookery book he could learn to cook one new meal every week.

Then came the little girl with her ball and she was still with the older man who was wearing his white robes. They were playing together just having a lot of fun. He was throwing the ball in the air for her to catch and she was throwing it higher than he could reach and it kept on going behind him. The little girl spoke first."

"He lets me just play whenever I want to and whatever game I like. Sometimes I am just tired and he lets me just be. He joins in and is my best friend. But he lets me be. He will tell you."

"Yes, she's great company and makes me smile especially when I miss the ball and fall over. Do you want to play too?"

"I would love to but I'm meeting a few others." Robby said.

"Well we are always here if you just want to be with us."

"Next came the young man who had been dressed in the Karate kit. He was now dressed in ordinary blue jeans, a t-shirt and he was carrying a book."

"What's with the book?" Robby asked the young man.

"It's one I'm writing. It's about how to avoid getting in to conflict with others. It's about how to be wise and avoid fighting at all costs. It's about being at peace with others but also about being detached."

Robby recognised this as the person he had become since leaving the RAF. He sensed that he was now not so reactive and thought much more before he spoke.

Then Robby was surprised by what happened next. A new figure appeared. It was a man dressed in a yellow jump suit. Robby thought he was being very funny, like a comedian. He was going from being sad and angry to being happy. He was mocking but also paying Robby compliments.

Robby couldn't work him out so he asked his talisman. The talisman said that the man was a jester but also a fool who was really the wise man. It said the wise fool was trying to tell Robby about how he was feeling and he represented Robby's feelings about everything. The Talisman said the fool would never tell a lie because he was about openness.

"When they have talked with each other, bring the talking to a close. Stand for a few moments in that bright part of the meadow with all of your sub-personalities and look at what you have found out. Look how what you have seen can help you change and grow. Look at a deeper meaning for you meeting and bringing these sub-personalities together."

When Robby invited them to stand around the edge of the bright area of the meadow, the little girl stood with the quiet man and the female doctor now joined them in the part about the Self. The earth mother stood with the female university lecturer in the body part and the boy with the book stood on his own in the area concerned with the mind. The jester stood in a new area called feelings. Robby stood there with them and wondered about what this had brought him. He wondered about how they could help him and he realised that they represent components which made him different at times. He saw that they had moved to areas which parts of him needed to move to. He could see that he did change and sometimes he was into the physical things and sometimes he thought too much. He then realised that he had probably been over thinking about everything.

He was aware of something deeper. He also had a very peculiar sense of completely losing sense of time. But most peculiarly he felt part of something more real and much bigger, as if he was part of everything. Robby felt moved by it.

"Soon this last meeting must end so you should now start to ask each person to return to the house. When they are back in the house close the door behind them and lay resting for a few minutes."

Robby thanked them and asked them if they would kindly like to return to the house.

"When you are ready, once again I want you to draw a circle and divide it up into segments like a cake. Put one sub-personality in each segment. Spend about fifteen minutes drawing and writing."

Twenty minutes had passed. Robby drew his second circle and divided it up into segments. When he had finished he sat back up in the chair and Vicky gave him a warm smile.

"Now let's look at what you saw."

Robby told Vicky exactly what he saw and what he heard. When he finished, Vicky was silent for a few seconds before she spoke.

"Words sometimes cannot describe some experiences. They are inadequate. Returning to the question of why you came here. It's perhaps not what it seems. You said on the phone that you wanted to come here to see what else you could do if you could not adopt a family. You said you were looking for forgiveness.

It seems like a new life is there for you and that it will enable you to heal yourself. But coming here has taken you further towards the path to your inner self. When you take one step towards the path, it moves towards you as well like a lover does. So things will probably start to move for you now very soon. When you are on the path, it can seem like it demands hard work and discipline to stay on it. But at other times it seems effortless. You said you were here to check out what your next step in forgiving yourself was. Maybe you are about to become like the girl with the wise man who has allowed herself to just be. Did you recognise her? Do you know who she is?"

"It's her. It's the Afghan girl. I see what Anita and my aunt meant about finding her. I've got to find her in me."

"Yes you'll be fine with the outer journey of adoption if that happens. But there's much more to this as you can now see. You are actually preparing yourself for the most profound journey any of us can ever take. Your sub-personalities are not the actual territory of you. They are just a map. They have aligned themselves for you to go deeper inside.

What you sense is much deeper in you, beyond your ego, your mind. It is the Self. This seems to be what you are really looking for, why you are here. You have already started to uncover it. When you said, 'It was much bigger than me,' the me you refer to is only your ego which is only the actual form of your thoughts. The ego is a bundle of thoughts and memories we think we are. But we are much more. The mind along with its ego is your personal memory, your story. The Self is more hidden, just waiting and wanting to be uncovered. This is what the Afghan girl showed you. When you accept that you are not the mind you will automatically sense acceptance for what happened in Afghanistan. Acceptance is forgiveness."

"How come you see this and I don't?"

"You are the one who saw it and showed me that you can see it. When you attempted suicide you were actually trying to kill your mind with its pain and stories. But these stories are about your mind, not your sense of the Self.

Something needed to die but it was your mind not your sense of your Self. Sometimes it is only through terrible pain that you can see the mind needs to be overcome and observed for what it is. It is no longer the most important aspect of you.

You are just beginning to uncover the Self. It's like slowly pulling back the blanket on a bed and finding there is someone underneath it. You don't suddenly see the Self but when you start pulling the blanket back you begin to see the Self and you can't stop. There will be times when you get caught up in the unreal world of the ego's thinking, but you will slowly learn that it is false and the self alone is real. That is seeing your true Self which has come searching for you and like being caught in the jaws of a tiger, it won't let you go."

"Is this all positive?"

"It's freedom from the known. Freedom from knowledge. It's not doing but being. It's the path of the Self. The Self refers to the 'ultimate reality' of a person's inner path which consists of the deepest values by which they live and feel connected to others, the wider world and the Universe. Traditionally, experience of the Self was part of religious experience but this is not necessarily the case anymore because of increased consciousness and the recent decline of organised religions which rely on doctrinal faiths."

"This may sound odd to you but how do I go about that?"

"There are lots of tools you can use to help find the Self. Some are meditation, mindfulness, contemplation, just being still, chanting, singing, or prayer. Participation in rituals as well as the celebration of festivals. Periods of abstinence or indulgence can sometimes wake you up to the Self. Consciousness of your Self may not necessarily involve a belief in a Supernatural God, Gods or Goddesses. It may be none of these but simply your own path and goal. It is significant that there may also be no difference between the goal and the path."

"Maybe that's why I have come here."

"Everything that is meant to be will be. There is no positive or negative about it. I can say one thing though. You seem to be going along the path further than most. It's only a few who can carry on the path you're on. Most people go downhill because it is easiest but you Robby; you are going up-hill. I think you will understand that on a life or death arduous march, many fall, but some are victorious. If in the future you want to re-visit the meadow, you can do it on your own, just like you have done today. But you may not need to. I think you have seen how you have been conditioned and moulded over time into becoming these sub-personalities. You no longer need someone like me to show you the way because you have three things which will always help you. You are compassionate, you keep things simple and you have humility."

"Anything else?"

"Follow the Afghan connection with the girl's look. If you make it you will be like her. Then you will have nothing to lose by dying. The you that you still know will be dead by egoside."

"I don't understand but it sounds like what my aunt talked about me going on the long journey. She said, 'Only when you let go of your old self, your mind, can you truly be your real Self. You have to unlearn to learn because learning is only learned ignorance.' I don't really get that."

"Your body and your mind are a form which you take. Your Self lives in it. You are beginning to sense something in you that is not just your mind. We all have this sense but in you it is strong. A wave in the sea is an expression, a manifestation of the sea but it is distinctly a wave. When it breaks up it is no longer a wave but part of the sea again. It is the same for us when we die."

Robby: Pocket Notebook Entry 13. The session I had was unimaginable before. I was taken by her as my guide to meet aspects of myself which I didn't realise actually existed. These sub-personalities had been expressing themselves through all sorts of things but I wasn't aware of them until today. I didn't know any of this until today. There were six of them and I met them twice. There were two males and four females. I am going to have another look at them and re-visit them on my own in the future. I want to see what changes. She said a lot of change was on its way.

+++CHAPTER 15.

"Is that Robby?"

"Yes. Hello"

"I'm Jamal."

"I'm sorry. Do I know you?"

"I'm the director at the Scottish Afghan Association. We were given information about you from the Imam. We would like to meet with you and discuss your offer. We have a family who might be interested."

"My offer?" Asked Robby.

"The Imam spoke to me and told me about you."

"You want to meet me? I can't believe it. The Imam said no one would be interested." He could hardly believe he was talking to someone like Jamal.

"We are here every day. We are open around eight in the morning and close at eight in the evening. I am here every day. Can you just bring some ID with you?"

"Tomorrow after lunch?"

"Yes. I'll be here."

Robby: Pocket Notebook Entry 14. I was taken by complete surprise by the phone call. So the Imam had kept his word and he was wrong. I wonder if this will come to anything. There is an Afghan family interested. I don't know what to think. I'm so excited. This could help me so much. If I thought there was a God I would thank him. I must take this as an ordinary but very good opportunity.

Robby found the Scottish Afghan Society in Glasgow straight away and managed to park around the back of the block. He was happy that his driving was normal but after weeks of physio he was frustrated that he still had a very slight limp on his left side. He approached the building with some fear as if approaching an old enemy. He walked through the two double sets of doors and found himself in a foyer.

He noticed in some corners there were groups of Afghan women with children. They were talking whilst sitting cross legged in a circle on the floor in traditional Afghan clothing. Most were dressed in black, which indicated to him that they were in mourning. There were others standing in small groups in western dresses and jeans. The men were separate and mainly at the back of the old office building. Robby noticed that the men were all dressed in western clothing. He instinctively walked slowly through all the people and right to the back of the building where two men and a woman sat around an old veneered office desk.

"I'm Robby."

"Jamal." Jamal was in his mid forties, roughly shaven with a moustache and a half balding head. He was skinny and dressed in a shirt and tie with black trousers. It was now that Robby became self conscious as he noticed that he was the only person wearing shoes. He shook hands with Jamal and then he slowly took his shoes off.

"Thanks for seeing me," Robby said standing in his socks. He felt a little anxious about Afghan people and he noticed his palms were sweating. Then he realised that the room was very well heated and he relaxed. The thought flashed across his mind that he was meeting with people who only months ago used to be the enemy; but now he knew they might be his saviour.

"It's our pleasure. Tea?" Jamal noticed Robby looked strangely nervous. "Come, sit and take a place with us." He beckoned Robby to sit with the others, cross legged on the carpeted floor.

"Ok, yes. Thank you, but sorry. It's been a while since I was with any Afghans and then I was not in the same situation I am now."

"It's ok. Come sit with us. Things have changed for us too. Most of us never believed we would ever be here in the UK," said Jamal pointing to some cushions on the floor. Have you had Afghan tea before Robby?"

"No."

"Then try it. It's different. Go on."

"It's very aromatic," Robby said. "What's in it?"

"Darjeeling tea and cardamoms."

"I understand now." Next he was given a peeled orange and a piece of flat pita bread which had been cooked with spinach in the middle.

"Try," said Jamal.

"Yes," Robby replied and broke it in quarters then broke each quarter in half.

"You've had this before?"

"Yes in Afghanistan."

"You like?" Asked Jamal.

"Yes. Very different," answered Robby.

"This is my friend Jamila." Said Jamal pointing to the woman who came and sat beside him. "Jamila particularly looks after the women's interests at the Society. She was a headmistress and teacher in Afghanistan." Jamila had a serious look just like a headmistress. She was about thirty and wore a black skirt, black socks and a black top. Robby thought she was in mourning. She held her hand out and shook hands with Robby.

"And this is Khalid." Jamal said gesturing to a man who came and sat on a cushion next to Jamila. "Who like me was also a lawyer in Afghanistan." Robby shook hands with Khalid who smiled. Khalid looked like a younger version of Jamal but more overweight and with a full head of black hair.

"You have the eyes of a kind man Robby." Jamal said.

"Thanks but these eyes have also seen their share of blood on both sides."

"I hope you can understand that we have not done this before. We have never introduced someone to a westerner to house them before. And no one has ever offered to do this for us. So please excuse us if we seem in any way hesitant. It is new to us. The Imam said it could be a good opportunity for someone to settle in the countryside. Maybe you can elaborate about yourself for us. We would like to know more how you see things. We wouldn't want to introduce a family to a monster or a sexual pervert. Please tell us about you."

Robby took ten minutes to summarise his life. Finally he said, "My aunt died recently and so I took over her farm. I think it is a way that I can repay the death of the girl." Then he waited.

"You have unusual wisdom. Maybe you are on a journey which may eventually help others on both sides. We have come to your country for help and now you come to us for help. It can only be a good thing. What religion are you?" Jamal asked.

"None. I learned to believe in me when I was around twelve. My parent's religion didn't help them because they had no discipline."

"You come with the best pedigree of contacts in Scotland. From the Imam himself. There is no higher authority for us. He has asked us to help you to help some of us. But we have never been asked if we would consider placing a whole family. We have not done this before," Jamal added.

"Why not?" Asked Robby.

"Simply because no one has ever asked us before. You are the first." Jamal laughed and continued. "Have some more tea."

"Do you have no children?" asked Jamal.

"No."

"Married?" asked Khalid.

"No. I'm twenty three and left the forces just over a year ago."

"Why should we trust you? You might be a British spy trying to see what trouble we are up to?" Khalid said.

"I'm done fighting... being part of anything like that," Robby said.

"How do we know we can trust you?" Jamal said, pouring Robby some more tea.

"What you see is what I am. I'm a bit worn but keen to run my aunt's croft, which is a farm. It has a lot of sheep. You are welcome to come and see it."

"That will not be necessary. We have seen enough. We also have sheep in Afghanistan. They can do well in cold weather.

My father had Afghan Arabi sheep which are good for carpets and meat. We are all shepherds. But now I don't care if I never see another sheep in my life." Everyone laughed appreciating the seriousness of his humour. Jamil clearly liked Robby so did Jamila and Khalid. They looked at him expectantly.

"Well I'm just in training." Robby said.

"Us too. Anyone who says they are not is more dead than alive," said Jamila.

"Now Robby. The Imam himself has told us to trust you. He said it was a good sign that you had approached him. He was shocked when we told him that we had a family that is interested," said Jamal. "We think we may have a family who you may be able to help and they may be able to help you. But it is probably not what you were expecting."

"Yes." Then Robby was silent. He dropped his head with humility.

"During the last few weeks we've been looking after a girl and her aunt who is twenty. Like the girl you met in Afghanistan they are also from Helmand Province. They managed to get out via Pakistan. They have been through Hell. They're still being processed by the Home Office so they've not been offered anywhere to live. But what they will be offered is so far down what you call the economic ladder that they will struggle for years if not for their whole lives to regain what their family once had.

"What happened to them?" Robby asked.

"They will tell you. Jamila will go and find them for you. The girl is called Khatira and her aunt is called Asheena." There was a silence and after a minute a young woman walked in holding the hand of a small child. Robby, Jamal, Jamila and Khalid all stood up and made room for the young woman and the child. Khatira was in a small pair of denims and had a pink jumper. Asheena was tall and very skinny. She managed a nod of the head and a small smile. She wore a multicoloured skirt, a thickly knitted cardigan with a headscarf which made her look much older.

"Asheena this is Robby. Robby this is Asheena and Khatira."

"Pleased to meet you both," Robby said and bowed his head like a large nod. He could see that Asheena was cautious and held Khatira close. What he found striking about them both was that they had fair skin, fair hair and green eyes. Robby thought that they looked like mother and daughter. He had only seen fair skinned fair haired Afghans once in Afghanistan.

"We are pleased to meet you." Asheena said. She managed a polite but frail smile. She sat down on the floor cross legged with Khatira in her lap.

"Asheena was a teacher in Helmand Province, teaching girls English." Jamila said. "Asheena. Robby is looking to house a family who are in need in exchange for looking after his farm. There will be the opportunity to eventually own your own business. Are you interested?" Jamila said.

"We have nothing but ourselves. Our lives are over forever in Afghanistan."

"Can you tell Robby about Khatira and yourself?"

"Yes of course." Asheena tried to hold her head up high and speak proudly. "We are from a village called Heratyan in the Sangin district of Helmand province in the South West." She stopped. "I was living." Her voice sounded fragile. "I was living in our family house with my younger eighteen year old sister Nahid who was Khatira's Mother; her husband, my two younger brothers, Jamil and Naseer who were eleven and twelve. It was my grandfather's house. When my parents got married they were invited to live there with his parents but they had died. My family were all there. So there were seven of us together under one roof. We were not Taliban. We were not terrorists.

We were farmers and had always been farmers. I had learned English and taught it to girls at our makeshift schools. Most of the time I tended the sheep and I earned some extra money doing some translation work a few times for journalists. I did not know I was called 'traitor' for doing this because it was for foreign journalists.

It was a Wednesday evening. It was on the 8th of May. We had a herd of sheep. My mother was just getting supper ready. I had to go and check the sheep at around seven in the evening. I took Khatira with me as Nahid was tired." Khatira stirred from her silence as soon as she heard her mother's name.

"When I got to the flock, I started checking the sheep. They were fine but disturbed by some people. I became frightened because I could see soldiers in small groups. They were huddled down on the ground waiting for something. There were definitely American. They all looked very young. Younger than me. Then I remember the two American planes. One of them dropped something which picked up speed. I gasped as I saw it enter one end of the house in the middle. The house exploded in to a massive cloud of small pieces of dust. I think you call it being vaporised. There were no screams. The bomb took them all before they could look up. They would have known nothing, felt nothing, become nothing. I lost my two parents, my two brothers, my sister and her husband. So my family were suddenly gone forever. All the animals at the side of the house were killed as well. Everything was vaporised.

I cuddled Khatira who was crying and we went back. It took ten minutes to get to the house to see if there was anything left of our family... but there were not even body parts. Everything inside and outside the house was blown to very small pieces. By the time I got there all the little pieces that could burn had already burnt to ash. There was really in truth nothing left. They had evaporated in a second into thin air. I couldn't even take a memento; there wasn't one. Everything had gone. All I knew was we had to get out of there and out of that country for ever. All of our family's papers were kept away from the house under a large rock in a plastic bag with a few photographs and a little money. I took them all. The best way out was through Pakistan. We walked for weeks. Trucks gave us lifts. We had lots of trouble but some people helped us. Then we went by sea to a port called Felixstowe and again by lorry to London. We were detained as we thought. I applied for asylum on the basis that I'm regarded as a traitor for working with foreign journalists as a translator. My life would be threatened if I returned to Afghanistan. Because of my English, I was told that I might be able to get a job translating for the Home Office or for doctors."

"Robby is there anything you want to ask Asheena?" Jamila said. She saw him thinking for a few moments. He was horrified to hear her story but he also knew it happened all the time in Helmand Province.

"And what about religion? Are you Muslim?"

"Most women have completely lost faith. Me as well. The Mujahedeen and the Taliban reversed all the things that the prophet Allah introduced to make women equal. Our rights were taken from us. We weren't even supposed to have any education. If you have seen what I have seen you would not follow any religion. A god would not have let my whole family die like that."

"What about Khatira?"

"I will not bring her up to suffer under the name of a religion like I did." Khatira looked straight at Robby.

"How old are you?" He asked Khatira who hid her face by looking down. Then she looked up straight at him.

"I'm seven." She looked down again and sucked her thumb trying to hide behind her bright fair hair.

"When are you going to be eight?"

"At my next birthday," she answered and everyone laughed.

"You're very clever," Robby said, smiling at her. Then he turned to Asheena. "Has it taken you all this time to get here since May?"

"Yes. It was with the help of some journalists in Karachi that I found a way out. I still pinch myself because I can't believe we made it alive."

"How has Khatira been?"

"Khatira is well. She's all I have left of my family."

"Did you apply for political asylum as aunt and niece or mother and daughter?"

"Mother and daughter. The names on our papers are the same surname."

Jamal then began to rustle some pages from a notebook. He looked up at Asheena and nodded as though to say that she had done the right thing by keeping Khatira as her daughter instead of her niece. That way the Home Office was less likely to deport Khatira.

"Robby has something to put to you." Jamal turned around and nodded at Robby. "Robby."

"Asheena, I hold no secret that I was in the British armed forces. My life was also torn apart by this war. I killed a child, a young Afghan girl. It caused psychological problems for me which are now better. I want to be able to make it up to that girl and I need to be able to forgive myself. I believe my only way of doing this is to support and bring up a family from there." He could see Asheena was looking carefully at what he was saying.

"What is your job?" Asheena asked.

"I was in the RAF."

"And now?"

"I have a small sheep farm."

"Ha!" Shouted Asheena as she shook her head. "Sheep again." And she laughed. "I can't believe it!" Asheena laughed again. "I've come all this way to look after sheep again." Everyone laughed even louder than Asheena. Then there was a silence.

"I have two separate houses up in the hills. I have a lot sheep that need looking after. The house and expenses are free. The opportunity is to build up your own flock of sheep."

After a long silence Asheena spoke. "It's better than surfing. I am fed up with it."

"You're fed up with surfing. In Glasgow?" Robby was perplexed and so were the others.

"Yes I have had enough of it."

"How do you mean?"

"Surfing is not as good as people think it is."

"I don't understand?" Robby said.

"There is too much moving about all over the place."

"There isn't any surfing that I know of in Glasgow."

"Yes there is."

"I'm sorry but that's impossible. You're saying that you go surfing and you are fed up with it because it's not exciting because there is too much movement all over the place."

"I have been told on very good authority that I have been surfing for the last few weeks. Anyone here will tell you I have been sofa surfing, going from one person's house to another each night and sleeping on the sofa." Everyone laughed. In her keenness to adjust to her new country and fit in, Asheena was learning and using all the new terms for things she came across.

"And the sheep?" Robby asked. Now Asheena laughed.

"It will not be the first time that sheep have saved Khatira's life and mine. So I guess I will have to like sheep." She laughed. "Did you know that they have noses on their feet?"

"That's got to be the craziest thing I've heard... saying sheep have noses on their feet. You're crazier than me."

"But it's true. Isn't that right Jamila?"

"Well yes it is. Sheep do have sensory, olfactory glands on their feet, the same as in our noses. This enables them to find their way back along trails distant from their farms."

"I give up. These women are too intelligent for me." Robby said accepting that they were very bright and quick witted.

"You're perfectly right Robby. They are too clever for me too." Jamal gave him a big smile laughing at how the women were smarter. "Do you want to give it a trial Asheena?" Asked Jamal.

"Yes you could come over for a day and see what you think."

"No trial."

"But you have a serious offer to consider." Jamil added.

"I'm serious." Robby said. "I'm not joking."

"I know when you joke." Asheena said. "Definitely no."

"Are you sure?" Jamal said.

"I am sure."

"Well... what are we to do?" Asked Jamal. I thought she was interested.

"I am sure. I do not need a trial. I will of course take up the offer. I have no other option but to eventually live in one room given to us by the home office under threat of being deported. What I'm being offered is stability. It's as if I'm being helped from a God above."

"What do you say Robby?" Asheena said.

"Yes I agree."

"Then that is a deal Robby and Asheena." Jamal shook everyone's hand. When he had finished he once again became more serious. " So when could you take them Robby?"

"If it's ok and you want to, I could come and collect you this time tomorrow."

"I accept." Asheena said clearly to Robby.

"Then it's done." Jamal said. "Are you happy with this Jamila?"

"Yes. These two make me laugh. I hope they make each other laugh too. They are funny because they misread each other so much," she said and nodded.

"This is a good thing for everyone." Jamal said. "We know there are lots of cultural differences, perhaps funny ones but there is no other kinder offer possible. It's a gift for all three of them. The Home Office will take any pressure off you because you've found somewhere to live by yourself. That means that your application for asylum will be a lot easier." Jamal clapped his hands, and then they all joined in signalling that it was all accepted and now it was being congratulated.

"Tomorrow at ten then?" Jamal said to Asheena.

"Yes." She replied.

"Ten in the morning?" Robby smiled.

"Yes ten am." Answered Asheena.

"Is this a done deal then?" Jamal said looking from Robby to Asheena and then to Jamila.

"Yes!" Robby said.

+++CHAPTER 16.

It was an unusual day for Robby because he felt as if he had changed and his world was suddenly moving at a faster pace. As he cleaned the whole of the guest cottage rooms, he found himself thinking half the time about Ian and Eleanor's generosity and half the time about Khatira and Asheena who were moving into the cottage tomorrow. He remembered that he was the last person to stay in the guest cottage just before he joined the RAF and he looked back at himself as a selfish rebellious young man. He worked nonstop, packing up stuff, putting clean sheets on Asheena's and Khatira's beds and all the general cleaning he could do. He cleaned the kitchen stove, washed all the pots and pans under hot water, mopped the floor and finally gave all the surfaces a wipe down to clear the dust.

He decided to give Khatira the large room and Asheena the smaller room. He swept, dusted and vacuumed the whole cottage and after he finished he realised that he hadn't done any shopping. He was too tired so he decided to do it in the morning. He would buy what every Afghan eats and that was chicken and rice. That's what he would get to start with.

"Hi Robby." There was a knock on the back door.

"Hello."

"Thought you might need this." Thomas said handing Robby a large hessian sack.

"What is it?"

"Take a look."

"It's some toys. How did you know?"

"Fearghas told me after you spoke to him."

"She'll love these." Robby looked carefully in the sack. "I've made her a bed so I'll put these beside it. Thanks."

"You're welcome."

"I hadn't thought about details like this. Thomas, you were right about an Afghan family. I just couldn't get my head around it at first. Now nothing could seem more obvious. I was pretty blind," he said raising his hands.

"Robby a lot has happened to you in the last year. A lot is happening for you right now. A lot must be happening to that young woman and child."

"Yes. I'm all too aware of that. I've been thinking of them. They must be nervous tonight."

"How are you feeling about tomorrow?"

"I'm very nervous. I'm really looking forward to getting them both back here. I haven't got a clue how I'll feel after that. I'm going to take it as it comes. I've got no plans."

"And what about their religion?"

"I decided that I would accept whatever religion they are. It will be more difficult for me and for them if they are Muslim because there will be some discontent amongst the locals, especially those who have children or loved ones fighting in Afghanistan. But I'm fighting on their side, whatever religion they are. It took me a long time and it was a struggle to get my head around this but I have to be unconditional about accepting what they are like." There was another knock on the door.

"Hey Robby."

"Hello." Fearghas came in and looked around.

"Robby you're a much better cleaner than me. The place looks spotless. Whoever the wee girl is, she'll be happy here. I've brought you something you might need." From behind his back he presented Robby with a child's car seat.

"I hadn't thought of that either. Thanks Fearghas. I'll be needing that tomorrow."

"We won't stay." said Fearghas. "You've probably got a lot to get on with for tomorrow. I hope it all goes well."

When they had left, Robby went back up to Eleanor's house and sat in Eleanor's arm chair, reflecting on the day.

Robby: Pocket Notebook Entry 15. Change is all I seem to be getting these days. But it's also sudden fast change, some expected others are expected. I feel so positive after meeting Khatira and Asheena today. This whole place is a blessing. I couldn't believe that there is a large Afghan community in Scotland. The two girls I met today have a far worse history than me. They have had everything taken away from them. What Eleanor and Thomas said I needed has come to me, even though I was stubborn about it. I'll be glad when everything stops changing and I feel more settled with a normal life.

I'm sure there are going to be a lot of cross-cultural differences with religion, food, schools and everything I haven't thought of yet, simply because things have moved so fast. I'm only just keeping up with things.

In the morning Robby drove to the Co-op in Aberfeldy and bought two free-range chickens, a large bag of rice, eggs, butter, milk, oil and flour. He stopped and looked at the children's isle and saw packets of pink children's socks and also packets of blue children's socks. He thought about how pink used to trigger his flashbacks and he was aware of the how he had changed, and just how damaged his mind had been at that time. He briefly thought about Lyneham, Kinloss, Brize, C17 Globemasters, Afghanistan, the girl, Tatyana, Kessingland, Southampton Hospital, Anita, Eleanor, Vicky and about right now, then he found himself happily buying the pink socks.

After he bagged it all up he put the shopping in the boot of the Land Cruiser and managed to get out of Aberfeldy by seven thirty to miss the local traffic. Half way down to Glasgow he pulled over in to a lay-by to take stock of everything. He felt he needed to think one more time about his own journey, uninterrupted by the driving. He couldn't find anything which he could look at which looked out of place.

He arrived a few minutes before ten o'clock and he went through the front door of the centre. Asheena was waiting holding hands with Khatira with a small bag over her shoulder. He could see that all Asheena and Khatira had was each other and a small bag of clothes. It was a moment he sensed was so very serious for Asheena Khatira and himself. Jamila was standing next to Khatira and next to Jamila was Jamal and Khalid.

"Robby," Asheena said, her eyes lighting up with happiness.

"Robby," Jamal said.

"Hello everyone," he answered.

"We're just here to say that you and your family are now also part of our family." Jamal held out his hand. "Robby we'll see you soon."

"Robby take care of yourself," Khalid said, shaking Robby's hand.

"Thank you Robby. We will think of you," Jamal said as she kissed Khatira and hugged Asheena. She then hugged Robby.

"Are you ready?" Robby asked Asheena nervously.

"More than ever," Asheena answered, smiling but also nervous. "Here let me take that bag." Robby lifted the bag from Asheena's shoulders. It was even lighter than he thought for a bag containing all the possessions of two people.

"Thanks. It's easier with one hand free." Her other arm held Khatira.

"Maybe from now on you'll have both hands free." Robby added.

"You are funny," laughed Asheena. "You are picking me up and I don't even know where you live." Asheena turned to face Jamila, Jamal and Khalid. "Thank you for all your help. Soon we'll meet."

Robby put Asheena's bag in the boot, then came back to her and leant forwards kissing Khatira on the forehead. He tried to pluck her from Asheena who was at first slightly hesitant about letting go of Khatira. "Careful," she said, eventually seeing that she really had to let Robby put Khatira in the car seat. He carefully placed Khatira in the child's car seat behind the passenger seat and did up the straps so that Khatira looked comfortable but he had trouble getting the buckles right. He saw Khatira's eyes were wide open as if she was taking every detail in. He pointed to the front passenger seat for Asheena.

"No I must sit with Khatira."

"Whatever." Robby said. "Less bumpy in the front."

Asheena got in the back seat and did her seat belt up but for the first time she felt slightly awkward sitting in the back beside

Khatira as she had noticed that most people put their children in the back of cars. She realised that she would have to accept change and sit in the front.

"She'll get used to you sitting in the front. She'll get used to seeing you and me together talking and find her own space in the back."

"It's just that all the trucks we have travelled in so far, she has been with me. I feel a bit awkward sitting in the back when everyone else with children sits in the front."

"When you're ready to sit in the front let me know." But half way up to Aberfeldy Robby pulled into a lay-by.

"What is it Robby?"

"It's doing my head in trying to talk to you with you behind me. I've got to rest my neck for a bit."

"Khatira's asleep so I will try sitting in the front." Asheena got out of the back, opened the passenger door and sat in the passenger seat. "How's that?"

"That makes me happier and I won't get a wry neck."

"What's that?"

"It's when you get neck pain from either stress or using it in a bad posture for a while." He now turned easily to see her in the passenger seat and he could see she was more comfortable and more relaxed. Robby moved out of the lay-by.

"Does anyone else live on your farm?"

"Just sheep." He looked over at Asheena who looked as if she was happy and smiling.

"How long have you lived there?"

"Just a few weeks."

"A few weeks. You are joking me... yes?"

"I'm not good at joking."

"So am I new like the house? Another possession? I'm joking with you."

"Let me explain. I used to visit there every holiday when I was a child. I always stayed in the guest cottage where you are staying. A few years ago I stayed there before I joined the RAF. This was my first visit back since I left the RAF. My aunt lived there until just a few weeks ago, she died of cancer."

"I'm very sorry. I hope I didn't hurt your feelings."

"No not at all. I came here expecting to stay a few days with my aunt. I didn't know she was ill and she died only a few hours after I got here. That was just a few weeks ago. So it's pretty new for it being my home too. I'm still very surprised what's happened to me. She left me what she had which is the house and farm. I'm surprised about that. I'm surprised about you. But please don't get me wrong. I'm happy about all of these things, except the death of my aunt."

"Why did you leave the RAF?"

"Because of the Afghan girl I told you about."

"Can I ask you something about her?"

"Sure."

"Why did you kill her?"

"She was coming at me at and my two crew with a grenade which she was pulling the pin out of. We would probably all have been killed."

"You didn't say that before."

"She wouldn't have done that unless like you she had lost everything. She was so little, she was too open to influence."

"I've seen children who have been turned many times. It's wrong."

"Here they don't turn them; they trick them into lots of travel in a foreign land. They seduce you into a disciplined lifestyle where all of your needs are taken care of. All you have to do is carry a gun and obey orders, including killing if the lawyers ok you to kill."

"There is a difference in the people who give the orders to kill and the children who have been tricked into doing it. The people, who give the orders, give orders from the safety of a political bunker and are cowards." Asheena said. "In my county they promise the children freedom in heaven."

"In the east they promise you a place in heaven. Here they promise you heaven on earth. They say you will have money, alcohol, travel, holidays and a pension. What is the difference between their promises? "

"I have heard of this. There is none."

"I was really only a child and I knew almost nothing of life. But it all came so fast." Robby answered.

"We all have to grow up and it seems that for you and for me it has been painful. What did you do in the RAF?"

"First I was a medic but I didn't like the sight of blood."

"Why did you become a medic then?"

"I hadn't seen a lot of blood before."

"What! You really do make me laugh. You hadn't seen blood?"

"No I hadn't."

"Then what made you want to be a medic?" Asheena asked more seriously.

"My Uncle was a medic in the Army."

"Oh I see. So what did you do after that?"

"I became a loadie, a loadmaster."

"What's that?"

"The RAF has two types of very large Cargo planes; Hercules with the four propellers and Globemasters with the four jets."

"I have seen both many times flying above us in Afghanistan. One is noisy the other one with jets is quiet, very quiet."

"Yes the quiet one is the Globemaster. They have two pilots and a loadmaster. The loadmaster or loadie as they're known is in charge of the loading and unloading of the cargo. The planes carry troops, food and ordnance to theatre."

"Theatre! Why take them to the theatre? Why would you go there when there is a war on?"

"Theatre is a military term meaning somewhere usually abroad where the armed forces are fighting."

"Oh I see now. And what is this ordnance cargo?"

"It's actually all military supplies but it's mainly guns and ammunition, tanks helicopters."

"So if you were this loadie, how did you end up killing this girl?"

"Our plane, this Globemaster had an engine fault so we couldn't fly for a few days. The three of us from this Globemaster went for a day trip… "

"Then you were crazy even before killing the girl."

"How do you mean?"

"Not even Afghans do day trips in Helmand. Didn't you know it was dangerous?"

"Yes of course I know that now. At the time it was only taking a small risk because things had been quiet for a while. It's only important that I'm alive and she's dead. That's what needs readdressing."

"So we are now your conscience?"

"No, I am paying for what I did."

"Well you're stuck with us now. We are as good as family." Asheena turned around to look at Khatira who was asleep.

"Maybe you're stuck with me." Robby said, and they both smiled and looked at each other.

"Where in Scotland is your home?"

"In Strathtay. In the Highlands near Aberfeldy."

"I don't know any of those places. Is it mountains?"

"Yes, with a beautiful lake, a river and forests. Yes very hilly but not what you would call mountains in Afghanistan." There was a pause as Asheena sighed and then yawned. "How are you feeling?" Robby asked.

"Tired. I got up early to pack and to say goodbye to everyone. And I am a little bit nervous."

"Why are you nervous?"

"Are you crazy? You are a stranger. How could I not be nervous? Maybe I'm excited more than nervous."

As they headed to the hills, Asheena could see by the low mid morning sun behind them that they were heading north.

"We'll be there in a few minutes." Robby said. They crossed the second bridge just before Strathtay then turned left along the River Tay for two miles before turning right up the hill. Asheena was quiet as they headed up the tortuous track to the croft.

+++CHAPTER 17.

"This is it," Robby said. But Asheena was very quiet. Robby gave her space to let her just be. Asheena stared ahead for twenty seconds then she got out of the car, knelt on the ground and then slowly leant forwards and put both hands on the ground in front of her. She stretched out her legs and then she stretched out her hands in front of her. She felt the ground and prostrating, kissed it. She lay there for a few moments, then she rose up and looked at Robby.

"What was that?" Robby asked

"I was saying thank you to mother earth for bringing me here."

"I understand that," Robby said.

"Can we go in?" Asheena undid the seat belt around Khatira and plucked her from the seat. Khatira woke up and looked bewildered.

"Where are we?" She asked

"Home," Asheena said. "We are living here now." She picked up her bag and turned to face Robby.

"Here this way," Robby said, pointing to the path down to the guest cottage. "There are two cottages. My aunt's one is just up here where I live and the guest cottage down the path where you live. You go first Asheena. The door is open."

"No please. Where I come from a man always goes first and leads the way."

"Ok." Robby turned and kept looking back at Khatira and Asheena as he walked down the path to the guest cottage. He opened the door and then held it open to let Khatira and Asheena in first. Asheena walked to the other side of the kitchen and looked back at Robby. "This is well... home." Robby said.

"You sound hesitant." Asheena said, patting Khatira on the back, encouraging her to wander off to explore the house.

"Well in my heart it's been kind of home for me all my life but I've only been living here a short time."

"Where did you live before that?"

"After I left the RAF last year, I became homeless."

"You are joking me. You mean like all the people on the streets?

"No. I'm not joking. I was homeless."

"But where did you live?"

"At first I did live on the street. But most of the time, especially in the summer, I lived rough in a tent." Robby looked deadly serious.

"You! But I've seen those people in Glasgow. They sleep on pavements in cardboard boxes. Most take drugs or bad alcohol. How did you get off being on the street?"

"I hung myself." Robby still looked serious and Asheena could tell.

"What! You are crazy."

"I was."

"How could you hang yourself and be here now?"

"The branch broke." Robby still looked serious.

"Then you were really crazy!"

"Yes."

"And now are you still crazy?"

"Hanging myself ended what I had become. I was refused help and I faced the truth about myself."

"What you said reminds me of a funny story about hanging."

"There's nothing funny about hanging."

"Oh yes there is. You don't know about Afghan humour."

"What can be funny about hanging?"

"Nasrudin."

"Who?"

"Nasrudin. Have you never heard of him? He is very famous."

"Who?" Robby looked very puzzled.

"Nasrudin. He's a legendary Mulla. Every country says that he was born there. Afghanistan, Iran, Turkey, India, Greece and

Russia. In the Middle Ages Nasrudin tales were used to mock authority. Are you sure you've never heard of this man?"

"Absolutely not."

"You reminded me of a story about him about truth and hanging. But it's no joke. Do you want me to tell it to you?"

"Yes."

"Right then. One day, the Mulla Nasrudin was with the King who was trying to show off his knowledge. The king was a show-off.

'Laws make better people.' said the King. 'No. Laws do not make people better,' said Nasrudin. 'Laws do not make people more truthful.' Answered Nasrudin.

'I can make people practise truthfulnesss,' said the King boastfully hoping to impress Nasrudin.

The King built a gallows on the only bridge entering the city and the next day he announced. Nasrudin was eager to find out what the gallows were for because they looked very frightening on the bridge.

'What are the gallows for?' Nasrudin said to the king.

'Everyone who wants to come into the city will be questioned. If they tell the truth they can enter but if they lie they will be hanged.' Nasrudin made sure he was the first person to try and enter the City and walked towards the gallows.

'Where are going?' asked the chief guard standing right in front of Nasrudin so the king could see.

'I'm going to be hanged.'

'I don't believe you,' said the guard.

'If I have lied, then hang me.'

'But if we hang you for lying, we make what you said true.'

'Perhaps what you know as truth is only your truth.'

That's the story," said Asheena.

"He wasn't only clever and cunning... but very funny." Robby said smiling.

"Yes. I'll tell you more sometime if you like?"

"Ok."

"You were just like some people I used to see in Afghanistan."

"How do you mean?"

"It's common there. Someone sees something or has to do something like what you did. Slowly over time it becomes bigger in their head until it takes over. They become split from reality and wander around just staring ahead."

"I've learnt it's called the thousand yard stare or dissociation in psychology."

"We know this very well in Afghanistan. I've seen several men and women also just like that. You must have been the same because we were told that they start taking opium or kill themselves to escape."

"That's exactly what happened to me. I did try to kill myself but here I am."

"Then my God you must be special."

"I don't see how. But you're the second person to say that to me recently."

"Who was the other person?"

"My aunt."

"But you said she was dead? And you said she told you this recently. You really do sound crazy the way you talk. I have moved in with a crazy man. I have heard that at times like this the Italians say Mama Mia!"

"My aunt really died a few weeks ago in this house," Robby said again looking slightly more serious.

"I'm so sorry." Asheena held her had to her mouth. "Don't worry. A lot is happening to both of us at the moment."

"So what happened after the branch broke?"

"It fell on me and broke my leg."

"I can't believe it!" Asheena had to hold her hand to her mouth to conceal her laughter. "You are making a joke. Yes? No. You're not are you? I don't know anymore."

"It really broke my leg." Asheena's laughter settled down just a little.

"What happened then?"

"A dog woke me up."

"A dog! How could a dog wake you up? They don't talk and are not alarm clocks. What were you doing with a dog? You must have still been very crazy to think that."

"When I jumped. The rope tightened around my neck and either that or the pain of the broken leg made me lose consciousness. When I regained consciousness, I had a dog licking my face and slobbering all over me trying to wake me up." Asheena couldn't help laughing but soon contained her giggles.

"Next," but she was sobbing in laugher. "I can't believe what I'm hearing."

"The owner of the dog called an ambulance. They lifted the branch off my leg."

"And then what?"

"Then I ended up in hospital with a broken leg."

"I know it was serious but it sounds so funny. Jumping from a tree, the branch saving you instead of killing you. But breaking your leg and being woken by a dog is so funny."

"When it was mended I was sent to the mental hospital."

"What is mental hospital? Is a hospital that thinks?"

"No not at all. It's a place for crazy people like me. Mental means crazy so a mental hospital is a hospital for mental people." Robby couldn't help seeing how stupid what he just said must have seemed to Asheena. She began to laugh so deeply again, but this time tears of laughter came down her cheeks. "You are a real comedian," Robby said, now laughing. "I don't think anyone has made me laugh before like you do."

"No it's you who are the comedian. My stomach hurts from laughing so much. I can't remember when I last laughed. In Afghanistan we don't have these mental hospitals. We are told that when you are sad that laughter is better than going to see the doctor."

"Going to see the doctor here when you have a mental problem here can be a big waste of time, at least in my experience with the RAF. I was unlucky. I had two female RAF doctors who had no compassion. And yes we too in some ways believe what you said about laughing. We have a saying, 'Laughter is the best medicine.'

"What does it mean that they didn't have compassion?"

"It's feeling distressed and pity for the suffering of others. In the military there is a thing called compassion fatigue which is very common in doctors."

"What's compassion fatigue?"

"It's when someone is unable to react with sympathy to someone's crisis because they've been over exposed to one crisis after another so eventually they think this is normal. It's very common in military doctors."

"In our country if you are in the military, you have to be crazy to see a military doctor."

"Why's that?"

"They are usually the people involved in torture. It's the same in Turkey, in India, in Iran and even the Americans in Guantanamo Bay. They are the supervisors. You will have some military doctors in your country who also collude with torture. The worst ones. They treat the detainee but then advise the interrogators how to manipulate them and exploit their phobias. You will find that your secret services and military doctors do exactly the same. They are the same in America. It's the same with psychologists. They work with the doctors and with the torturers. People like this are only into political power because they know that torture never works. It is there as a psychological lever to make ordinary people frightened."

"It's strange how the doctors and psychologists also end up trying to help these people who are victims of their own professional knowledge and instruments. It's the same in war when you end up treating casualties you've created. It happened to me."

"What?"

"Helping someone I had just beaten very badly because he would not let go of a knife. I haven't thought about it until now because, fighting was automatic to me then."

"I will tell you another Nasrudin story."

"I would love that. But before you do, let me show you around and where everything is." Khatira came into the kitchen smiling.

"I've got toys on my bed... soft toys and a bear."

"Ok," Asheena said, "You'll have to show me."

"I'll show you the way to the bedroom."

"Come on. I'll show you the rest." Robby walked backwards with Khatira.

"She must like you because she usually doesn't go easily with strangers."

"I hope I won't be a stranger for long."

"I'm sorry. I didn't mean to hurt your feelings. It's me who is the stranger in this place, not you."

"Don't worry or be sorry. We've spent less than two hours in each other's company so we are both strangers to each other. This is the bathroom. The water is heated by the wood burning stove in the kitchen and partly by the fire in the sitting room."

"Where do you get the wood from? I noticed a large stack outside."

"The house owns some planted pine forest. There's no shortage of wood."

"How do you get upstairs?" Asheena asked.

"Through here." Robby opened a door opposite the sitting room and bathroom. It looks like a cupboard but it's the stairs." Asheena followed him up the stairs. This is Khatira's room and this is your room."

"It is very relaxing," said Asheena feeling how springy the mattress was with her hand.

Robby showing her across the hall. Then he led her down the stairs.

"Let me show you around the other cottage where I live. They are very similar." Robby led the way to Eleanor's cottage and took them upstairs. Then he took them into the lounge.

"What a beautiful chair."

"Thanks. It was my aunt's"

"Did she die in it?"

"Yes. She did die in that chair. Why do you ask?"

"It looks like a very relaxing chair. It looks like the best place in the house. Can I try it?"

"Of course." Asheena said.

"Yes I was right," Asheena said; sitting back.

"How is it?"

"It feels warm."

"How do you mean warm?"

"It feels like I like it." Asheena said looking as if she was at home." Robby showed them around the back of the house then back to the guest cottage. He took the carrier bags out of the back of the Land Cruiser down to their cottage and put them on the kitchen table.

"The fridge is over here. There is some bread, some cold meats and there is some fruit over there if you and Khatira are hungry. I must go now."

"Don't you want to have something to eat?"

No, I've got to go out and do some errands."

+++CHAPTER 18.

Robby was a lot longer and so Asheena decided she would cook some of the food he had brought back with him. She cooked Persian rice with chicken. When Robby returned, he was surprised at the smell coming from the kitchen.

"What have you cooked? He asked smiling at Asheena.

"Persian rice with chicken. I'll show you." Asheena opened the oven door and brought out a large oval stainless steel platter dish. She placed it in the middle of the table then she took the silver foil off the top. There was white rice and yellow saffron rice mixed with all sorts of colourful ingredients.

"I know it is any Afghan's favourite meal but how did you make it? I like cooking but I'm not good at it," Robby said half licking his lips with his tongue.

"You half boil the rice, drain it then add some butter to gently cook it for half an hour until the rice at the bottom starts to go hard and crispy as it's fried by the butter. The crispy rice at the bottom is called Tadiq and it's always given to guests as it's the most prized part of the meal. When it's ready, you add small pieces of shredded roast or fried chicken and you can add things like nuts and fruit. You add whatever food you have that day. It's a meal in one."

"But there is enough food for five or six people there."

"Afghans always cook more than we need just in case an unexpected guest turns up. It can be reheated and eaten for breakfast. I hope you like it."

"It looks so good. Can I start?" Robby scooped up a ladle of rice on his plate. "Can I serve you?"

"Yes if you want to."

"It smells good." He tasted a mouthful of rice with chicken. "It's very aromatic. You'll have to show me how to make this." He took another mouthful. "How are you feeling?"

"Very tired. I was awake early with excitement. Is it ok to give her a bath?"

"Of course." Robby said. There are towels in the cupboard opposite the bath."

"Yes I saw them. I had a look around at everything when you were out to learn where everything is. I noticed the shed at the back of your house. Do you get power cuts here?"

"Yes. But I had completely forgotten about that. I remember when I last stayed here there were a few, but there don't seem to be any now. They tend to happen in storms when the power lines come down. Why do you ask?"

"I noticed you have two generators in the shed at the back. We had no mains electricity in Afghanistan where we lived so we relied on generators."

"I haven't looked in that shed yet. I don't know why. I don't know if the generators work."

"They do. I started them both. Your aunt must have been very practical. One is diesel, the other petrol and they are both quiet."

"Your life must have been so very different in Afghanistan from here."

"I had a lot of family, but I wasn't married like my sister. My sister would be so proud that I have got Khatira out of Afghanistan. Thank you for asking."

"Remember you never have to say thank you. I'm doing what I have to do. I'm making up for what I did."

"Ok. But I had to say it once. I worked with sheep every day. We all lived in a straightforward house like this. I had to prepare food, cook, clean, go to the village, help slaughter the sheep, cut the wool, make carpets and sell the meat and rugs. We all lived in the one large area, my two parents, my two grandparents, my sister and her husband and our two brothers. My family... they are gone forever. But all of that life, it's gone. It cannot come back. It's over. I hope to improve my English and maybe I can teach you some Pashto. But now I'm here with you and Khatira. I've given up planning tomorrow. It may never come; so there is only today."

"I'm so sorry for you losing all of your family."

"I've been too busy trying to save Khatira's life and mine. We have been on the run, travelling, surviving, dealing with all sorts of people, some nice, some crooks and the Home Office. I've had to deal with social workers and counsellors from the United Nations High Commission for Refugees. The Scottish Afghan Society helped me and I've been looking for somewhere to live and now finally we are here with you. I know I have not given my family enough thought. I have had no time to but they are all I dream about."

"I really hope you are happy here."

"I'm happy and I'm content. But yes I know I have to work through my loss. What about you. Are you happy?"

"I'm very happy that you're here, that I'm actually able to help you and Khatira. This is part of my healing of how I'm getting myself back together again. It already feels right and I'm feeling better. But I don't want to keep you up as you look very tired. You probably need a lot of rest and sleep after coming so far." Asheena agreed and a few minutes later she tucked Khatira up in her bed.

Robby walked back to his house and sat in the kitchen at the table writing with a pencil in his notebook. He was also tired but wanted to keep track of what had happened to him.

Robby: Pocket Notebook Entry 16. I collected Asheena and Khatira from Glasgow and I feel really good that they are both here. Khatira is a beautiful girl with green eyes and fair skin and fair skin just like her aunt. In Afghanistan I once saw some Afghans who were fair skinned, fair haired with blue eyes.

Asheena is a good woman. She loves and cares for Khatira as if she were her own daughter. She's so proud that she got Khatira out of Afghanistan. I see the seriousness of her look when she talks of home. But she's not wallowing in grief. Outwardly she seems to have moved on but I should expect that when she has settled, maybe the grief will resurface. She does seem happy to be here but she must be emotionally exhausted and in need of a lot of rest.

She's clever and very funny. Her English is really very good except for some words which she has never come across before. This has already led to some very funny misunderstandings. She has a good sense of humour and was clearly very well brought up as she knows how things work. Not just how politicians and doctors work, but generators. She's very practical.

I feel as if they have already filled in that awful space in me, which was my fault. It was like a hole that kept on repeatedly tripping me up. I now have to help Asheena with whatever she needs to bring up Khatira. But it's early. I haven't even asked her yet if she has any ambitions to study or work or to get married or even travel. I don't know if she can drive a car or ride a bike. I'm sure the next few days will show us a lot about each other. There is one thing I know about her. She can cook really well. Tonight our meal was like a banquet. She says that I'm a blessing, but it's her and Khatira who are the blessing.

She has shown me one thing about herself which we seem to share. Like Asheena, I live only in the present, but wasn't so aware of it until she said it about herself. I don't seem to be able to get in to tomorrow because I'm so busy with today. It's as if I am some kind of prisoner of today. But I've known so many people who are prisoners of tomorrow and can't stay in the present moment of today. So I shouldn't moan about being where I am. I just notice that most people aren't happy with the present and I suppose I think I'm a bit odd in that way. I'm not unhappy with it and it's a relief to be with someone who feels the same way about the future. It's less of a pressure.

+++CHAPTER 19.

Robby: Pocket Notebook Entry 17. I am feeling very content with Asheena. Life has been up and down to me since I visited my aunt just before she died. Khatira and Asheena have settled in much more easily than I had imagined. We go shopping together and she is showing me some cooking. Khatira is settling in and plays by herself and is very content. Her eyes are only just beginning to open up to the world and she seems to be growing. Asheena is having driving lessons so that if I'm ill she will be able do any shopping or any errands. She has her test tomorrow.

I felt a twang of guilt last night after telling Asheena about who had helped me through my difficult times. She was surprised that I hadn't written to them to tell them how I was. I realised that I hadn't written to Sam and I never wrote to that woman Tatyana, who ran Vinny's in Norwich. I remember fending off an escaped prisoner who was attacking her. Asheena said these were really important people in my life as they had helped me to survive. She said that I needed to say thank you. I wonder if Tatyana ever found out about her father.

When I knew them, I was in such a mess. But now I'm better than I was even before I signed up with the RAF. I'll start with Sam.

Dear Sam,

I'm just writing to say thanks for all you did for me during that summer. You were right I needed help in the end. I got and I'm better.

I hope you're well and you've met someone. I still think about all those crazy people in those crazy planes.

If you are ever passing this way let me know. Come and stay.
With fondest wishes

Robby

At lunch time, Robby went into Aberfeldy with Khatira and Asheena to post the letters.

"I think you are a man whose debts are all paid now Robby," Asheena said.

"I'm not sure."

"How do you mean?"

"It's just an uncertainty."

"About what?"

"Nothing in particular, just a niggling feeling that something is left undone, but I'm not quite sure what. It's nothing to do with anyone or anything I've done. I suppose it's a niggling thing that I've got more to do yet. It's come up recently. It's a bit odd."

"The main thing is you've done everything you can think of to make things right."

"For the last few months, there always seems one more hurdle to get over, just when I'm not expecting it."

"This is life itself." Asheena said.

That evening after Khatira and Asheena had both gone to bed Robby looked back at the last day and wrote down what he thought had happened.

Robby: Pocket Notebook Entry 18. After discussing things with Asheena last night, I felt happy enough to share my happiness with those who have helped me through difficult times. I suppose that means a phase of my life has finished and a new one is free to begin.

Here I am. I'm happy here with two delightful girls who light up my life and make me happy. I feel as if I have got past a difficult point, past an important point. I feel happy enough in my own forgiveness that I can now share this.

What comes next? I don't know. I'm in some way in awe of the look on Eleanor's face and the look on the Afghan girl. It comes from somewhere. I know I need to find that place in me. Not just when I am dying but in my life I want to find that place of happiness.

But tomorrow I'll start fixing some things around the house and garden that need doing. I'll collect more wood for the fire and I'll see if any of the furniture needs repairing. I'll repair the walled garden's walls so that the garden is ready to take some vegetables for the spring. And maybe I'll clean the windows of the green house and replace a couple of cracked panes of glass.

+++CHAPTER 20.

The next morning Robby drove to Pitlochry to get some glass to replace the broken glass in the green house roof. He was talking to the friendly Scottish girl about wrapping the glass when he felt someone grab his arm. He turned around as whoever it was had gripped his upper arm firmly.

"Robby... is it you?"

"Tatyana! What are you doing here?" Robby looked into her eyes which seemed to sparkle. He took half a step and put his arms around her and brought his face against hers, then he kissed her lips. She tightened her arms around his neck and kissed him back. The girl who was serving Robby blushed and went into the back room.

"Wow!" Robby said as he let go of Tatyana. He couldn't help noticing her smile was beaming at him. "It's so amazing to see you."

"I can't believe you're here. What a surprise. But what the heck are you doing up here?"

"I live half an hour away in Aberfeldy. And you?"

"I moved up here to a house left to me by an old Ukrainian friend of my father. It's in Strathgary; half an hour away."

"That's incredible. You look so different. I mean happy and smiling."

"I could say the same for you. I left Vinny's a couple of weeks after you. My father died a month later and I spent weeks trying to find out about him and any relatives."

"Sorry to hear that. I remember you mentioning him to me."

"And you?"

"Well, it's almost the same for me. I used to come up and see my aunt. She died a few weeks ago. She left me her house so

I'm living there." He looked at Tatyana. "And you... did you find out about your father?"

"Yeah I did but it's a very long story. Too long for a chance meeting in a hardware shop." Robby opened the door of the hardware shop to let Tatyana out first.

"I want to hear it. Do you want to have lunch or supper some time?"

"Is that a date?" Tatyana blushed.

"Yes I fancy you like crazy."

"How about tomorrow lunch. Early?"

"Early is best for me. Shall we meet here... I mean because Pitlochry's about the same distance for both of us."

"Right here at twelve for lunch." Tatyana put her arms around Robby's neck and gently kissed him on the lips, sending a small shiver from the base of his spine to his neck and scalp.

The next day they were both on time and they gave each other a kiss on the cheek and a hug. It was a blustery autumn afternoon as the two of them walked up the main street of Pitlochry and because neither of them had eaten out in the few weeks they had been in Scotland, they settled for an Indian meal.

"So what you doing up here?" Robby asked eagerly.

"No you first," Tatyana said, sitting up straight revealing her cleavage through white cotton blouse.

"Ok, I know I must have seemed quiet and a bit odd but I wasn't very well at the time. You seemed to know what was happening to me, as you said you had seen it happening to your father. I wanted to forget and you wanted to know.

When I left Norwich, at first I didn't cope very well and my memories almost cost me my life. The luck you wished me must have come true as I was very lucky and I also had a lot of help with what was bothering me then.

I now realise I can't forget what happened but I've slowly come to terms with it and I realise that the memories will always be with me. The treatment I had helped me more than I thought it could and it took away the fear and guilt away from my memories. The things I remember don't make me jumpy or too frightened to sleep. They don't wake me up or suddenly intrude into where I am. They no longer take over my reality. All these are still getting better. I'm a lot like the me I used to be.

I've come to terms with being in the military. I joined when I was really young and I wasn't prepared for the war. I volunteered to do what I thought was a respectable job helping people. But in reality, in theatre, when the shit hit the fan, I acted as a paid killer in someone else's county. I wasn't prepared for what I had to do until someone tried to kill me. She was a young girl, maybe seven or eight with a grenade. I had to kill her.

I didn't know until then, that when I started my job, it came with a hidden invitation to Hell. The Hell there can't be accurately described to warn you. I wouldn't encourage anyone to go and be in that Hell because it leaves you with invisible wounds. It was luck which brought me help in the end. Maybe it was the luck you wished me because I survived trying hang myself."

"Robby, I had no idea it was that bad for you. I knew you were away somewhere else in your head, but I didn't know it was that bad."

"But hey, now for the more positive things that have happened to me." He took hold of her hand and gently moved his hand around hers, each finger acting like a separate hand stroking and exploring her skin. "I've begun to understand what my life has been about and what I need now. I am living where I am because I'm coping well with living here having a simple life. Maybe it's only because of where I have been that I love it here so very much. I've learnt a lot of things very quickly and I've taken over my auntie's croft."

"That's big stuff. I mean you've been to Hell got the T-shirt, the video the tattoo and come back alive. That's very tough stuff."

"And you?" Robby noticed Tatyana had become very serious as she listened to him. But now he saw her face brightened up and she smiled as she responded to his hand by squeezing his.

"My story is not so bad at all. My father and I used to come and stay with Nicholai, a Ukrainian friend of his just outside

Pitlochry in Strathgary. I used to come up here every summer and I was very close to him. He was like my uncle. When he died he had no relatives and left me his house. But just before he got sick he helped me find all about my father. He fought with my father during the Second World War. He was able to talk about the war freely but my dad never could. I think it was because he was so damaged by it all."

"Yeah, wars affect people differently."

"Well, seeing you that last day. And the man who came in to Vinny's who you saved me from. It made me get off my backside and really spurred me on to search into my father's past. You left me some mess to clean up to cover your tracks. The police were mystified who had stopped that psycho. They said whoever did it left him in as much pain as it was possible to be in. They said whoever did it took him to the very edge. They asked me if I knew if anyone who came in was trained in any martial arts. He had a broken throat, two broken hands, a broken arm, several broken ribs, and his balls were mashed up. They also said it was done so expertly that not a drop of blood was spilt. They said it was a specialist."

"Not me. I did Tai Chi and ran a lot to keep fit. I only took him as far as he needed to be taken to be stopped. And yes it was a long way because he didn't want to stop. But hey, whatever it takes."

"When Nicholai died two months ago and left me his house, I put my father's house in Norwich on the market and moved up here because I've got so many fond memories of being up here as a child. I miss them both so much, but it's getting easier."

"Yeah it gets easier but I still miss my aunt and uncle. I used to come up here to escape my family in Bristol."

"Oh Bristol? I studied in Bristol and I came up here once or twice a year, usually at half term. But yesterday, I was so shocked to run into you. I wasn't sure at first. I thought it was a double of you. And you're living just a few miles away."

"Yeah it's me." He squeezed her hand and she responded with a beaming smile.

"Your father. What did you find out about him?"

"His parents were killed by the Communist regime and he started life as a baby in an orphanage. He was brought up in the orphanage. When he was about fourteen he was picked up by the Germans. It's a long story how he got here after the war. But he would never talk about it. He was always quiet but jumpy."

"What a journey. He must have felt so scared."

"So you see, I was brought up with my father in that frightened state. He always thought that there was a possibility of him being sent back to Russia. He lived in fear with all his memories of the war. My mother died when I was six from breast cancer so he had a huge influence on me. It was secure but not really that happy."

"That must have been hard."

"I think I learnt to accept that some people can't trust other people and they can suffer for that. I now know that is how I really became interested in working with homeless people who on the whole don't trust people because they are mowed down by them all the time. I still love that work."

"How did you find all this stuff out about your father?"

"I followed what you said. You said someone from his past would remember him. I put an advertisement in a British Ukrainian newspaper. I spent two weeks in the Ukraine and got nowhere except from finding people with the same surname who only wanted money to buy a new tractor or a new car. When I came back to the UK there was a reply to the advertisement from a man called Stefan who lived in the same village in the Ukraine where my father had worked. He put me in touch with other Ukrainian veterans who were living in Canada and the UK who I've written to. I've now built up a whole story of my father's life. I understand after all this time what he went through."

"Sounds like it should be a book."

"I can't tell you what it was like. I've met all kinds of Ukrainians and went through so many emotions about that country, my parents and myself. I've kept it as a diary just in case I ever have children and they want to know where I come from. But for right now, I'm leaving the diary open. And you

Robby. You seem as if a black cloud has been completely lifted from you."

"When I came up here my aunt said I could only forgive myself by bringing up a Muslim girl. I thought she was wrong and fought against it until I realised there was a strange wisdom in what she had said. I went to see the Imam in Glasgow and he contacted the Scottish Afghan Society who eventually discovered Khatira and Asheena in Glasgow. They live in one of the two cottages on the croft and Asheena is looking after the sheep."

"I thought something dreadful had happened to you. And are you happy?"

"That's the worst question you could ask me. I know it seems as if I should be and in almost all aspects I am. Khatira and Asheena have healed a wound in me. They have let me find forgiveness but only to reveal that I'm aware that in my own self I lack something. I can't put my finger on it but I'm aware of not being fulfilled in myself. My aunt saw it and I've felt it more since Asheena and Khatira have been around. There is just a gap. It's not another person, a relationship. There is time for that. It's me. In a few weeks I'm going to South India to a mountain my aunt and uncle used to visit. I'm going there to scatter my aunt's ashes on the mountain but also to see if I can find the solution to this... well... inner hunger."

"So you are still looking for your own truth?"

"I feel so close to it. I'm right on it but I just can't see it."

"I've got something to ask you," Tatyana said seriously.

"Fire away." Robby sat upright in keen expectation of anything she was going to say.

"When I met you at Vinny's Robby, I was doing what I loved, what I was good at. Ok, not the cooking. I feel a bit selfish bringing this subject up but I need this. I need to get my teeth into something. I need some help in setting something up."

"You were good at cooking. You just got distracted by the clients," Robby said, which made Tatyana smile.

"I was only there for them and sometimes it made a difference. The day you left, I realised I needed to move on too. I left Vinny's because when my father died I had to go and find if I had any family back in the Ukraine. I had to hand it over to someone. I needed a few months off. I needed to get over Dad's death as well."

"Any word from Vinny's?"

"I hear from Jenny and Mike who took over from me every now and again and Vinny's is doing alright. Actually it's doing better than when I was there. You see I was overstretched as I was doing the manager's job which was a full time job and I was also doing the cooking every morning. I learnt really quickly that it was only the relationships with everyone who needed the food that was keeping me going."

"I don't see where you're going with this."

"That's what I want to talk to you two about. You see, you have a lot of meaning in your life with Asheena and Khatira and I am so pleased for you. Robby, you've forgiven yourself. But I'm afraid there is also a needy part of me which needs feeding. I need nurturing. I did my time studying art and I still draw and paint. But I only used to find inspiration to draw and paint in the people I saw at Vinny's. There's still work for me to do in a place like that. There are people and emotions I want to draw. I want you to help me set up a Vinny's here."

"What?"

"I've been looking around Pitlochry and Aberfeldy and I think I've found somewhere which might be suitable. I just need some reassurance that the building is alright and that I'm doing the right thing."

"Are you crazy? You could be seriously wrong," Robby said.

"Wow that's a big reaction."

"The locals here are good people but very conservative. The last thing they are going to want is drawing in a homeless population. It's ok in a city but it could be very out of place here. It sounds strange for someone like me to say that but I think that is how it might be. Don't get me wrong, I mean I'm one hundred percent with you about it, but that is the one obstacle which might make it a risk. How are you going to pay for it?"

"Same as Norwich. In Edinburgh I met the Catholic bishop, the Chief Hindu priest, the Chief Rabbi, the Imam and the

Head Monk at the Buddhist temple. I've done the same here and they're all keen to put money into the project. It is going to be a non-denominational subsidised cafe for the homeless who are passing through the very heart of Scotland. They are ready to give me set up funds to get going whenever I think I've found the right place. Because of the economy I told them that within a year it will be self funding."

"I didn't know you had done that to get Vinny's going. What about the local Council?"

"What about them?"

"Did you approach them?"

"They told me if they could they would block it. They can only block any new planning permission or changed use of premises."

"But they represent the people who will probably object."

"Don't tell me. I've already had hate letters, saying Nicholai would turn in his grave and that I should go back to England. That's usual. It happened in Norwich."

"How do you reason with them?"

"I don't. Homeless people have needs like you and me for food, shelter, warmth, health, friendship and love. Because there is no national organisation, it's left up to each area to help these people. If there's nothing set up they have to beg on the streets. That's always a sign that things are wrong. People of all ages begging on the street makes everyone think, things shouldn't be like that. People are begging all over this county from Perth to Pitlochry. This is not a poor part of the world and it shouldn't happen. I'm hoping to get the local people to help these people and change things. But it's going to take a long time."

"Right. I'm with you now. But how will people hear about it?"

"When I set up Vinny's in Norwich, the locals told any homeless person they came across about it. How did you hear about Vinny's?"

"I heard about it from an article in the local paper. You were being interviewed by a reporter. People were raising funds. The article was trying to raise awareness of Vinny's as well as funds. I went there one morning to see what the food was like. What kept me going was that I felt normal there. I could just be whatever I was. I wasn't very well but it was a place where I felt safe. You were a master of silence and seemed to know that I needed to just be alone."

"There were all sorts there. About one in ten were ex-armed forces like you. There were men and women who had just lost their homes for one reason or another. About one in ten were women or men who had been abused by their partner and had enough pain. Some took drugs, some drank and some like you just survived fighting all the stuff that was going on in their heads. There were refugees who were asylum seekers from Iran, Iraq, Somalia and Turkey. It's a long list. Everyone was looking to move on, to get a home. No one ever wants to be homeless. It's not a choice. It's always a time of crisis."

"I know well enough. Not happy times. Having someone like you Tatyana, just being there without any expectations is the biggest help. It's somewhere to get silently helped while you are also getting some shelter and some food. What people don't realise is that when you've got a load of shit going around in your head, whether it's bad memories or whatever, you don't need someone talking a load of therapy to you."

"That's essentially what Vinny's was about. Understanding people's neediness and trying to help them to work it out for themselves. That's what feeds me. It's what I do. Getting to somewhere like Vinny's is like getting a second chance to look at things on your own and that's rare. Maybe you get to look back over your childhood and look at your parents. We all have a sense of our parents being good or bad. Some are too selfish and don't give us enough love. Some are smother mothers. Some are over controlling helicopter mums and some are 'where are you mums' because they are never there for you. Whatever we had, we seem to sense what was missing because something in us knows. We automatically try and find what was missing and we don't necessarily need to be very verbal about it. Some of us can spend our whole life trying to make up for what our parents didn't do for us. But if we are lucky, there is a time when the games up and we become conscious of it and we can just get on with our life. Occasionally someone else points it out to us. But that's only one of a load of problems."

"You said it in one. I'm a believer. I'll look at the building and I'll even help you now and then with cooking if you like. But I'll leave the customers to you," Robby said in a soft voice.

"That sounds good."

"I can cook while you are doing other things. That's providing there is no trouble with the sheep and it's not lambing. The other thing is I need to go to India."

"Do you want to come and see it tomorrow after breakfast?"

"I'm convinced," said Robby.

The next morning, Robby met Tatyana at the estate agents and walked round to the empty property in Aberfeldy.

"Too dark." Robby said.

"Yes. Ceiling's too low," Tatyana said as she looked up.

"It needs a few days work. The wooden tables and chairs look in good condition."

"We could paint the walls an off white like gardenia and cover the wooden floor boards with some rugs. Did you ever come in here when it was a Persian restaurant?"

"Never been one for eating in fancy restaurants. Remember I was homeless when we met. I used to eat out a lot... out on the street."

"How we met in Vinny's and how we are now here in this place, seems like it's been waiting for me. It seems strange but familiar."

"It's going to be strange cooking breakfasts for homeless people." Robby said out aloud to himself.

"The cooking is incidental and that's what seemed strange to me at first. Like me, you might find you are distracted by the customers too. You soon see that cooked food is a way to a person's mind and heart, which is what life itself is all about."

"Maybe I'll just make hot food because I'm happy to stay in the back ground and cook. How much do they want for this place?"

"The estate agent says I have to pay the full rent even though I am going to register it as a charity. But because it's down an alley way off the main street, the rent is only half of what it would be right in the middle of town."

"That's good." Robby said as Tatyana disappeared through a doorway. "What sort of restaurant was this?"

"A Persian kebab restaurant. It's a really good kitchen. It's got professional sinks, two cookers and air conditioning." Robby followed her through the door. "There's a chip fryer and one of those vertical gas grills for making doner kebabs. There are a few large pots and a stack of plates. I don't think the last owner was going to open another restaurant otherwise none of this would be here."

"I used to like kebabs but was put off by a health and safety officer in the RAF."

"How would a health and safety officer put you off?"

"She said that the public health officers always did late afternoon random checks on Kebab shops during the summer."

"Why the afternoon?"

"That was the best time to see the flies eggs from the night before which had hatched into maggots on the kebab meat."

"Yuk. That makes me feel sick."

"Haven't had one since." They both continued inspecting the kitchen.

"Do you think I should rent it Robby?" Asked Tatyana opening a door which revealed a small garden with two chairs. "This must catch a few rays in the summer. I could put a couple of tables out here."

"Are you sure you want to do this again?"

"It's in my bones and in my blood now. I don't want to be a professional. I just want to do basic stuff with people."

"I know. I'm not so sure I'll be so good at that but I can cook breakfast with hot beans."

"Those cold beans were the moment I knew you were moving on. I knew when I sensed you were not coming back again that it was time for me to move on too. Even as a child I was too distracted by people to concentrate on cooking. When my mum died, my father use to joke about me completely forgetting to cook one part of the meal. At Vinny's it was the same. That's how come I served you those cold beans."

"I know. Please don't be offended but you can be a bit scatty. If you rent this place, it would be ready in a week. We would need to get some second hand rugs and a lot of paint. We would need to do a few trips to the local rubbish dump to get rid of some of the junk. But that's all it needs."

"There are two things I want to add which Vinny's didn't have. It's a gents and a ladies, each with a sink and a hot shower. Stuart the builders said it will take a plumber a couple of days to convert the gents and ladies to two shower rooms. The other thing is a washing machine and a dryer."

"That will make a lot of difference to the number of people coming. Some would come just to have a shave or wash their hair or clothes once a week. The thing I missed the most was not being able to wash my hair when I wanted. That made me look a bit wild."

"I thought your hair really suited you long and a bit wild." Robby was stuck for words but heard where Tatyana was coming from.

"Hang on a moment while I get a chair and see what's above the roof tiles."

"It is a really drab ceiling but probably fire proof," Tatyana said as Robby lifted up a tile.

"Well that's a surprise."

"What is?"

"The roof has eight large glass windows in it. The light is dazzling above the tiles. I'll show you."

"The last owner must have wanted a cosy intimate atmosphere with slightly dimmed lights and no light from the sun or the moon," Tatyana said as Robby removed three tiles from their aluminium frames. "I see what you mean by dazzling. This place could be so light."

"If you take this, the homeless will be able to eat in the light. When I was homeless I didn't like eating in the dark. I needed to be able to see what I was eating. Funny how most people with enough money to eat out eat in darkened rooms. Is it the atmosphere or are they hiding something?"

"I should take it."

"I know." Robby looked into Tatyana's green eyes and wondered what she was thinking. Tatyana tilted her head to one side and smiled. When she tilted her head, he felt she had opened the door just a little for him. He moved towards her and she felt his right arm on her left shoulder, then his left arm go around her waist. He moved closer and gently pulled her to him. As their lips met she put both arms around his neck and welcomed his kiss by kissing him back. After a minute of deeply passionate kissing, Robby pulled back.

"This might sound a little crazy but, I want to wait until I'm back from India. You've got things to do, so have I. We would distract each other too much. I can wait. Can you?"

"It doesn't look as if I've got a choice." Robby could see Tatyana was annoyed.

"I'm sorry but I've got to take my aunt's ashes there and you've got to get all of this up and running. Can you wait?"

"No I can't. It's a bloody cheek. Kissing me and then telling me I've got to wait. I don't know for how long. Do you know you're right. Perhaps you will be my reward."

"Well I hope I make a good present."

"You little devil. It's probably going to drive us both crazy." They came together deeply happy. They were smiling, kissing and hugging each other in acknowledgement of their agreement about a future together.

+++CHAPTER 21.

By lunch time Tatyana had signed and paid for a lease for one year whilst Robby had bought a hundred litres of off white gardenia paint. They spent an hour in Aberfeldy's second hand centre and bought twelve second hand Persian rugs and eight large mirrors which had been acquired from a bankrupt gym. Robby ordered a skip to be delivered by Stuart's builders and by five o'clock the whole of the false ceiling, its aluminium framework and lighting were in the skip. Four days later the painting was finished and the tables and chairs were returned to a floor covered in Persian rugs. Each of the eight mirrors was fastened to the walls just above the skirting board at an angle to reflect light from the eight windows in the ceiling. On the sixth day the food was delivered and 'Vinny's Cafe' was officially opened on the seventh day.

A week passed and no one had come to have a subsidised breakfast. On the eighth day Tatyana went to the supermarket in Aberfeldy to get some fresh milk whilst Robby had prepared the kitchen in case any customers turned up. On the brief walk to the supermarket Tatyana was confronted by three local women.

"Bloody bringing down the tone of our town," said one woman who was in her forties. "Just go home back where you came from."

"Why don't you go back down South where all the homeless people come from instead of bringing all your muck up here? We've got enough trouble with people on alcohol and people on the whacky backy," said the younger woman beside her.

"We don't want people from down south coming up here and taking heroin or crack. The next thing we'll be having drug dealers living here and then there'll be the crime. Go back home and don't bring any of that rubbish from down south up here. Go home," shouted the oldest woman in the middle.

"Three selfish bullies. Could be you, your son or daughter who is on the street next!" Tatyana said as she passed them but she walked on because she was so angry. Tears of anger came down her face as she took refuge by walking straight into the exit of the supermarket. Tatyana noticed that one of the two female cashiers saw her tears. She wandered around the supermarket trying to calm down. She bought two pints of milk and was beginning to doubt if she had done the right thing by setting up a cafe for the homeless in a place like Aberfeldy. She was still questioning herself when she went to the cashier to pay.

"I admire you. What you're doing is great. We know about the homeless up here. We know about the deaths from cold from suicide, from drugs and alcohol. I'm Helen."

"I'm Tatyana." They shook hands as a sign of mutual understanding. Don't mean to bash your ears but I just had a some harsh words from a group of women. Told me to go back down south as if I was bringing a drug problem up here."

"I saw them having a go at you through the door. People like them have got closed eyes. They're selfish and don't care about what happens to other people. Maybe they haven't had a lot of pain in their lives. They're a lot of us women who think you're very brave and would like to help you. We've all been a bit intimidated by the local council. But we've been talking about it."

"Thanks for your support. It means a lot to me. Maybe you could tell your friends to tell their husbands that one in ten of homeless people are ex forces, most of them army. They were once warriors but now are worriers. Most of them are just over twenty and in desperate need of support and help. A cafe is a non threatening way for them to at least get some basic care. No one wants to be homeless. It's not a choice, it's a crisis and so many of them die very young. If they've fought for our country we owe them a lot."

"Have you had any help so far from any one local?"

"The only help we've had so far is from the religious community and the local GPs. That is where we will probably get a lot of our customers from. It would be good to get some more support."

"I'll tell my husband and some of the girls I know because a lot of men up here served in the army and they're very proud of it. That might open their eyes and get you a bit more support." Tatyana noticed a tear well up in Helen's eyes and she waited for her to say what it was.

"My brother Kieran is homeless in Manchester," Helen said quietly.

"Any contact?" Tatyana asked.

"I used to get a text once a month usually from a stranger about him. It's been a year since I went to find him in Manchester. We met but he's showing no sign of moving on. He had a breakdown and left. Just took off. If he comes this way he could drop in here. He came back here six months ago. He wouldn't come and stay. He was sleeping rough. A few people saw him but then he was gone again. You couldn't miss him. Six three with ginger hair and soft brown eyes. Was in insurance. Will you let me know if you see him?"

"I wouldn't miss him and I'll let you know if we see him," Tatyana reassured her.

"Anything else?"

"Our mum died a month ago but neither of the two people who usually text me about him have responded. Maybe he's moved somewhere else. I wouldn't think anything bad has happened to him because he is such a big man. He could probably look after himself. The thing is he doesn't know about mum. If he shows up, don't tell him. Just let me know and I'll come and get him."

"I won't forget."

+++CHAPTER 22.

It had been the first cold night of the year and the stove was hot, ready to cook if anyone came. Robby made himself a mug of tea and was about to sit and drink it when a figure silently appeared in the door way.

"Open?" Said the figure in a soft voice.

"Yes we're open. Come in." Robby was curious about the young man who was about twenty two and had a small day pack slung across one shoulder. He was unshaven and his hair was dishevelled as if he had just woken up. Robby noticed he made no eye contact and he had a very slight limp.

"Chance of a brew?" The young man asked softly. Robby instantly recognised the military term 'brew' for a cup of tea, which usually meant a break and a chance to think through things.

"Yeah. Sugar?"

"Two."

"While you wait for the kettle, there's a toilet with a sink and a hot shower through in the men's shower room. There's a free washing machine which takes forty five minutes. We do free breakfast with the tea."

"Any sausages and bread?"

"Yeah. I'll do some for you." The young man took his worn walking jacket off and carried his daypack to the shower room. He had made no eye contact with Robby and Robby noticed that he was underweight. Robby grilled the whole packet of eight pork sausages and buttered eight slices of bread. He put the sausages and slices of bread on two plates and covered each plate in foil to keep them hot.

The young man emerged from the shower after ten minutes having shaved, showered and washed his hair. He had changed into a clean pair of jeans and a different shirt. He collected his tea, a plate of sausages and bread and left the right amount of money on the counter but gave no eye contact to Robby. Robby noticed the young man make two sausage sandwiches which were gone in two minutes.

"More brew and sausages?"

"Please." Came the monosyllabic reply. As Robby made the mug of tea and put the plate of sausages on the counter, he knew what was going through the young man's head. He was sitting looking straight ahead through one of the mirrors. Robby could see he was seeing things from his past. He didn't disturb him because he knew it could be dangerous. After a few minutes he came to the counter and collected the tea and sausages. He ate them and left.

When Tatyana returned with the milk she looked at Robby who seemed a bit distracted and distant. She could smell the aroma of the cooked sausages which lingered in the air as Robby hadn't switched the kitchen fan on.

"A visitor?"

"We had our first one."

"Male or female?"

"Male. Ex-forces. Army. Had a limp, no eye contact, living rough in a tent. He was having flashbacks. Sat as far away as he could so I wouldn't notice him. I used to know where he is. I used to live where he is in his head. It seems a lifetime away but it was only months back."

The next morning he was back. This time Robby was mopping the floor and Tatyana cooked the sausages and buttered the bread. Robby took the tea and sausages over to him with an extra cup of tea for himself. He sat down and looked at the young man.

"I'm Robby," he said offering his hand.

"Dave," he answered shaking Robby's hand. Robby noticed his quick glancing eye contact.

"You at the camp site?" Robby took a sip of tea from his mug.

"Yeah. Six weeks now."

"Getting a bit cold?"

"Yeah."

"When were you deployed?"

"How did you know?"

"I had a problem in Helmand. You?"

"I was there two years ago. My best friend had got shot during a contact a month before we were due to leave. I wasn't with him when he got shot. We had a row the last time we spoke. His mother wouldn't let me go to the funeral. She just wanted family, no soldiers. Then our Land Rover got blown up by an IED. I was top cover and I got blown out. Cracked my pelvis in two places, shrapnel in my arm and four broken ribs. I keep on seeing my sergeant sitting in the passenger seat. The metal plate from the IED came through the floor. Came up and cut off all the front part of his head just in front of his ears. His jaw was gone I could see behind where his face had been. The front part of my sergeant's brain had been sucked out of his skull by the suction force of the steel plate. There was mud and blood everywhere. I heard him gasping before he choked to death. The driver lost both legs and his eyes. I thought he was dead too."

"What help did you get?"

"I was in Headley Court for two months. The pelvis took a few months to get right. I saw a Senior Medical Officer who recognised what was going on. He sent me to see the Community Psychiatric Nurse who recommended some treatment. Problem was it was going to bring up all the memories again. That was too much. So I didn't go. I got a reminder once a month for three months, but no-one bothered to phone me or came to see me. To them it was just paperwork. Eventually I told the doc I was better and I was leaving. That's what they wrote in my notes. I got a clean bill of health with my discharge."

"But the truth is... " Robby said.

"Yeah. I know. I'm getting flashbacks, bad dreams and I'm getting more irritable."

"Was the treatment called EMDR?"

"Yeah."

"I think there has been a very regrettable mistake. There must have been some miscommunication to you. You see I nosedived when I left. I had EMDR after I lost control of all the memories. When you have flashbacks and nightmares, you avoid anything you think will bring them up, especially therapy. Avoidance is the most dangerous thing about it. You not only avoid people who bring up the flashbacks but also you avoid the very people who can help you. Part of the problem, as you said, is they don't chase you up. It can end up in a real mess."

"Yeah see what you mean."

"EMDR doesn't bring up all the terrible memories. It processes them. Somehow you were given the wrong message about how the treatment works which has scared you away from it. It doesn't open a hatch where all the memories come from. It simply processes them. I think you may have got really anxious that the memories were going to overwhelm you. But the thing is they will if you don't process them. They are so dangerous they can make you want to kill yourself." There was a silence and then Dave got up and left, still not giving any eye contact to Robby.

"That was full on," Tatyana said.

"I couldn't let him go where I went. I had to let him know. It was easier to stop that psychopath from killing you in Vincent's than it was for me to help Dave stop wanting to kill himself. I've been so well and happy; I almost forgot how relentless and deadly those memories are. I feel a bit shaky after that. It's odd but I remember so very clearly how I used to feel. I think I'll leave the talking to you. I'll stick with the cooking."

"You helped him more that I could. You couldn't have helped him anymore."

"I could have told him what happened to me, but it might have sounded a bit like a competition. I remember Anita saying not to get into guilt with those words; coulda, woulda and shoulda."

"I'll tell him if you think it might help."

"Whatever you think. You know."

The next morning he was back.

Robby made the tea and sausages with bread for Dave and started preparing a full English breakfast for another visitor.

Tatyana took the tea and sausages over to Dave who sat quietly at a far away table.

"What happened to him? The big guy."

"Killed a little girl who was a suicide bomber who was coming at him in Afghanistan. Ended up trying to kill himself but he was very lucky."

"I can see myself going there if I don't get out of here. How do you get the treatment he had as a civilian?"

"It's easy. You can go and see the local GP here and register as a temporary resident. Down the street and left just before the mini golf course. If you say we suggested you go there, they will take your case up. They have a therapist who does trauma therapy and who uses the thing Robby had called EMDR. They cover this centre and any visitors as temporary residents so there is no drama about getting help there. Ask to see Dr T." Dave nodded in appreciation. He had listened to every word Tatyana had said.

"I didn't know any of that before. After breakfast I'm going straight over to the GP's surgery to get some help." When he finished his sausage sandwiches he walked down the row of tables and as he passed the counter where Robby was cooking breakfast he took a sideways look at Robby. Robby caught the eye contact in the corner of his eye and raised his hand giving Dave the thumbs up sign. Dave raised his chin and gave Robby a thumbs up sign back. Dave held the door open for a couple of people who walked up to the counter to order breakfast.

Robby took the tea over to a woman who was sitting in the middle of a row of tables. She had spread some of the contents of her small rucksack onto some of the chairs on either side to sort them out.

"I'm Robby. There is a sink and a hot shower in the ladies shower room if you need any hot water. There's a free washing machine with powder in the room between the ladies and gents. Takes about forty five minutes. Breakfast will be another ten minutes if you're hungry."

"Very helpful. Thanks. I saw you do full English. Can I have one?" She stuffed what looked like clothes back into separate carrier bags which she then forced into the small rucksack. "I just need to wash a couple of things."

"I'm Robby. Breakfast is no trouble. Where've you come from today?"

"I'm Jane." Her brown eyes looked up at Robby. "Camping on the site at Kenmore. Lost my husband from cancer two years ago. Got very depressed. Took two overdoses. I lost my job last year and my flat in London this year. Being a woman at fifty five; the streets are too tough there. Had to get away. I was being threatened with being attacked. That young man over there's on the same site in Kenmore. He's very nice but very quiet. I've been up in Applecross. It's been warm all summer. It's dropping a few degrees, getting uncomfortable. Going to be a bad winter and my chest always gets bad in the cold. I need to find a hostel for the winter. I'm heading south. Cornwall... warmer there." She took her rucksack to the shower room.

"There's free breakfast with a mug of tea." Tatyana said to the couple.

"Oh that's good love. We're a bit short. Hey Harry what ya want for breakfast?"

"The lot."

"And yourself?" Asked Tatyana.

"I'll have scrambled eggs with beans on toast love." Tatyana filled two mugs with tea.

"Do you want sugar? Is that a London accent?"

"Yeah. Two love. East End but not proper Cockney. Came up here in spring. Got our flat re-possessed. Pension's worth nothing and couldn't afford to rent anything there. We've been staying on the caravan site. We'll make it through the winter. Just a bit colder up here this time of year. Heard the food was cheap here and lots of it so we thought we'd come in for a meal and try it."

"Well if you're staying up here, we've got two hot shower rooms and a free washing machine with power."

"That will help as it gets colder. We have to boil water in a kettle for everything. Hot water bottles, washing up and the washing."

"Take a seat and I'll bring the food over. It will be about ten minutes."

Robby handed the kitchen over to Tatyana whilst he delivered the full English breakfast to Jane. He sat down opposite her and gave her another mug of tea and sipped at his own mug of tea.

"Do you know Cornwall?" He asked her.

"I went there once as a child. Happy days."

"There are homeless centres in Truro, Camborne and Penzance. The breakfasts are best in Penzance but the weather can be full on there. There's not much accommodation and it's too cold to tent it even in the winter. There's no work after September when all the tourists have left. It may sound easier there but it's not necessarily the case. The people up here are different and have a bit more money. But they don't like to see others suffering. It's a good community."

"Sounds like it might be better staying here."

"The days are a bit longer and warmer in Cornwall but it can be rough. Not as rough as London. Me, I wouldn't rush down there just yet. There's a bit more warm weather here. But it does get very cold here. You might even find somewhere to stay." Suddenly there was ferocious barking.

"Dogs." Jane said as she got up, grabbing one of her sausages and opened the door where she had tied her collie up to a lamp post. A young couple with a toddler were talking at the counter with Tatyana. They had tied their Labrador puppy to an old metal boot cleaner outside the door. Jane broke the sausage in two and gave the two dogs half each, which silenced them both.

"There is a sink and hot showers in the shower room." The girl looked up at the man she was with as if she was relieved to get some help. "There's a washing machine in the middle room which is free to use. You get a free meal with a mug of tea of coffee." Tatyana now noticed the man who looked about twenty five looked as if he was a little tipsy from alcohol.

"Two coffees, a water and three breakfasts." The young woman said, looking self conscious of her appearance. Tatyana thought she looked sixteen, underweight with bags under her eyes. She thought she must have had the child when she was about fourteen.

"Bear wants lemonade?" The girl said looking up at Tatyana.

"Would your bear like a straw?"

"Yes pink one."

"Does your bear have a name?"

"Rocky."

"What a lovely name. What's your name?"

"Izzy."

"Here's Rocky's lemonade. If he drinks it all up he can have another one." But Tatyana now noticed that the man she was with also looked pale and unwell.

"It'll be ten minutes if you want to use the shower rooms." Tatyana said. The young man walked quickly into the male shower rooms. "Is he alright?"

"I'll wait until he's out. He's not been well," the young woman said, taking off her small rucksack.

"I'm Suzie." Tatyana noticed how small she was.

"I'm Tatyana. Where have you come from today?"

"We got a ride with a lorry from Dundee. The tourists are dropping so no good for getting money on the street now."

"Been together long?" Tatyana knew the answer.

"A while."

"Yeah."

"Well... two weeks. But he seems really cool. He's kind. We met in Aberdeen. My mum left when I was ten and my dad abused me from then until I left a year ago. He got me pregnant and Izzy was the result. This is better than being with him at home. Billy's better than being on my own."

"What's he on?"

"He said it's stress from... I don't know, but I think it's the grog."

"How much?

"Half a dozen ciders in the day, maybe a bottle of vodka from lunch until... " there was a sound of someone being sick and it was coming from the gents.

"Want me to go?" Tatyana asked.

"No I'll be alright." Suzie was slight in build with dyed black hair.

"Is he alright?" Robby asked Tatyana. "He looked as pale as a ghost."

"Not sure. She's gone to look."

"I'll knock and take a look." But just as Robby was about to knock, the door opened and Robby could see Suzie was slowly keeling over backwards towards him as she started to faint.

"Billy." She softly said.

Robby saw her partner had collapsed after vomiting up blood in the toilet and was lying on his side with blood around his mouth. He caught Suzie with one hand under her knees and one hand under her neck, lifted her whilst swinging her around, showing her to Tatyana whilst he gently put her on her side behind the counter. "Water on the face. Call 999. Shock due to blood loss. Ask for blues and two's," he said. Tatyana scooped a clean towel soaking in a bowl of water to soften it up and placed it over Suzie's head for a second. She came around slowly whilst Tatyana dialled 999.

"A collapse in Vinny's in Aberfeldy. Someone's in shock due to blood loss. Requesting blues and two's an emergency."

"A crew's should be passing through on its way home. They'll pull in to you... arrival time one minute."

"Can you hear me?" Robby said. There was no reply. Robby lifted Billy's feet up putting one foot on the toilet seat and the other on a stainless steel bin to increase the blood volume returning to Billy's heart. "Can you hear me?" Robby said louder, pinching Billy's ear lobe, but still nothing. "Can you hear me?" He repeated again, rubbing his knuckles down Billy's sternum. This time Billy tried to raise his head but there was no other response to pain. Robby could see there was a lot of blood in the lavatory. He took Billy's pulse which was faint and racing at over a hundred and fifty beats a minute. Robby registered that Billy looked even paler than he did when he walked in. What worried Robby was that now Billy was cold and clammy.

"There's two paramedics coming through the front door," Tatyana shouted.

"Send them straight in." The female paramedic was in first then her partner both dressed in bright green overhauls and white trainers.

"I was a forces paramedic. He's in acute shock. Pulse over one fifty."

"Glasgow coma score?" Said the dark haired female paramedic.

"One out of six. No decent response."

"Right. Anything else on him?"

"I think he's had a big bleed from a varicose vein in his oesophagus. Can't say how much is in the pan. Can't rouse him so his gullet's probably bleeding freely into his stomach. Might be another one or two in there, so he's in big trouble. Handing over to you, right."

"Right," said the female paramedic. "Time check; eight thirty am." She cut up Billy's clothes from the wrists to above the elbow whist her male partner put a large intravenous needle into each arm to give him fluids to expand his blood volume. Two minutes later the paramedic had forcefully squeezed two litre bags of plasma substitute into Billy. Billy didn't open his eyes but he swore under his breath. Robby was not convinced he was that much better.

"Ok, lift after three. One, two, three," shouted the female paramedic. "Anyone with him?"

"His girlfriend." Tatyana said. "Suzie and her daughter Izzy."

"Can someone give them a lift? Perth. Time check eight thirty five. Sorry about the mess," said the female paramedic. Robby knew Billy was on the edge of his life.

"You go Tatyana." Robby said. Tatyana put her arm around Suzie as they followed the paramedics to the ambulance. Dave who had just come back from making an appointment at the local GP, held the door open for the stretcher and then for Tatyana and Suzie.

"What's happened?" Asked Dave giving Robby full eye contact. "He looked bad. She looked distraught."

"He's very sick."

"Yeah. Funny how you never get used to the sight of blood."

"It's not a good thing to. Did you get sorted over the road?"

"Mate. Ta. I owe you one if ever I can help."

"You want a brew?"

"Yeah. Any chance of some more sausages and bread?"

"Yeah, take a seat. We seem to have a lot of sausages at the moment." Robby gave Dave the tea, the sausages and bread. He cleaned the kitchen whilst waiting to hear from Tatyana. At ten the call came through.

"Didn't make it," Tatyana said solemnly. "They lost his pulse in the ambulance and his heart stopped. Couldn't get him back. Tried to resuscitate in A&E but that didn't work. They shocked him at least six times. I'm bringing Suzie and Izzy back."

Robby refocused and thought about what he was supposed to be doing. He realised that everyone who had had breakfast was still there. He went up to Jane and the Cockney couple and took more orders for tea coffee and breakfast. He realised again how polite they were in not asking for more.

"I'm very sorry." Robby said as Tatyana brought Suzie and Izzy to the counter. "Tatyana will help you." Robby said this because he knew Tatyana would probably have some experience of this.

"You are still going to need some food and tea or coffee. It doesn't look like you've had a good meal for ages," Tatyana said. "Come and sit over her whilst I work out somewhere for you to stay."

"Where are you going to send them?" Robby asked.

"Robby, I don't know, anywhere. I thought all the way back in the car. She's in a very difficult place. She can't go home because she's only got a dad who abused her. No other relatives and she is in grief about the unexpected death of her boyfriend. And Izzy is only two. We are going to have to call the crisis intervention team. She's going to need a lot more help than we can give her. It's beyond what we can do. Help is going to have to come from social services. I'm going to call them. They usually respond in an hour or two."

"She's going to need some time and some human input as well as a roof. And that little girl needs some kind of life."

"Her mum's got a mind of her own," said Sam the duty social worker. Sam was a thirty year old softly spoken Glaswegian who had trained in social work in Glasgow but wanted an easier life in the hills. "She needs emergency housing today which we can do and we can pick her case up from there. But that's just going to be her next step in housing. Essentially she's homeless on benefits and got involved with a guy who's done time for assault. He was in the forces. We found him because of his dog tags. Ex infantry, honourably discharged. Was on a death wish with alcohol. Doesn't look like we'll ever find out any more."

"So where are they going to stay."

"There's a B and B we use in town which is alright for a week or two. She can stay there until she gets her life sorted. If not she'll be on the street within a week. Here's the B and B card. Oh and I've told her to ring the GP in town. She says she's with you guys. Said you will look after her. Is that right?"

"That's the way it is." Tatyana said taking the card. "I'll be in touch in a day or two."

"You've got an unusual technique of acquiring new business," Robby remarked.

"That is funny Robby." They smiled at each other. "That was a first for me. No-one's collapsed and actually died on me." Tatyana said.

"She's going to need someone to be with and to talk to today and over the next few days."

"Looks like she found someone or rather someone's found her. Dave has gone over to her."

"He's switched on. Funny how you can be as messed up like I was and he is. Yet you can still focus on other people's problems. It's not uncommon in civilians who are medics and fire fighters. We must be crazy."

"I'm not going there about you being crazy." Tatyana laughed.

"I'm amazed at how well behaved everyone is."

"People in the forces are very polite and very rarely rude. That's because of discipline but these people are polite because they are needy. Ten minutes after being nice to someone a soldier could be shooting someone. Same here. Someone here could sell someone down the line ten minutes after you've served them breakfast. Every type of person, class, of all religions can so easily be homeless. It can happen so fast. Occasionally two unconnected things can happen to someone, which seem bad luck, like an illness, an accident or a bad debt and suddenly you're on the street. No possessions, no shelter, no food, no job, no family, no friends, no holidays and no future."

"You just reminded me of a dream I used to have. I used to call it the Corridor Dream. All those things were written on the doors leading to the end door. But gone now. The difference between me in Norwich and now is just huge."

"We're both different. Looks like we have five customers who might be regulars during the winter. They behave well because they see this as their potential home. Look how they left their dogs outside without asking. The dogs behave and the owners all wiped their feet. They bring their plates and mugs back to the counter."

"They are all going to run into big problems up here," Robby said.

"Yeah. I can see it already," added Tatyana. That woman Jane's got a bad chest. Dave is undernourished and underweight. He's fragile. That couple living in the caravan just don't look well and Suzie, well I'm not sure where to start with her. She's into drifting and has so far avoided being raped or having to get into prostitution. That's such an easy way out to where she is. She needs some very straight forward planning and is going to need a lot of input."

"Do you think many more will appear before the winter sets in?" Robby asked.

"It's quiet. But there could be a last minute rush as the weather gets cold. Another couple of weeks and anyone here will be staying the winter but the rest will have gone south. You get a feeling that everyone senses the freezing weather comes in after Halloween. So I reckon we might have ten people."

"The weather is a really worry."

"I'm worried about the weather too. The work is ok as long as it's the mornings only. There are other things to do to keep the place going. Fundraising. Checking out if the people here really are ok. A visit to the camp site in Kenmore to see if there is anyone else sleeping rough there or anywhere else. It's worth chatting to everyone because it's amazing what they notice about strangers and tell you. How well or badly they are dressed. If they look well, anxious, depressed, spaced out or looking for an eye-opener. There can be all sorts of odd leads that need following up to make sure there is no-one out there completely unsupported."

"What's an eye-opener?"

"It's an early drink someone has to have just after they get up so they can actually get going and start the day. A very low point. They're usually in so much physical and mental trouble at that time; they can't function beyond getting more alcohol. They're usually vitamin B deficient which means they can't think properly. They don't even think about how much they are drinking any more. So they need vitamins and good food. But it's another thing trying to get them to spend money on anything else other than alcohol."

A familiar woman walked in and put two carrier bags on the counter.

"Helen from the supermarket."

"Hey there." Tatyana said. "This is Robby. What's this?"

"These are a few things which will be out of date tomorrow. They're not out of date yet but no one's going to buy them with the same day expiry date." Robby looked through the two bags.

"There are four cans of beaked beans, four packets of sausages, packets of bacon, two boxes of eggs four pints of milk and two loaves of bread. This is almost all we use. There's pasta as well. Cans and cans of everything. This is really great."

"If it helps you keep your costs down, I can give this to you once or twice a week. It's difficult to get the ordering right this time of year and we usually have this amount past it's sell by date."

"That is brilliant. Thank you so much." Tatyana went up to Helen and kissed her on the cheek.

"Thank you for this." Robby said.

"I'll be back in a day or two." Thomas the priest held the door open for her, and then he walked up to the counter with Fearghas.

"Hey Tatyana, hey Robby how is it all going?" Thomas said. "Earlier a young man asked us the way to Dr T's. Too polite; looked ex-forces. Seems like you're busy."

"It's not too busy," Tatyana said.

"Where are all these people staying?" asked Fearghas, raising his bushy eyebrows with an inquisitive smile.

"The older couple are in a caravan at Kenmore. The middle aged woman, and there's the young man you met, are camping at Kenmore. The young girl's going into emergency accommodation with her daughter. The young girl actually lost her boyfriend Billy today to the drink. It's just getting cold and I'm pretty sure not one of them has anywhere else to go."

"They don't look too hardy or healthy any of them." Fearghas eyed them up as he would eye up his sheep to see what shape they were in. "Are you saying that they are going to be here for the winter?" Fearghas asked Tatyana.

"Yes. I know what you're thinking about. The cold. I think it's a bit too late for them to go south and find anything now. Most hostels will have filled up for the winter. Most homeless people don't travel this time of year. The problem is that everyone here is new at being homeless and new here. They don't know how bad the winter gets. Bad enough in a city but up here... I've began to wonder if I've done the wrong thing by opening the cafe at this time of year."

"You've done well to get it open at all considering all the flack you've taken. I know. I've had a few heated discussions with people. This place needs a facility for the people who pass through it. There are a lot of people in the community who are proud of what you've done. Weren't at first but they are now. Some folk near us were snowed in for over two weeks last year. None of your customers would even be able to get here from Kenmore when the transport's out. Alone on that caravan site in a good tent or a caravan would be dangerous."

"I know and I realise I might be responsible for them staying up here."

"What you've done is really good for all of us here. We are all being less selfish. Come up to my place tomorrow with Robby before it gets dark. I want to put something to you."

"Alright. We'll both be there." Fearghas took one last look at the individuals seated at the tables and then left with Thomas the priest.

Straight after lunch the next day, Tatyana and Robby drove up to Fearghas's farmhouse.

"So Fearghas, what have you got to tell us."

"Nothing. I've got something to show you. Come with me." The three of them walked past Robby's car down the lane towards a long building with several doors which were all shut with bolts.

"What's this building?" Tatyana asked.

"These used to be the stables for the horses that worked the farm. There are eight stables, a large tack room and the room for the wagons which is half full of bales of hay." He opened the door to the first stable.

"Come inside and look. Dry as you can get. There's an old wood fuelled boiler which still works in the tack room. Each stable has its own heating. My dad loved horses and he looked after them like family."

"It's warmer inside than out." Tatyana observed, "And it's got a window in the roof. It seems very soundproof."

"Come and see the tack room." Fearghas let Tatyana out then bolted the door and led them in front of the other seven ·stables into the tack room. "There's the boiler. There's a toilet and here's the sink. We used to hose the horses down here. See the drains. Could easily put a couple of cubicle showers here. Got the hot water and the drainage."

"What are you saying Fearghas?"

"In a couple of week's time, those customers of yours will freeze to death on that camp site. I know. I lose enough sheep every year to the cold. If you want, you can tell them they can come and camp in these stables. They're dry and very warm. Minus thirteen degrees last year here. Can't have you being responsible for them actually perishing in these parts. It wouldn't go down well. I can fix another toilet. And believe me it gets hot in here with the wood burner boiler. Anyway it's just a suggestion. You don't have to worry about land use as I'm registered with the Caravan club and the local council for using the land for camping."

"I don't know what to say. It's a life saver Fearghas. I had been worrying the last few days about all of the customers and I know there are going to be problems if they stay on at the caravan site. So yes, it's a wonderful offer to which I could never say no. Thank you so much for thinking of them. Can I help in any way?"

"No it will be ready in a week."

"Why are you doing this Fearghas?" Tatyana asked.

"I don't want to find any more dead bodies on the farm. In my time I've found two. Both were in their twenties and were missing from home. I remember finding the first one just sitting up straight against a fence. Frozen with a light covering of snow on his hands. I still think about what a horrible way to go. But more what a terrible thing for man to let happen to a brother. The young woman was... I don't want to talk about it. I just don't think it should happen on my watch."

"You have my total respect Fearghas," Tatyana said. "That young girl you saw yesterday. Her friend Billy was in Vinny's one minute and gone the next. They are so fragile. They don't have any of the emotional the support we have. Most are deficient in nutrition so they are not as hardy as the rest of us. They are very vulnerable."

"I know there are some old hospital beds going for free which would keep them off the floor for better warmth. The food you provide them with will be just enough for them. I know it is not sophisticated but they won't die in here because there is water and it is warm. I thought of evening meals, but with the sheep we're unreliable because we can get very busy."

"Fearghas, they will be ok with one big meal. We can always prepare a sandwich supper or flask of soup for each person. Shelter really is the main thing for them and you've given them that. Food's a lot easier to do than shelter. They are going to be very much in your debt and grateful when they see what the weather is like up here."

The next morning Tatyana gave the good news about the stables to Dave, Suzie, Izzy, Jane, the East End couple, and two new single women who had lost their jobs and then their homes. By the end of the week the last of the winter family had joined them; the six foot three red haired man called Kieran and a woman who lost everything she had gambling on the internet. Billy's puppy and Jane's Collie had even been allocated a stable for themselves.

+++CHAPTER 23.

"I'm thinking about going soon."

"I could sense it was near." Asheena answered. "Do you know how long you might go for?"

"I've got an open ticket. I want to see the Hill my uncle and aunt visited. I've got to scatter her ashes there. I suppose the biblical time of forty days and forty nights in the desert might be enough. So six weeks is what I think I'll need. I know I'm going there to take Eleanor's ashes but I want to look into what Ian did there. I feel bad about leaving you and Asheena even though you will be alright. I also feel bad about leaving Tatyana with her homeless customers at the cafe. But again I know she'll be alright."

"I thought you might need longer."

"I've got to go. Something I've got to do."

"For the first time I'm worried about what I've got to do."

"How do you mean? It's not me is it?"

"That is kind and so funny. Well... I feel very settled here but I know I've got things to look at. When you are away it will be time to face up to my grief properly. I need to spend time thinking about my family. I didn't have a chance to say goodbye to them. They were just gone. So many things I should have said, could have said."

"I remember using those words when I was getting help. Coulda, woulda and shoulda. Boy was I guilty. Guilt and survivor guilt. Both difficult."

"I know them. I feel I need to weep, to scream, to write, to just think about them for a while. I need be in grief fully. So much left undone. I'll take time when you are away to do this."

"That sounds like going through Hell."

"The time of forty days and forty nights you mentioned, I remember learning about this too. It's the time it takes to heal surgical wounds."

"Where did you hear that?"

"My mother used to say it to us when we got injured or cut ourselves."

"There are no victors in slaughter of the innocent, only victims. Even the torturer eventually becomes a victim. There really is nowhere to go to escape. Temporary vacations from reality with drugs or alcohol only delay the inevitable."

"I've watched you become more yourself over the last few months."

"Sort of began when you arrived here. I felt free to move on."

"The next step for both of us is as you say... inevitable. I need to feel more free too. I need to put my family somewhere in myself where I feel comfortable with them. Somewhere I can relate to them. Do you know what you are looking for in India?"

"My aunt gave me some clues and some advice. When she was dying she was trying to show me."

"Do you know what?"

"It's not easy to show you. I don't know if you've ever been with anyone who is dying. A week or two before they die, sometimes just in their last hours they seem to be in a state of bliss. They seem to have shed off all the cares of the material world and are just at home in themselves, whether you glimpse them on their own, with others or when you are talking to them, they have a look of complete happiness, which is what I see as bliss. The girl I shot in Afghanistan had that look of peace. It was the same as my aunt's look. But my aunt had that look for years. Her and Ian my uncle both had it."

"I feel completely settled here and I don't even want to travel south again. But now I've heard what you've seen and what you've said, you've got to go. I can see that."

"I'm going to go soon. I had to get a six month visa which arrived this morning. I've just got to buy a return ticket to Chennai. I'll be back within six weeks."

"There is one thing I need to do and that is visit the Mosque to say thank you. Will you take me?"

"Is the morning ok?"

"It's the best day because it's Friday."

+++CHAPTER 24

Robby parked the Land Cruiser outside the Glasgow Central Mosque and turned to look at Asheena. She looked confident.

"Do you want to come in with me?"

"No. I'll wait here. I met the Imam once."

"Ok then. I'll be straight back. I know there is always a queue to see him. Even though I'm not religious I have to do this. It was our family's way. We must always acknowledge when someone helps us."

"Take as long as you like. I'll be here." Asheena took Khatira by the hand and headed straight up the steps towards the Mosque. Robby turned on the radio in the car. He reclined the seat and closed his eyes. He dozed off and but then he was suddenly woken by a knocking on the window.

"Robby! Hey Robby! Hey Robby, Robby!"

"Jamal. Jamila," Robby said as he opened the door. Jamila threw her arms around him and gave him a hug. Jamal shook his hand. "What are you doing here?" Robby asked.

"What do you mean? We come here every Friday. It is a day for praying. The important thing is what are you doing here? Have you decided to convert?"

"Me, no. Asheena and Khatira wanted to pay a visit and thank the Imam for introducing us."

"Have you seen inside a Mosque before?"

"Me, no. Not religious. Not my thing. Been in the office but not the mosque."

"Then you must see what a Mosque is like and come and pray." Jamal grabbed Robby by the elbow and walked on the outside with Jamila on the inside.

"Well ok but that will be interesting because I don't believe in god," Robby said as he went along with them half heartedly. It was a cold day and Robby felt the early morning chill.

"Not to worry. It's always a good space to be in. It's warm too. And it looks like you could do with some warmth." Jamal and Robby walked into the mosque and removed their shoes and put them with dozens of other pairs of shoes. Jamila walked off in the direction of the other women who were meeting separate from the men. The mosque was warm and Robby took off his coat and followed Jamal. He looked up at the mosque ceiling and he realised it was much bigger than he had thought.

"It can hold two and a half thousand people. It is the biggest mosque in Scotland and also the biggest community centre in Strathclyde. Come we must pray. I will show you. Don't look so nervous. No one knows you here. Just relax. You kneel here like this. Here is a prayer mat for you." Robby awkwardly knelt down on the mat on one knee and then the other. "Just copy me... Allah be praised, Allah be praised, Allah be praised," Jamal said as he prostrated three times. Robby copied him, then sat cross legged on the marble floor. He looked around and saw a familiar figure coming towards him. He kept on looking at him and as soon as he recognised him he stood up.

"You are the last person I ever expected to see praying here," the Imam said. Robby saw that he was dressed casually in black trousers and a white shirt.

"More of a gesture really," Robby said trying to excuse himself. Jamal politely wandered off our of respect for the Imam's approach to Robby so as to leave the two men to talk.

"All gestures are taken very seriously by an Imam and by god."

"I'm here because Jamal and Jamila saw me waiting for Asheena and Khatira in the car."

"She is a formidable woman to have come overland on her own." He looked deeply at Robby. "She does not have faith in a God anymore, just like you." He grinned and looked Robby eye to eye. "Come let's walk around the Mosque." The two began a slow paced walk around the inside of the building.

"And you?"

"What do you ask?"

"Do you believe in God?"

"No one has ever put that to me."

"And?"

"No. I mean in the way you asked the question. It would be impossible for me to believe in a supreme god after all I have seen, heard and had to witness. I have retreated into my inner world and I found that it was there where I found what I would think of as God. That sense of our inner self is the real God, only it is covered up for most people."

"My uncle's friend is like you. He's a priest but says it's all psychology and doesn't believe in a God anymore either. Not after what he saw in the first Gulf War. I understand him and I'm getting a sense of that myself in a very roundabout way."

"How do you mean?"

"I got a sense from the Afghan girl I had to kill, from my Aunt, from a therapist, from my friend and now from you. It's a bit like whatever I do, wherever I go some people keep on saying exactly the same things to me."

"Like?"

"They say it's the inner self. I just don't get it."

"How come?"

"I shot an eight year old girl. I went crazy. I became a tramp. I tried to hang myself but the branch broke. I had therapy. My best friend my aunt died. I've somehow got forgiveness but I'm still stuck."

"And you don't see it do you?"

"What for heaven's sake. I'm so mad at everyone who keeps on saying that to me. What do you really mean?"

"I can't tell you, about you, with authority. I can only tell you about me with authority."

"Do you understand guilt and forgiveness?"

"Completely." The Imam spoke slowly. "That is why I helped you. I didn't want you to end up like me." He grabbed Robby's forearm tightly, then let go. "Eventually you'll see the only place you can find happiness is inside. One day you will open your eyes. One day you will wake up."

"You're a holy man. You couldn't have done anything as bad as I did by killing a child."

"I have two children. A girl Angela who is four and a boy Mahmud who is three. My wife Parvin had an affair two years ago. She was twenty four. The affair only lasted a few weeks. I understood because I had been paying everyone else too much attention. I was always faithful but I was a lousy husband. I got home late. I was away a lot. I didn't do the little things for her. I know now that a good relationship is like a part time job, say one evening a week. Doing the washing up. A meal out. A holiday. Flowers. Chocolates. Some new clothes. Yes I had no idea women appreciate that. For a man to buy a woman some clothes is difficult and it means he cares because he has had to put himself out to do it. But I was the Imam. She went off with a very wealthy man. They were killed in a car accident a year ago."

"How you can continue?"

"The children. A few weeks ago, on the anniversary of her leaving, that day I swore that I would stop teaching religion. I have not taught since that day and I really ceased being an Imam last month. The other two Imams now lead the prayer. They understand why I am leaving."

"What are you going to do?"

"I can't stand being in that system any more. So to earn an income I have got a job teaching in a local school at the beginning of next term."

"I see how you know about guilt and forgiveness."

"I am also lucky. I had some very good years with Parvin and I have her children. Asheena is lucky because she came here and now has a life. You are lucky because you have overcome everything that was put in your way. The only thing for you to do is to realise your self. You will find a way and like me it is not through religion."

+++CHAPTER 25.

"I'm missing him already," Tatyana said. "I could see part of him felt badly about going."

"I miss him too but we all have things, what you call stuff we have to work on. That's why I'm here. I wonder if you could look after Khatira for a couple of hours?"

"Of course. What are you up to?"

"I want to use some of the time whilst Robby is away to work on some unfinished business. It's about my family. I just need some quiet time to think about them."

"Of course. I understand. I'm not sure how I would have coped if I lost all my family. I've never asked you about this. I was waiting to see if you wanted do talk about it because... "

"I'm not sure I've really coped. I've just carried on living a day to day existence. I need to get through my pain and come out the other side. I need to move on without so much pain. It hurts so much. I want to bring Khatira up to be happy, not to be thinking about her poor old aunt."

"Come here let me give you a hug." Tatyana held on to Asheena whilst Khatira walked around the kitchen. "I love having Khatira around. You can leave her here any day all day any time. You make sure you take as much time as you need."

"You are my best friend. Thank you for giving me this time. I'll be, maybe a couple of hours."

Asheena walked back to the house with intent. She had to let out her feelings about her family because she needed to let go of them. But she didn't make it to the door. Half collapsing, half kneeling she fell sideways onto the path. She curled up in a ball and hugged herself. She didn't want to cry but she hadn't cried on her own or with Khatira. Tears were squeezed out between the closed eyelids. Noises came from her stomach as it contracted and her breathing was in gasps, small at first then huge gasps. She opened her eyes and the floodgates of her saved tears emptied onto the ground. She lay there until she noticed light from the sun flickering through some leaves into her blurred vision. It was if something in the light was calling to her.

She gathered herself back up on her legs and feet, walked into the house and sat on the floor. There were some old fashioned matching envelopes and writing paper and she was just about to start writing when the postman came. It was all uninteresting mail which was only to do with the local council. She held the ball point pen wondering where to start when there was a knock on the door. It was Fearghas.

"Can't stop Asheena but here are the eggs I said you should try," said Fearghas. "They're from my neighbour and free range. Everything alright?"

"Yes. Khatira's down playing at Tatyana's cafe."

"Did Robby get on the train alright?"

"Yes, he was excited about the whole trip. He's got Eleanor's ashes. She'll finally be resting with Ian where she always wanted to be the most. Let me know if you hear from him. I'll pop in and see you in a few days. Call me if you need anything."

Asheena took a big breath and looked straight ahead. She was scared to close her eyes. She closed them and she remembered looking for a couple of seconds before the bomb entered the end of the house. Tears ran down her cheeks as she wailed and sobbed. When her tears stopped she wanted to talk but she could only write. She picked up the pen and she began.

My Family,

Since many months I have not seen you. I miss you like I'm not able to say in words... My heart has been in pain since the day you all vanished. This emptiness is all that was left when you went.

Nahid, My sister and friend.

Khatira. She is alive. She's well and happy. You would cry with tears of joy if you could only see her. She has all of your looks. She's stubborn too. She has your eyes and nose. She's getting bigger. I was so light of heart before. Here they say happy go lucky. I am now a mother like you were of your only child. I have grown up. I am no longer just your lovely little sister and I will forever be your little sister Nahid. I'll always be your little sister... but I am older. God... I hurt so much without you.

Papa, I have had to take care of what little is left of our family. All our memories, stories, and the songs you sang. The strength you showed me, I have kept going. I'll show it to your beautiful granddaughter Khatira. I miss you so much, I cry when I think of you.

Mama, I am still looking after sheep, but not to make carpets. I have a driving licence and live in a place which would not be too strange. There are hills. But there is not you... Sometimes I don't want to live any more without you all. Khatira only keeps me going. She makes me smile too and yes I would not get up from my bed if she wasn't there.

Jamil, I miss you my brother, You are always smiling for me, when I think of you. I will not be able to grow up without you growing up beside me and walking with me amongst the sheep. I remember us calling to each other.

Naseer, I still think of your naughty grin when I think of you. You are still taller than me even though you are gone. I have so many memories of you in my head.

But Mama and Papa, Nahid, Jamil, Naseer, I have to confess to you that I cry about you all the time. But it's always worse when the sun goes down like it did at home. It's then that I feel you around me the most, but I miss you because I can't see you. And some of the time when I cry I can't remember what your faces are like when you were with me. I cry because I am terrified I am forgetting you, or that I ever will forget you. I can still smell the earthy smell of each of you, of our house. The smell of the food cooking, the fire, the air outside.

Why did I have to live? Why? If I had died I wouldn't have the heavy pain that weighs me down on me like I'm very old. How do I get rid of this pain? I can't get rid of the memories because that's all I have of you and yet they cause me so much pain. I want to think about you but it hurts so much when I do. But I have to move on with you in what's left of my life. Somehow I have to carry the wonderful memories of you with me. These memories which make me miss you so much it hurts me like a knife in my stomach. I have to let Khatira have her life here to make up for all of you not being here.

I don't know why they bombed our house but I saw that they bombed every one of the eight houses in our village so probably only Khatira and I survived from the whole community. I left but didn't see any of our old friends, because there was nothing left of their houses. All the animals were killed in the explosions of the houses. It was just flat. All the buildings were just gone. There wasn't even a pile of rubble anywhere. The bombs were so powerful and so hot that they burnt everything. I don't think you suffered because the plane bombed all eight houses in just a few seconds. They disappeared as fast as they came.

It's like I am locked out of that life before that moment. It has all gone. I have got on though. I have walked. I have been driven. I have applied for what I can and I was sent up to Scotland. Afghans, Iranians and Iraqis have helped Khatira and me otherwise we would have lost the will to carry on. The Scottish Afghan Society finally helped me to find Robby. He is a like an old fashioned knight in shining armour the way he simply rescued us and plucked us out of the middle of Glasgow.

I am waiting to get political asylum in the UK. It's only then that I have any real protection. I know Robby would never let Khatira or me be sent back. He has suffered in the forces having to kill a girl who was going to blow herself up and kill him and his two pilots. He's making up for her death by looking after Khatira and me. We both suffered in different ways. But it seems to be working. Without saying it, we are in our own ways helping each other. He is trying to get his head back together again after becoming one of those who stares a thousand yards. From what he says he's much better. The guilt and pain of what he did made him try to kill himself like lots of the boys back home. He has been lucky to survive.

I like him because he's calm. He has the strength of two men. Sometimes he says strange things which I don't understand and sometimes I say things because of my English that he doesn't understand, and we both laugh as we are both strangers to this new culture that the other person has. He's aware of what death is, but not just because of the girl. His uncle was killed in an accident and only weeks ago he lost his aunt to cancer. We both have to pick up and carry on with our lives. I have Khatira. He has us. We have him too and if it were not for Robby we would be still sofa surfing or we would be living in a one room apartment in the centre of a city.

So here I am in Scotland with a sheep farmer. It's not just like that and so simple and yet it is. I have my translation work I could do but I know you would want to me to study something, to become something, so that I can help Khatira become something. But my first thing is to love her and bring her up as you would have brought her up if we were all still together. I could go to Glasgow to be with other Afghans but I like it here. Glasgow is not only a long way but I need to mix with the local people here who have been so kind.

So far I know Tatyana; is an old friend of Robby's from when he was ill. Tatyana is great. She lives in an old house an hour away which belonged to a friend of her fathers. She's always positive. Then there is Fearghas and his wife. Fearghas was Robby's aunt's brother, the aunt that died. Fearghas is a quiet man with a beard and he is a sheep farmer who lives about a mile away. They have a daughter Alice and a son Andrew who are both Robby's age. Alice is about to have a baby and is living in the town Aberfeldy. Her husband Jim and her brother Andrew work for Fearghas. Andrew is going out with the daughter of another farmer.

Everyone is quite close here. When something happens, everyone knows about it and I have been welcomed into the community. People know that Robby was in the war and they know I was in the war, but they don't ask any questions about that. They are not nosey. Then there is Thomas the local priest. Well… he assists the local priest. He's more like a psychologist and is clever. He's good to people and like Robby was in the RAF but he retired because he got his leg blown off.

I spend my days doing a mixture of things. I look after the house, the food and cooking. I look after the sheep and just keep an eye on them when Robby is not here. I go for walks with Khatira. I see Tatyana. I go into Aberfeldy and Pitlochry to do shopping and see the health visitor to make sure Khatira has all her injections. They have lots of injections here. I have had to have them too. They keep on checking me, taking my blood pressure, making sure I am happy and not depressed. They worry a great deal about themselves when most of the time there is nothing to worry about. When they worry so much Papa, they remind me of you telling me not to worry.

The people who live here are a mixture of Scottish and English, although there are a lot of Polish and other Eastern Europeans. So I don't stick out like the only foreign person here. I suppose I do stick out though because I am the only person whose family has just been destroyed and taken away so suddenly. I wonder if it shows on my face or with how I get on with people. Sometimes I wonder if they can tell I have lost my family in the war. I don't think they can sense it but I think they know because that's what they would have been told.

Tomorrow we're going into Aberfeldy to get the photographs copied that were with our papers and money. We're going to hang the one of the whole family in our bedroom so that Khatira can see a picture of her mother. We are going to get one of you copied Nahid which I am going to get blown up and put it above Khatira's bed. I am going to get one miniaturised and put it in a locket around her neck. It's so that you will always be with her Nahid.

I feel for the first time since you were taken that I can communicate all of this with you all. Perhaps my life is beginning to settle down here just a little bit and that's why I can open up a little about what I am feeling about you all. Perhaps that's why I have time for quiet times now. Tatyana is looking after Khatira for me so I must go now. I will be back to talk to you.

It was odd trying to get up from this sofa after writing to you. I felt as if there was something which I had not done. I couldn't work it out and then it dawned on me. I hadn't thought of posting this letter. But now I have, I am going to post this letter and wait for it to arrive. I am going to post it to myself and then I'll think about the reply. I'll write the reply on your behalf to me.
I will never stop loving you.

Asheena

The next day the letter arrived for Asheena. She had just finished putting a picture of her whole family up over Khatira's bed together with a large picture of Nahid at the foot of the bed. She felt that from the foot end of the bed that Nahid would always be watching over her little girl whilst she slept.

Asheena went down the stairs and looked at the letter on the floor. She turned it over. The address was written in her own hand writing. After she drove to Aberfeldy and gave Khatira to Tatyana she stole away with the letter back to the house. Then she opened the envelope and read. She sat looking into space for twenty minutes before she wrote the letters of reply.

Dear Asheena,

I handed you Khatira and lay down to rest and sleep. It was time for you to go and tend to the sheep and you insisted that you take Khatira with you. I am so glad you did that to give me a rest, a rest which I so much needed. You've both survived because of this. I knew nothing and felt nothing. One minute my head was comfortable, the next second there was nothing. But you... you go on, but are not the same. You've worked to keep Khatira alive. You've moved country and have taken a leap we dreamed about. I wish I was there with you and we had travelled together. I know I didn't make it to Britain with you, like one day I said I would Asheena, but Khatira has.

Despite the pain Asheena, be strong. Be wise. You are the only one looking out for her.
All my love forever.
Your sister

Nahid

My little ones,

You've made it to a new life. Well done. I am sorry that we never had enough money to move out of Afghanistan during the war. I wasn't trained well enough in money and never had enough and I am sorry for being a simple farmer. I am your best friend and I am sorry for your loss of me and Mama, Nahid, Jamil and Nasser.

Even though you are in pain you've achieved what all of our dreams were. Two of the family have got away, survived and you have a great future. Please always remember that although I was simple and didn't know about money that I always loved you with every part of my heart. Apart from our self, all we have is love and friendship. Give both whilst you can.

I'll always be with you watching over you, making sure you never get hurt.

Love Papa

My little girl,

Asheena, how I want to see you so much and little Khatira. I don't know if you were lucky, just following your daily routine, wise, or angels looked after you but you've saved us all by looking after little Khatira. I am glad you don't hate sheep! I always said never undervalue them. And this man Robby! Who is he? He has helped you save the whole family. In fact the whole village because the two of you are all that survived. He's so important, make sure you truly look after him like you would all of us. Asheena, be happy, and then you are truly alive.
We will grow in you and in Khatira each day.
All my love

Mama

Hey Asheena,

It's me. I stopped growing…
But you've got taller and Khatira is talking and walking. Hey you won't forget me will you?
When you are with the sheep, I'll always be with you, listening for you calling out to me. I'll never stop listening for you calling out to me to check neither of us has drifted off.
Don't stop calling.

Jamil

Hey, Asheena,

Are you still reading this, keeping a check on me. You know I'm smarter than you, so just get on with what you got to do today. I'll be seeing you all the time.

Nasser

Asheena put the five letters in an envelope, addressed it, and then added a second class stamp. She needed more time to process what she was thinking. Five days later the letter arrived. Tatyana was very accommodating by looking after Khatira and knew that Asheena needed her quiet time. Asheena knew she must carry on with this routine for everyone's sake.

On the floor, she opened the letters; read them, then looked ahead, wondering about them all. Then she wrote replies to all the letters.

Dear Nahid,

Thank you. Your words reassured me that you didn't suffer. Oh how I wish you were here. I miss you so much. Khatira is beautiful like you. One day when she's a little older I'll tell her all about you. You will always be her mother and when she hears all about you that will honour you. I love you little sister.

Asheena

Dearest Papa,

In not being able to give me some material things, you were able to give me so much more. You gave me insight and determination. You made me trust my instincts. Thank you for the incredible love and the friendship you gave me. You are always in my heart.
Forever your loving daughter,

Asheena

Dearest Mama,

Your little ones are safe. Khatira is great and one day I'll tell her all about you. You would cry if you saw how beautiful and how happy she is. I smile every day when I think of you. You keep me positive.
Forever your little one

Asheena

Hey Jamil,

*I hear you calling back to me every day when I am outside. I miss you.
Your sister forever*

Asheena

Hey Nasser,
*You, the smart one. You are always in the corner of my eye. I miss you.
Your sister forever.*

Asheena

Asheena put all five letters in an envelope and whilst she
was writing her own address she began to weep. There was no
funeral. There would never be one. She knew there was no end
to this. They vanished forever. It was over in an instant and she
hadn't been able to work through it apart from in her dreams.
She had to keep moving with Khatira to keep them both alive.
There was no time to stop until now. She wept so deeply she
was unable to cry any more. As her breathing settled down she
realised that she was letting go of each one of them in herself.
She felt her heart aching with pain as she saw each one of them
was now moving on in her mind. The realisation that she was
saying goodbye to all of them made her want to always keep
them very close in her heart.

As she sat on the floor, for the first time she didn't feel so
alone. She felt she needed to thank everyone who had helped
her, in the same way that she encouraged Robby to write the
letters to the people who had helped him. Before she collected
Khatira from Tatyana, she wrote a letter to Tatyana and to her
old friends at the Scottish Afghan Society.

My Dearest Tatyana,

*I just wanted to thank you for helping me since I have been here.
You've been true like a sister to me. You've lifted me up when I've*

been down. You've helped me understand the British and to understand Robby. You've taken loving care of Khatira. You've helped me with all sorts of little things. For that my heart is happier and lighter.
Thank you my sister.

From Asheena

Dear Jamal and Jamila

I am just writing to say thank you for everything you each did for me. Emotionally and physically you picked me up when I arrived from Afghanistan. You showed me some of the ways of the British and you helped me keep my spirits up so I could look after Khatira safely.

You are like a family to me and I would not be where I am now if it wasn't for each one of you. I am well and Khatira is happy. She's learning Pashto and English like her mother and I did. When the weather breaks a little we will all come and see you. Thank you for all of your help.
Love from

Asheena and Khatira

After two hours she came down and went to collect Khatira from Tatyana. She gave the note to Tatyana. Tatyana read the note and looked out of the window and she was about to thank Asheena when Asheena said, "You miss Robby, don't you?"

"Yes. He's not the same. Nor am I. When we first met, we both had big problems with the past. Now he offers so much security. He's changed so much since I met him in Norwich."

"He has also changed a lot since I have been here. He seems at peace in an odd way, like how he talks about his aunt."

"Yes, he described how peaceful she was before she died and I agree he actually seems that peaceful. He used to have a thousand yard stare when he was taken over by his memories from the war. Now he's got another stare, but different. It's a stare straight ahead, through everything like he's awake to everything but not part of it."

+++CHAPTER 26.

Robby: Pocket Notebook Entry 19. I've become very down hearted in India. It must have been so very different when Ian and Eleanor were out here because I've found the place almost the opposite from what I had expected. The town with the holy mountain is a spiritual centre but I haven't been able to find a single person who could communicate with me what it was all about.

But why does a place like this attract so very many derelicts like me? Maybe because only the sick need a doctor. And who am I to say that I am anything other than that. That is why I've come here. Healthy normal people wouldn't want to come here because they aren't needy in the same way for some kind of inner cure. But now I'm not sure what I've got from being here. A part of me secretly feels like dropping out like a lot of the people here. It would be so easy. I would have no responsibilities and life could easily be so stress free in this humid jungle heat. But I know it would be worse than being homeless because I wasn't fully conscious when I was homeless. I was too distracted by thoughts. I came here in search of something and I'm unsure if I've seen it, found it, or missed it. I really don't know. I've got to admit that right now I feel more lost by coming here.

Compared with all of the people living around the hill, I seem to have come out the other end from a long dark journey. I've never met so many people in my life who are on a dark journey. Nearly all the people living around the hill have had terrible experiences and are still trying to heal their wounds. It felt a bit like my time in hospital where everyone was trying to get well. There are people who've been sexually abused as children, people who've had other terrible things in their childhoods. Some had cracked up studying, some had got addicted to drugs or alcohol as a psychological pain killer. There are semi-reformed hedonists who are still dabbling.

There are two other people I've met who have had similar experiences to me. Neither of them were lucky enough to have had the EMDR that I did and they still seemed a little jumpy about their time in the forces. Looking at what happened to them, I was definitely the worst with a full blown traumatic stress syndrome. Bill the Pill was with the US air force as a chopper pilot and got shot down and captured for a week before getting rescued. He got a discharge on medical grounds. He was taking loads of painkillers for his back pain, then realised he didn't have back pain but still kept on taking them. He was so doped up he couldn't see it until he had a car crash. He had no injuries and it took the hospital a couple of weeks to figure him out. After he left he never took another pill.

Big Jimmy is a Scot who thought he was battle hardened on his third tour of Afghanistan until he found himself covered in two other friends' body parts after being the only survivor from being blown up by an IED. He hadn't had a drink for four months since getting to the mountain. Seeing these people reminded me of the ingredients of what got me well. I was in so much pain I took the ultimate painkiller which was to end the pain by death. The people on the mountain made me see that I've worked through what happened to me and I'm now just getting on with simple daily life. I suppose, trying to kill myself was the signal that people like me have to show in order to get help because what was going on in my head was invisible.

One thing I noticed was that the more damaged people; I suppose like me, definitely Bill the Pill and Big Jimmy, we seem to be a bit more relaxed than a lot of the other visitors. I'm still working on this.

+++CHAPTER 27

In her positive enthusiasm to move on, Asheena started to do a winter clean of Robby's house so that no dust would settle whilst he was away. She decided she would sort out some of Eleanor's old furniture and see if anything needed gluing, oiling or repairing. She started with the rickety squeaking old armchair which she pulled away from the hearth of the fire and swung it around so that the back was facing the fireplace. Robby had kept the place clean and vacuumed regularly so there was little dust and no rubbish underneath the chair. Asheena had an interest in practical things and was curious as to why the otherwise solidly liking chair felt a little bit wobbly and made a noise.

She held both of the arms and tried to push them apart and pull them together, but the chair was solidly constructed and didn't feel rickety at all. She couldn't work out why it squeaked and didn't feel as stable as it should. She tried to think why when she sat in it; it felt as though it was coming apart. She started blindly exploring the upholstery to find the joints in the wooden legs but there was nothing loose at the back or at the sides. She then sat down in the chair and tired to feel what felt odd about the chair. It was certainly comfortable and she rested her down turned palms on the arm-rests. She moved her back around a bit and then she was certain it was the actual seat that was a little unstable.

She decided to look at the large seat area and knelt on the floor to see if it was in need of repair. She slipped her fingers under the front of the cushioned area and found that there was a hollow space just below the area where her calves had been touching. There was a small but definite gap of about half an inch which her finger went through. Very carefully she moved her fingers along the inner edge of the gap, being careful not to cut it in case she came across a rusty staple or nail. In the centre she came to an obstruction. It was a small piece of metal which her fingers moved to one side. It seemed like a catch on the inside of the gap. She gently bounced on the seat to see if anything happened and the piece of metal squeaked. When she moved the piece of metal a bit more to the side, there was a click and the cushioned panel at the front of the chair simply fell forwards. It was the front of a concealed area beneath her chair. Robby's aunt had a secret hiding place.

She looked at the front panel which was simply padded the same as the rest of the chair and bent down to look into the concealed area. She could see there were two groups of papers. The first one she removed consisted of some old school exercise books. Beside these was a small pile of letters which had been tied with string around the middle. She didn't undo them but noticed that they all had Indian stamps on them. She glimpsed at the exercise books which had bright yellow or bright orange covers.

She thought of Robby's aunt and how she had hidden these so that he would not find these immediately, as this wasn't a place you would explore. She wondered if she hadn't wanted him to find this right away for a reason. She thought that although they were quite well hidden, his aunt had wanted him to find them. Then she remembered Robby had mentioned something about his uncle's notebook and his father's diaries.

She opened the first exercise book, which had a small embossed area on the cover saying 'Made in India.' Inside was a letter simply addressed, 'To Robby.' It was dated only a few weeks before she had died.

Asheena knew that Robby had been very curious as to where the notebook and diaries were and she remembered him being concerned that they had important information in them for him. She put them in a waterproof lunchbox with a short note and sent them to him at the Postal address he had given her.

+++CHAPTER 28.

When Robby collected the parcel from his daily visit to the post office his heart was pounding. What was this something that Asheena needed to tell him about? He opened the parcel.

Dear Robby,

I hope this finds you well and enjoying that heat!

I was doing a winter spring clean on your aunt's house today and oiling the doors and sorting out creaking furniture. Your aunt's chair puzzled me because I couldn't work out why it was so solid but it also seemed a little fragile and had a squeak. I investigated it and found a catch which opened the front of the chair to reveal a secret space. There was this letter from your aunt to you and I think these are the notebooks and diaries you looked for everywhere.

We are all missing you and excited about seeing you soon.

Love from Asheena and Khatira

My Dearest Robby,

You know that when you find this, I will have been gone for a little while. What a delight you have been for me and Ian in our short lives. And it's this I am writing to you about.

I saw how well you were but how there was something else. I am sure you will find the answer whilst you are here. It will lie with the Afghan girl. It will be her look. When that is done you will be able to find not just inner peace but you will have inner happiness.

I also noticed that you do have that look that your uncle had. It's a certain look from someone who needs to know. Your uncle had it until the Gulf War. Then when we came back from India he had the look that he knew. All I can show you is what he showed me in my search for happiness. My favourite thing he used to say was, "Just be."

The hill wasn't only precious to us, it was a great refuge. Ian's father Scott went there after he was tortured by the Japanese in WW11.

Here is Ian's diary of the time he spent in India after the First Gulf War. Please also have Ian's notebook. Read these and find your own 'Inner path.'
Your loving aunt

Eleanor

Robby wasn't sure what to think or to feel. His aunt had probably written this a few hours before she died. This was a letter from beyond the grave, from the person who had cared about him the most. He found himself overcome by emotion with streams of tears pouring down his face because he missed her so much.

When the tears dried, he was surprised that what he read was true about him. He had found forgiveness and Eleanor had simply confirmed now that he had to move on again. He recognised this as the uneasiness he had sensed since Asheena and Khatira had arrived. He felt he wasn't the first one to be where he was. He felt Ian and his father Scott had been where he was now and he felt he was being shown a way forwards. He felt in their company and he felt part of what they were part of. He felt like it was another coming home.

He wondered how his aunt could have seen this in him without him mentioning it. Was it just a look he had? Whatever it was that portrayed what was going on, it certainly felt true for him. He read the letter several times. Then he opened the top diary. On the facing page were two words.

Just be.

He turned the page and in the middle of the first page were some words which had also been written with a blue biro. He remembered Ian's father Scott. Robby now saw that Ian and Scott had similar temperaments. They seemed very calm. At times almost too calm. Sometimes as if they were on a much more serene level of consciousness than anyone else he had met. He remembered Scott as a frail old man when he was a young child.

Ian's Diary: Page 1. Happiness is deep inside you. Nothing outside will make you happy. It doesn't come from anywhere else. What happens in your life obscures it from vision but it's always there. It's your essential state of consciousness. The conditioning we experience early on makes our mind extraverted so that we constantly look outwards. We rarely look inwards and see our true state of being, which is simple happiness. It's a state of just being. It is consciousness which is... bliss.

The paragraph about happiness seemed to open up a door in himself about understanding his own path. It wasn't that the logic of the words that just seemed true. He could see he was saying that he had to look within.

The communication from Ian's father and Eleanor right at this time gave Robby a renewed sense of a truth which he had not been able to identify, but which he sensed was there all along. He was filled with a new sense of hope, a sense that there was something positive there to get in touch with. Ian had confirmed it wasn't something out there, but rather something he had sensed which was inside himself. But from there he was stuck. He would have to read more of the notebook and diaries.

+++CHAPTER 29.

The next afternoon Robby picked up the diaries and looked at the exercise book marked with the number '1'. He quietly sat on a cushion on the floor. He laid the diaries out on the floor in front of him sensing that this was a special moment.

He briefly flicked the pages of two of the school exercise books. Each school book had a little handwriting on each page and there were also a few hand drawn pictures dotted throughout some of the school books.

Robby began reading the same exercise book from his aunt's armchair which he had first opened. He opened the first one, exposing the empty inside cover. The cover was blank but on the facing page were again the two words.

Just Be.

Then he noticed that at the bottom of this page were some words in faintly written in pencil.

Don't be this or that, just be.

Robby knew this was something along what he had been sensing in himself and he saw this as a step to opening the next page, but he waited a while. He sat on the floor on a cushion and put the book on his lap. He looked ahead and saw what 'Just Be' meant. He felt this was a huge moment in his life because these diaries had not just fallen into his hands. They had been saved for years just for him. He had a new sense of purpose, a sense of becoming.

Slowly he turned the facing page to page one. For the second time he read the writing which began just like a short monologue as if trying to give helpful instructions.

Ian's Diary: Page 1. Happiness is deep inside you. Nothing outside will make you happy. It doesn't come from anywhere else. What happens in your life obscures happiness from vision but it's always there. It's your essential state of consciousness. The conditioning we experience early on makes our mind extraverted so that we constantly look outwards. We rarely look inwards and see our true state of being, which is simple happiness. It's a state of just being. It is consciousness which is... bliss.

Again it made sense to him. He turned and read the next page.

Ian's Diary: Page 2. Although you may see that you must travel, the travel is not outwards. It's travelling inwards. It's the great single journey of discovering the inner self. You may think that you want to detach from the world but travelling inwards will finally and permanently unite you with everything of the world in a state of bliss.

Robby recognised that the journey was inwards from Eleanor's death. She had gone inwards even more than ever in her last day. He now recognised that Ian had gone inwards when he had come back from the Gulf War. He knew this as the path he had to take and he turned the page.

Ian's Diary: Page 3. There is nothing wrong with wanting to be happy, to be in a state of bliss. Every living thing strives to be happy and it is natural. Happiness does not lie in the pleasures of the senses. These are simply desires like a child's toys. When the desire is satisfied there is pleasure but it's only temporary. Another toy is required for this kind of happiness and then another. This kind of happiness is temporary. It's not to be pursued beyond the basic necessities and comforts.

This confirmed what he knew which was that all along he had been trying to live a simple life. After leaving the RAF he tried to look for happiness inside himself and not in the outside world but he was too disturbed by the images. He remembered how very simple he kept his life when he was homeless. He turned to the next page.

Ian's Diary: Page 4. After you've seen suffering in your life, you realise that there is a self inside you which is somehow hidden. It's not what you just call your Self; it is the Self. You also see that this is where the source of happiness is. But how do you get there and get in touch with your natural state of happiness? Getting there is simple and it needs frequent practice. The Self is simply covered and concealed by a curtain which is the mind with all its thinking. This curtain of thinking has to be removed and only then can the Self be revealed. It's simply removing our ignorance to show what we truly are.

Robby knew that he had already begun the journey on his inner path. Simply accepting what the words said confirmed to him that he was on this path. It was now a matter of practicalities and how the journey was to be carried on with the least interference to everyone else's lives.

He reflected on the last few months when he had tried to stop his thinking by killing himself. Forgiveness for what he did was taking place with him looking after Khatira and Asheena. But that was not it. He sensed that there was much more to what he now was and what he was reading confirmed this. He had seen Eleanor's state the last day he had seen her. She was in a state of bliss and she told him he could find this. He believed her and he was now focused on Ian's diary. He knew somewhere in himself that it was there. He just had to find out how to tap into it. He read on looking for a technique, the key to stopping his thinking.

Ian's Diary: Page 5. The only way to see this is to just be. Just be still. There is nothing to be done. By just being and not thinking the self will be seen. Just be still. Even when you are busy, the work can be done but you don't have to be attached to it.

When he was in Norwich he couldn't get rid of the effect his painful thoughts were having on him. Now they were not painful; they were just in the way of him seeing himself. Robby smiled as he read this because he knew what it said was true. But he was puzzled by how could he actually learn to stop thinking and just be.

Ian's Diary: Page 6. To be still, requires vigilance not to let thoughts intrude on this state of just being. It is better to have your eyes open some of the time but you don't have to close your eyes or have them open. You can just stare ahead with them open or closed. You will find yourself suddenly thinking about this or that in some detail, such as a person, food or being somewhere and doing something completely different.

Automatically these thoughts branch out like braches from a tree into all sorts of associated thoughts. The trick is to stop the first root (thought) becoming the trunk of a tree through which all branches of thoughts spring. At first when your awareness is not acute, you will have to work backwards from the braches to the trunk to get to the root. It's as if thoughts are more attractive than the inner self and so you are easily lured off by them. They lead you away from just being, from experiencing the bliss.

Being lured off by a train of thought may happen three or four times or even a dozen times or more each time you sit. It doesn't matter because all the time the direction is actually inwards and all the time progress is being made, even though it may seem to you as if you are slipping backward or getting nowhere. The sense of lightness which you experience during the days continues, no matter what the apparent degree of one pointedness achieved. You have to just carry on and just be. You are already there… you now only have to pull back the covers to see yourself. Again, even when you are busy, the work can be done but you don't have to be attached to it. You can just be.

Robby thought how this didn't seem too overburdened with detail, just a simple instruction and so he turned the next page and read.

Ian's Diary: Page 7. By just being still, slowly you sense you are just being. With daily practice less and less thoughts intrude but they do continue. The length of time just being increases.

Soon through daily practice, the curtain begins to open at other times by itself without effort and a state of bliss arises, outside of this practice. Daily life should continue as usual, but with ten to twenty minutes to just be, most particularly on waking in the early morning.

Persevere with this for four days and progress will be made before the beginning of the fifth day. If you get stuck at day two or three come back to read this. Lastly, this is not meditation it is just being. All forms of meditation, especially mantra meditation should be put to the side. Simply learning how to just be still is the key to the self. If nothing appears to change in the first day or two don't be put off.

It's like riding a bicycle. You feel frustrated because you can't do it then suddenly you're doing it and can't remember exactly what it was that you learnt. Suddenly you will sense an inner silence. It is simply the art of being. That is all.

It is the way of the self as taught by religion's finest and also the way of the self as taught by masters in both East and West. Whether you call it spirituality or psychology it shows the self which is not the mind. The mind is the form of a bundle of thoughts. The mind is transient and like an illusion. The self always exists whether sought after or not, whether seen or not. Just be still. There is nothing more than being. When the 'Self' is seen, the ego is observed as just a bundle of thoughts only. It is then that we see the world with different eyes.

Day 1. Just being. Robby continued to sit on the cushion on the floor against the wall. He stretched out his legs and laid his hands on top of each other in his lap. He felt a little uncomfortable so he adjusted the position of his leg. He still felt uncomfortable so he adjusted the position of his back twice so that he felt better. He sat back, and then he closed his eyes. All he could think about were the different shades of light and dark in front of his eyes which distracted him and his thoughts focused on these. After a couple of minutes he opened his eyes for a few seconds. Then he closed his eyes and tried not to think but all he could do was think about not thinking. Then he found himself trying to remember when he had last had a cup of tea. He realised he'd gone way off on a train of thoughts leading to the subject of the tea. He wondered just how he'd got so distracted by his thoughts. He felt he had little or no control of his thoughts when he wanted to just be quiet.

He adjusted the cushion twice, his legs twice and his back twice. He looked straight ahead and tried to concentrate. He slowed his breathing down. He was quiet for a few moments but then he started thinking about yesterday and how hot the Indian food was and how he'd like some yoghurt next time. He then became aware that he was thinking about yesterday instead of trying to stay in the present. He tried to stay in the present. Then he found himself thinking about supper and how he could cook some scrambled eggs and how nice they would be with tomato sauce. Then he saw he had gone off on a train of thought. He saw that he was looking outwards rather than inwards. He was now aware that he'd been thinking along this useless path for quite some time. He tried to refocus on the present and not think but he was plagued by all sorts of minor thoughts now about if he was doing this properly, how should he proceed. He decided to open his eyes and see how much time had passed. He was surprised to see on his watch that exactly twenty minutes had passed.

Robby: Pocket Notebook Entry 20. Reading the diaries today what they reveal seems straightforward. I'm following the instructions and I can't say that I've noticed much. Except that my mind seems distracted when I try to focus on being quiet. My mind starts thinking of things and then suddenly I'm in the middle of some complicated scenario of thoughts. Being pulled by this kind of mental activity is powerful and it's like I have to wrench myself out of these thoughts to focus on the quietness. But the quietness only lasted perhaps five or ten seconds.

Day 2. Morning. Just being. Robby sat against the wall and looked straight ahead for half a minute. He looked at his watch which indicated it was five thirty am. He closed his eyes and was determined not to be overtaken by his thoughts. He would just be. He dropped his shoulders, stretched the back of his neck then looked straight ahead. His eyes just looked ahead whilst he tried to let himself just be and not let his mind jump into action thinking about anything. Again he slowed his breathing to make it come from his stomach.

He sat just being quiet for about twenty seconds and then without being aware of it, he started wondering about what he was going to have to eat for breakfast that day. What was breakfast going to be like? Would he have toast with butter and honey? He would then have coffee and maybe another piece of toast. Then suddenly he was aware he wasn't just being; he was thinking about breakfast. He realised he had gone off thinking for a while but didn't know how long so he looked at his watch. He had sat down at five thirty and taken perhaps a minute to settle. It was now five thirty four, so he had gone off thinking for four minutes. He covered his watch with his sleeve, dropped his shoulders, looked straight ahead and tried to just be without letting his mind run off thinking.

He waited and after only a few seconds found himself wondering about what good weather it was and how he was looking forward to a walk in the early morning sun. He thought of the sights he might see. He would see the hill and go and have a look up the gentle slopes. Then suddenly once again he became aware that his mind had taken him off in a tangent in one of the many braches it could find. He looked at his watch. It was now five thirty eight. He opened his eyes and assessed his progress. He could sense that he had remained just being twice perhaps for about five to ten seconds in the last four minutes. His quietness was overtaken by thoughts twice. Robby decided that he needed to apply more determination. He picked up the diary looking for further help and found just where he left off.

Ian's Diary: Page 8. At first when you try to be still and quiet, it will appear as if nothing is happening. Soon you will notice that you can only remain silent without thought for a few seconds only. You will suddenly find you've been carried away, often thinking about things in detail, whilst you actually were trying to sit still and just be quiet. Leave the thought you discover that you are having and gently turn to just being quiet inside. Having all these thoughts is normal. It is how our minds have become dominant. It will seem like a struggle at first, but you will suddenly be able to just be with ease. Don't struggle. Just be still.

Ian's Diary: Page 9. When after about four days you are able to have some time with no thoughts, you should start to enquire what the self is. You have to ask yourself who you are and what you are. You should ask yourself every time you sit and just be. You will see that you are not the body or the mind or any of the senses. Eventually when you ask the question 'Who am I?' you will see that you are just the self, the self that you experience when you sit and just be.

Eventually like suddenly being able to ride a bike, you will wake up and see it. This will help you to see thoughts arising at their root and branching out. That consciousness, that sense of just being is what you are. This state of consciousness will then start to come to you at other times. The ego will become silent by only a few minutes of 'just being still' every day. The state of just being is consciousness and is bliss.

Throughout the day Robby sensed his need to be more vigilant to watch out for this thinking springing into action when he was just trying to be. The entry on page nine had now told him what he was looking for. He knew what it was. He just had to try and stay with it.

He decided that he would try again to just be still in the afternoon. However he sensed his best time to sit and just be was early in the morning, a time when he knew his mind had not yet got fully running and taken over everything. But the afternoon was the time when everyone was quieter or asleep and not so active and therefore less likely to disturb him.

Day 2. Afternoon. Just being. He looked ahead. It was very quiet and he closed his eyes. There was silence and it was peaceful so he stayed with this. But then he found that he had let himself be taken off on a train of thought about his boots and the fact that he needed a new pair because his soles were worn. He slowly left further thoughts about his boots and was now quiet again. He sat waiting and expecting to be distracted again by his thoughts. He was and he missed the beginning of being distracted and found himself far down another trail of thought thinking about Khatira and Asheena.

Day 3. Morning. Just being. The next morning he woke at five thirty. He got up and walked over to the small cushion. He sat down and took a couple of shifts of posture of his leg and back to get comfortable. He kept his eyes open for just a few seconds, closed them and raised his head a little so his eyes, although closed were looking straight ahead. He was determined to make a stand against his thoughts taking him away with them. He dropped his shoulders and looked straight in front of him.

He could tell there were no thoughts. He kept on with being aware that this moment was thought free and peaceful. Then without any sense he was thinking about repairing a window in the toilet and how the best way to remove the broken glass was to pick out as much of the glass with some pliers and then prize open the frame with a thin knife or chisel. He would than measure the glass; replace it with polythene before going in to the village to get a new piece cut. He saw himself getting back home and eagerly setting about placing the new piece of glass in its frame. Now he realised he had been carried away by this thought for a while. He looked at his watch and it was now 5.34. He was surprised and very aware that his thoughts had again carried him off for a long time without him being aware.

He promised himself he would be more vigilant as he sank back into inner silence. Again he settled back into to dropping his shoulders and tried to just be. Four minutes later he realised he was thinking about the hill. It was now 5.38 and he could see that there was some regularity with which his mind distracted him. He reckoned that he could sit still in silence for about ten to twenty seconds and then his thoughts carried him off. He needed more help to stay in the present rather than get carried off with thoughts about the future.

Robby felt unusually peaceful and felt a positive sense of being much more part of the world. At the same time he felt less worried about himself and everything in the world. He was acutely aware of this good feeling and wondered if it could be the time he was having trying to get back to the moments of silence. He wondered if perhaps this was his first glimmer that there was a thread he was able to get hold of, even though it was extremely brief, intermittent and seemingly not under his control.

Day 3. Afternoon. Just being. Robby sat in his usual place. Then he closed his eyes. For the first time he was quiet without thoughts for some time but then he found himself distracted by thinking about where all this was leading him. He looked at this watch and six minutes had passed. He could tell that he had only been thinking about where this was leading him for about three minutes. He had spent about three minutes in silence and this made him feel as though he was getting a bit better and making a little progress. He tried to be quiet but soon found himself thinking about Eleanor and how much he was grateful to her. Then he realised he had gone off on a trail thinking about her. Twelve minutes had passed in all. He settled back into silence twice more and twice more thoughts came and distracted him along long trails of thinking.

Day 4. Morning. Just being. The next afternoon after his lunch, he sat looking straight ahead and he had a desire to close his eyes which didn't come from tiredness. There was no routine just that this was what he felt he now had to do.

Robby sat looking ahead. His shoulders dropped without any effort and as he looked straight ahead he closed his eyes. He sensed he wanted more of what he had experienced with no thoughts. He carefully looked out for thoughts taking him over as he sat looking ahead with his eyes closed. Again he sensed there were no thoughts and just appreciated this. But then, within the space of less than a minute he again found himself engrossed by thoughts. This time he had thoughts of insecurity and worried if what he was doing was right for him. He fretted about if he had taken the wrong path.

He was worrying about this when he became aware that he was actually on a train of thoughts. He opened then closed his eyes and dropped his shoulders but less automatically than before. But then he looked straight in front of him and the sense of being became more prominent. For the first time he was aware that it was there all the time, but that it was covered up and virtually concealed by his thought patterns. What the diary had said was true. This was his true self and he was surprised to see that it really was simply concealed by his mind. What a simple thing he realised. Robby could see that he needed to regularly remove these covers of the mind which concealed his true self. He knew it was the determination not to let thoughts take him over that was the path to this state of being.

Robby: Pocket Notebook Entry 21. I've noticed during the last two days that I feel a lot lighter and free of worrying. I feel happier in myself and a lot closer to other people and things generally. I feel more part of the world and not like an isolated person. The little time I am spending 'just being' is having an effect on me at other times. When I am being quiet, it's the pull of thoughts which distracts me but it's the return to that quiet state that seems to be changing me. Returning time and time again to that place which I can see is always the same. It is opening me up to accessing that space at other times when I am not just sitting being still. For example, I noticed tonight that I was in that silent space but I hadn't made an effort to get there and I wasn't thinking. I was 'just being.' I must go back to reading the notebook and diaries tomorrow.

+++CHAPTER 30.

One early morning before sunrise Robby woke and couldn't get back to sleep. As it was still cool he decided to go for a walk around the hill.

Robby: Pocket Notebook Entry 22. Early this morning I decided to go for a short walk before my breakfast of coffee and bananas. It was already very warm and I headed to the cooler most northern part of the road, going clockwise around the mountain. Around that part of the mountain are a few very small one roomed thatched mud huts where some of the poorest people in the district live. Everything about the village was so simple, it seemed as though the villagers were on the border between being civilised and being native.

It was nearly dawn and I was walking as close as I could get to the mountain without actually beginning to climb it, when I came across what I thought was a statue of a man wearing a white loin cloth. My eyes had acclimatised to the dark and I could make out some detail. There seemed to be nothing unusual about a statue in a place like this, as there were dozens of statues or shrines around the mountain. That's until I saw that it wasn't a statue. It was a real man whom I took to be a statue because he seemed to be perfectly still. In another country this could easily have scared me at this time just before dawn, but here it made me inquisitive. I couldn't make out his face because it still wasn't light enough, but from the shape and size of his body he looked like an average Tamil man, dark skinned, skinny but muscular.

As I looked at him from about fifteen feet, the man remained standing perfectly still with his arms by his sides and his feet two feet apart. He remained like this with his eyes closed for a few minutes. Then he spoke clearly but to himself.

"This is an ancient technique, taught for hundreds of years. You were told to keep your instruments sharp. There was no difference between

whether these were used for life or for death. Calligraphy, drawing and art were important to balance daily life."

I noticed his toes move up and down once, and then his big toes explored the red soil. His heal came off the ground and gently dug itself into the soil. Both feet rocked so that the outside of his feet rose up a little and then they too settled in the soil. As I watched I was wondering what on earth he was doing. Although his feet moved, he was still. Then I noticed his toes seemed to explore and bury themselves in the red soil. Something was happening inside this man, but I hadn't a clue what.

He stood still again with his head bending even lower as if he was in sorrow or praying. Then a tiny piece of light from the sun began to appear in the east and I could now see him a little more clearly. I noticed that his head slowly began to rise up until he was looking perfectly straight ahead with his eyes closed. There was a pause of maybe a minute as he stood there with his feet apart. The rays of light from the early morning sun were now striking the red mountain and his face. His arms slowly began to lift up from his sides and when they were higher than his shoulders, the palms of his hands turned upwards with the fingers spread apart, as if he was receiving something. His head now tilted back just a little as if he was looking up at the sky. He seemed in total control. His nostrils flared and his lips moved as if they were a pair of powerful muscles. He took a large breath which started to extend his tummy. Then he spoke again.

"If we can stand our ground in our own space, we can deal with everything. When we say yes, we mean yes and when we say no we mean no. If we do this every day of every week of every month of every year we can deal with life. Now this is an exercise that should lead to action so put energy into action and walk."

Looking at him from the side I could see his knees slowly begin to bend. As he slowly swayed towards the right, his weight transferred to that leg and his left foot came off the ground. Slowly he swung around and turned towards me. He opened his eyes and looking directly into my eyes, he smiled. He wasn't Tamil; he was Japanese, perhaps fifty five.

"That was unusual." I quietly said.

"Yes. Not many people know of this these days. Even in Japan."

"I've never seen anyone do this."

"I'm not surprised." He laughed.

"How come?"

"You see it's not taught."

"Is it a martial art?"

"It's much more and it's been hidden for years. The significance of the simple movements lies in the imagery that goes with them."

"Who did you learn it from?" I asked.

"It was part of my family tradition for many centuries as long as anyone can remember. My great grandfather and grandfather taught me when I was a boy and later my father showed it to me, time and time again."

"What tradition?"

"Long time ago, my family were Samurais. What you saw just now was the Samurai Warrior Grounding Technique. It's an ancient technique taught for hundreds of years. It has never been written down as it's an oral tradition. You were supposed to do it each morning of your life. You could use it as an emergency in times of great distress. You were told to keep your instruments sharp. There was no difference between whether these were used for life or for death. Calligraphy, drawing and art were important to balance daily life. These things are the same today."

There was a long silence as we both looked as the sun's rays shone over the top of the mountain lighting up other much smaller monoliths in the distance. For me it was as if this event of dawn over this mountain, which had occurred each morning for millions of years was a special event and had to be seen especially today. At first I was silenced by what he said but now he remained quiet because of the way the mountain was changing colour as it was bathed in the early rays of sunlight, which were red at first, then yellow, and finally full daylight. When the light seemed normal for me, he broke the tranquil silence.

"I come back here every year to the birthplace of most of the martial arts."

"You mean here in India?"

"Yes, just a few miles from here. There was a South Indian monk called Bodhidharma or Dharuma as we know him in Japan. He left Kanchipuram near Madras and arrived at the Songshad Shaolin Monastery over one and a half thousand years ago. He's thought to be the patriarch of Shaolin boxing and Zen Buddhism. He is therefore the patron of most Japanese Martial arts. He was very important because

he introduced the principle of wu-te, which is respect for human life. The term wu-te is a Chinese meaning martial virtue. It involves the qualities of humility, restraint, and discipline. Fundamentally it promoted spiritual development."

"So it didn't promote fighting?"

"No, wu-te promoted health not fighting. The best swordsman never has to use his sword. He avoids quarrelling and fighting. Like me, typically true martial arts masters are always also healers or doctors. Tamil Nadu is a very important place but this mountain is the centre of its spirituality and was in the time of Bodhidharma. That is why I'm here."

"Could I learn this grounding technique?" I said, quietly thinking he would probably simply refuse me.

"If you wish, I'll show you each day whilst I am still here. I leave in seven days," he replied. "Tomorrow before the sun rises I'll meet you here. I am Ki-ai."

"Ki-ai?"

"Yes, it's Japanese for spirit meeting. But is also the name of the cry given when you release a mortal blow."

"Well, I'm Robby. I'll be here at sunrise."

The next morning we met at the same place outside Ki-ai's hut in silence before sunrise. On the first day Ki-ai began to speak very slowly.

"This is an ancient technique, taught for hundreds of years. You were told to keep your instruments sharp. There was no difference between whether these were used for life or for death. Calligraphy, drawing and art were important to balance daily life."

I remembered these words from the day before and I understood now that he was repeating them for me so that I too should remember them. Then he continued.

"Stand with your eyes closed and your feet apart. Feel your toes and flex them up and down. Be aware of the ball of your foot and then the heel of your foot. Then be aware of the inside of our foot. And then where the outside of your foot touches the ground. Imagine your toes growing roots into the great Earth Mother, slowly exploring the earth and growing down like the roots of a tree."

I realised that this is what he was doing when I watched his feet moving the day before. As I followed his instructions, imagining pale roots growing into Mother Earth, I felt really different, as if there was a connection. I visualised my feet growing roots from the ends of my toes into the earth and it seemed as real as if my eyes were open. Then the centre of my attention completely changed when I continued to imagine what he suggested.

"The great nurturing Earth Mother who has taken everything since time began has accepted it and turned it around into the creative giving ground of the Earth. Everything that you've experienced good and bad; all the pain, grief, anger, loneliness and disappointments. Let this return to Mother Earth to her bosom by the roots which connect you through your feet. Be aware of all of this going down the root to Mother Earth."

For some time I stood there thinking of all the negative things in my life and then the good things too. My whole life seemed to appear in front of me. As I imagined all of this I tried to let go of it and give it back to the Earth. Something seemed to flow down out of my feet into the roots that went deep down into the soil of the earth. I didn't just feel grounded now, I felt cemented and glued fast to the Earth, as if I was part of the Earth as well, like a tree. I felt as if there was no separation or difference between myself and the Earth. Then my sense of direction changed once again as he continued.

"And at the same time, like the green sap rising up the new roots of a tree, imagine a new form of energy rising up through your roots from Mother Earth. Up through your toes, feet and legs to your pelvis, through the sexual organs to the stomach, to the heart centre. Be aware of the heart centre as the apex of a triangle. Be aware of the apex of another triangle from above with the apex coming from the Father in the heavens. As you become more aware of this other more masculine energy which provides all life with energy and light from the sun, feel your arms slowly rising like the branches of a tree. This energy pours in through your fingers, hands, arms, across your shoulders through the crown of

your head. Through your nostrils, sharpening your smell. Through your mouth, enabling you to control what you say and to your lungs, giving you awareness and control of your breath. And now its apex moves down to meet the apex of the other triangle in the heart. Experience the two triangles meeting, the two energies meeting in your body."

I now understood the small movements I remembered witnessing the day before which were unusual; the flaring nostrils, the moving lips, the big breath. They all made sense now as I acted them out.

"If we can stand our ground in our own space, we can deal with everything. When we say yes, we mean yes and when we say no we mean no. If we do this one day of every week of every month of every year we can deal with life. Now this is an exercise that should lead to action so put energy into action and walk."

Very slowly I put one foot in front of the other. As the sun rose and shone on the hill, it made it look a light red. We stopped and as he turned in the red light he stood perfectly still looking at me as if to speak.

"The best swordsman never uses his sword."

Somewhere I heard this. Maybe it was him. Maybe it was in me. Maybe I imagined it all. Then he wasn't there any more and I wasn't sure if he actually spoke at all. Next I was walking around the hill and I knew he wasn't there.

Robby: Pocket Notebook Entry 23. It's as if I've grown up and now actually have a tool box with some psychological tools in it. I had nothing before apart from my gut reactions. The Samurai teacher has shown me the grounding of myself and let me see the relationship and merging of the masculine and the feminine, the earth and the heavens. The therapy helped me get rid of the anxiety associated with the images in my head. Looking deeper into the mind with the sub-personalities helped me see the bigger picture of the components of my mind.

Listening to my aunt and talking with Thomas showed me there was more than I could see by taking in Khatira and Asheena. It didn't just restore balance, it began to show me how all this happened and hinted at what was happening to me.

But what I learnt from my aunt and from the notebook and diaries she left me has made me feel a sense of bliss I've never experienced before. I feel like I'm on an entirely different level of consciousness.

How has this happened? Most important is I see that sitting just being still and watching thoughts appear, then gently stopping them has slowly shown me that thoughts can be stopped and that a more peaceful state just of the self can be experienced. I've seen that I need to be vigilant and watch just how thoughts arise during the rest of the day. I had to be shown this because I wouldn't have seen it for myself. It exposes the self that is really always here but is covered by thinking.

Seeing my own self and the tools in my psychological toolbox makes me see how much more there is to me than just having a history, having a job and having knowledge. I'm not just my history, my mind or the ego. It's made me realise how in the west our psychological toolboxes have become depleted. These new tools have shown me my own relationship with the earth and with whatever is out there in the universe. I see my feet on the ground. But the big thing is I see the self… the self that I am. I can now see clearly the self that Eleanor was. For the first time I also see the self that Ian was.

+++CHAPTER 31.

Robby: Pocket Notebook Entry 24. When I look at the bigger picture. I'm not normal, whatever that means. And this place is not full of normal people. It's attracted people who are in some ways psychologically unwell. Whatever the problems they have, whether drugs, alcohol, abuse, torture or trying to leave a religion, they are all trying to move on from them. Even if they are stuck here they are better than being back in their old lives. I can't imagine being back in the armed forces. That's why I'm here in this steamy hot town in South India. I'm treading my own new path. It's very much an inner path and not some new trade or profession. And it's an improvement. I'm lucky I've got so much to go back home to.

Robby: Pocket Notebook Entry 25. This morning after a long night of heat, I woke early and decided to go for a slow walk around the hill. I'm glad I did because I met a man who had been here a long time.

I started walking slowly on the dusty eight mile route around the hill and after only twenty minutes, I came to a small village. It's a good place to rest, have a coffee, and just be, especially as I had all day to do the walk around the hill. I sat on a very basic wooden bench and waited for the owner to notice me so I could order my coffee. I thought I heard someone say, "Gidday" but I couldn't see anyone.

After a minute I thought I heard it again, "Gidday." I could now see that there was indeed someone sitting across the other side of the open fronted mud hut coffee house which was on the dark side because it was shaded under some coconut trees and it had no windows. He acknowledged me with a gentle smile and after I was given my coffee, he smiled again and I was just about to say who I was when he spoke again. "Mate, you're British aren't you?"

"Yes," I said. I could now see his tanned face and short cropped white hair.

"They say you've been living in the old compound, being pestered by all the Europeans. This place has swallowed a few of them up. I've been here many years."

"What's your name?" I asked.

"They call me Australian Swami, but I don't like all that Swami crap. I'm just an old man now. An old fool after years here. I've been lucky to be so happy here."

"You must know the people here well then?" I asked.

"Yes I seem to understand them. Not too bad for an old Australian fool who tends to the trees on the hill."

"You must have met some wise people here during that time."

"Many fools just the same as me. The old man who lived here and probably one or two visitors." The Australian seemed reflective and there was a silence. "By just being you uncover the inner self. Thoughts are in competition with the inner self for attention. If you sit still with your eyes closed and pay attention to the inner self, you will notice thoughts suddenly taking over your attention. But you also have to ask yourself who is having these thoughts. You sit there waiting and for a moment there are no thoughts; there is just silence. Then thoughts spring up uninvited. When you find that silence, you must ask who you are. You will see that you are not the body, not the mind, not the collection of thoughts or your ego. You are just this inner self. Soon you will find yourself increasingly in that state much of the time whatever you are doing. Where there are no thoughts is the true heart. It is a state of 'just being.' It is consciousness and a state of true happiness."

There was a silence. "I'm here after time in the war. I'm trying to find something in myself where I am just happy to be."

"I understand. You'll realise that you've come to the best place to be. You have to 'just be.' That's all. It's that simple. But I've got to go."

The Australian was very funny and indeed a very wise fool. He saw everything in a positive humorous way. He was almost like a happy child. I felt like I had known him as a friend since I was a boy. When I got back to my small house, I realised I had lost track of time as the sun was setting. I feel it has been a good day.

+++CHAPTER 32.

Robby: Pocket Notebook Entry 26. I went for another walk around the hill today. I stopped for a coffee at the same village and met the Australian again who goes by the name of Australian Swami, but who prefers to be known as the fool. I was so knocked out by what he said to me today that I wrote it down because I thought he told me so much. He has been here a long time and although he pretends to be a fool to everyone, it is only an act to keep westerners away. But the truth is he is the most switched on wise man here.

"How are you getting on with the westerners?" He asked me.

"I try and keep them at a distance. Well... they seem a little disconnected. Not very friendly."

"Then you've spotted something. You are right. Many of the people here are not friendly because they are caught up in their own problems. But one recurrent problem is that in trying to become non-attached to material things, they also become detached in relating to other people and they lose their compassion. Our heart is after all the only thing of any value that we have to share.

On a practical level, if a person still has profound issues which have not been resolved such as some past trauma, then it will be difficult for them to simply be calm inside themselves. Healing should be looked at by some sort of self examination, perhaps writing or talking to someone, even a friend. Spirituality is not a substitute for dealing with this and any kind of 'searching' is most likely to be just avoidant play which feeds the need of the mind to escape from their more 'needy' unpleasant reality. All this un-worked out stuff has to be processed, otherwise it bothers you and will block you. After the Second World War several people came and lived here who had been in POW camps and were either tortured or very shaken by what happened to them. They sorted themselves out here first and then they practised what the old man showed them about being still.

It's a fundamental reality check, which without exploring first, means you shouldn't look anywhere else. It's a hierarchy of needs check. Basically getting your priorities right. You may need to get off your cross because you need the wood for a fire to keep warm or cook your food. But these things have to actually be in place or action still has to be taken about them before any journey starts into the spiritual. Avoidant spirituality is common not just in India but everywhere in temples, therapy sessions and being with a guru."

"What about therapists, Gurus and priests? What function do you think they really have?"

"The main difficulty in looking at religion, spirituality and therapy seems to be sorting out of who is authentic from all of the religious leaders, gurus and therapists because all of them seem to have unexpected dark sides to them. Sorting out which one you may need, if you do, is another question which I spent years looking at before I came here. I've met a lot of people who've got lost with gurus, therapists and religious leaders. Now the reasons why seem much clearer to me. If it helps you not having to tread all the paths that these people have trod, then I'll explain.

Part of a religion's function was originally to unite and to keep certain groups of people together by providing each person with a shared sense of purpose and meaning. Rituals, religious mantras and rosaries mesmerise people and are the glue that binds them together. Every religion, even if it's just the belief of a small group of people, attempts to provide meaning about everything in life, from how to grow up, work and even what to eat and what not to eat. Religion provided a common explanation of everything in life and life's ultimate outcome by belief in a better fate for each person in the next life.

The focus of faith is largely based on fear. Through fear, religions have clearly kept a great sense of order in the World for a very long time. But they are institutions, in some ways like schools. And they have also been responsible for a lot of conflicts.

These days, people who seem lost don't look to religion; they come here. They come here because religion is the most obvious thing in India as it seems to be everywhere you turn, which is certainly not the case in the western world. There are thousands of different Gods and Goddesses. Most visitors look in India for something that's common to them all, something which unifies these, the essence of all religions. In India you soon realise that the unifying common denominator is not in the religions but in you. That is why people come to this place. It could easily be said that spirituality is all psychological and that God is really inside us.

Let me try and make this very clear for you because it is vital. The English poet Shakespeare said it when he wrote, 'To thine own self be true.' This is the same as the message from the old man to ask yourself 'Who am I.' There are two things written on the portals of the Temple of Adelphi in Greece, 'Know the Self' and 'Nothing to excess'. Christ said that the kingdom of God is within. What could be more plain and simple than that? They are from different cultures and ages but essentially saying the same thing.

But there are all sorts of levels of attainment. For most people in the world's larger traditional religions, their fundamental beliefs are really very much unchanged today from how they were two thousand years ago and they can go through their whole life accepting these ready-made explanations of life, God and the Universe. However, there are others who as we say in Australia are 'non-sheep.' These non-sheep are the most interesting. There is an old saying by the nineteenth century monk Vivekananda which says, 'It's a blessing to be born into a religion and a tragedy to die in one.'

Let me go a bit further and amplify this. It's a privilege to leave one and discover your own self and find out what you are."

"Do you think India is a good place to do that?"

"Yes, but only because by being in India you are so overwhelmed by the plethora of religious thought that eventually you are forced to give up all beliefs and all sets of rules. It's unique.

It's more to do with the discipline of attending to the inner self. And not an outer set of rules. It's inner discipline, not an outer theory about the inside like therapy and religion. It's like riding a bike. You have to get on it and start peddling. You can't sit on it and discuss it. You have to do it. You have to get going. You have to start having time to 'just be,' to be your inner self.

It requires repeated daily work and this is probably the modern day true spiritual path. This path can seem confusing and perhaps this is why the more modern gurus of the last two hundred years have apparently seemed so popular in recent years. In the last hundred years therapists have tried to take over their function, but unsuccessfully."

"You look at the mountain like a familiar friend," I commented.

"It is my best friend. I think 'good friends' are usually less risky and perhaps better than therapists because their only motivation to help you is because they like you. There is no investment in carrying on with you other than friendship. There is only enjoying being with you. They are not getting a sense of expanding their ego, power base or popularity by seeing you. I've often wondered if people who present to therapists only do so in many cases because they don't have 'good enough' friends.

I'm only telling you this because I have seen so much of the underlying reasons why people come here. There are lots of spiritual tourists who come here on a vacation out of an intellectual interest in what is here. But they are not interested in finding out about themselves. They don't actually try and 'just be' and find out who they really are.

I'm not sure I've met many normal people here. Many people who come here would probably be taking medication from their doctors if they weren't here. This place really does help them.

But you have to be cautious. Some people can become very unstable who are probably unstable anyway. I've see a lot of people become very strange and well… crazy. Some people appear to have breakdowns whilst they may actually be breaking through, away from what they have been. It can be as consuming as total devotion and the effects are probably the same. I have seen people pour themselves in to this and I now know that consciousness can be a painful thing for some people and it may be best left alone."

"Basically you're saying that some people shouldn't dabble?"

"Yes. Some people are probably best just to worship and devote themselves to a god, goddess, a mountain, a rock or a river but not to really question. This is another function of some gurus; to be devoted to. This might appear to be true for some therapists too. With some people a guru can appear to unconditionally accept a disciple's unspoken love for them, as well as their unspoken problems and faults or sins, and the devotee can then think that they are being given love back from the guru, without all of the basic human worldly things that would usually go with loving someone. The problem with this type of relationship is that the devotee projects on to the guru, god, statue or stone and these people have to largely imagine what they think they are receiving back in return. But sometimes this might be all a person needs in their life

at that time and their vulnerability may be reduced, which can be the whole point.

Others may feel that the only way they can show love is by giving money and that's why so many gurus or ashrams are very wealthy. Perhaps it's a sad thing to accept, but it's a fact that some people only see themselves as being able to give money in return for everything in life. But if money is their form of personal energy then it's probably a fair exchange. It probably only seems strange because the people who receive the money can look amusingly hypocritical by what they choose to spend it on. I'm sure you've seen them with their dozens of luxury cars.

If you don't ask about your life, or question yourself about how to lead it and you don't follow any religion, guru or therapist, you may appear to look happy. You may appear to be very fortunate and not be needy or vulnerable. But the truth is that we all know that this is not the case. Because as life progresses, it usually deals out a lot of pain. And a lot of this is accumulative. It gets to you more as you accumulate more.

If you are wealthy and overprotected by wealth you are usually cut off from the inner self. That's what the Bible meant by saying that it is more difficult for a rich man to get to heaven than to get a camel through the eye of a needle. In India God is seen as being the inner self and in Christianity, the self is the kingdom of heaven within. They are different ways of saying the same thing. Preoccupation with wealth and what it brings distract you from your real neediness, from what you can be. It is all simple.

After some time in India you begin to notice that people who seem to be in search of 'enlightenment' most commonly go in search of someone else to follow. They will look everywhere and repeatedly search out guru after guru, sometimes for years, but they won't look inside themselves and stick with that. It's the single most frustrating thing to observe in these people and after some time it can become an amusing thing as well. Any simple honest person would simply point a finger at them telling them to look inside themselves. The inner guru rather like the inner physician is to be always trusted above everyone else. You know when you've got a good doctor or a bad one. The same can be said for the self.

India is a good place to visit and explore this, but rather like a raft, it should only be used to cross a difficult river and not to actually live on. Once you get to the other side you have to discard it and walk away as there is no point in carrying a raft on your back on dry land. The same could be said for therapy. Sadly this is not seen by most people and they easily become slaves to their need for an external Guru or a therapist."

Robby: Pocket Notebook Entry 27. Listening to Australian Swami yesterday, I feel a lot clearer. He has spent years here seeing all sorts of people come and go trying to answer the same question, trying to find them. He says it's simple and you have to look within. You have to just be and get rid of the thoughts. I met him briefly this morning and again he was helpful.

"After experiencing a trauma in your life is it possible to be happy again?" I asked him.

"There is usually a change in your 'view of the world' after a trauma in your life and sometimes there's a turning away from what previously made you content. Some like me... like you... are left searching barehanded under a naked sky like Stone Age man. A sense of seriousness develops which needs nurturing. We have a scent for happiness, for meaning. It's as if there has been some kind of waking up. Invited or not we know we have to look inwards. That is how it happens. We call ourselves inwards."

"Can you be happy again?"

"Those who experience a lot of darkness are automatically on a path to balance it with light. There has to be balance. It's natural. Black can't exist without white so the imbalance leads you to look for more light in your life. You look for happiness. The capacity for happiness is increased. Some who are thrown into trauma have the capacity to become happier than others. You actually wake up. You wake into full consciousness. You get in touch with it."

"What happens as you get more in touch with it?" I asked him.

"Given the choice of being happy or thinking and talking about it, most people want to talk about it. But not here where you and I are. We see that thinking blocks your ability to just be. When you get through this, you can 'just be' and everything is but a dance in front of you... just be still."

Robby: Pocket Notebook Entry 28. Everything Scott and Ian learnt from India, they have passed on to me through Eleanor. The Australian Swami has said exactly the same things to me. 'Just be still' is the most important thing. Almost all the time now I am spending more time just being still. I've learnt so much from Ian, Scott, and the Aussie Swami.

+++CHAPTER 33.

Robby: Pocket Notebook Entry 29. I started my walk around the hill at six in the morning. The walk along the already hot road seemed like a whole day because it was so busy everywhere I walked or looked. After nearly six weeks living in a basic room, taking daily walks around the mountain and sometimes climbing up it, it is almost time for me to leave. I feel it in my bones that it's time to get back to my life in Scotland.

After fifteen minutes walking today I felt I had walked off my breakfast of idlis and samba from the Aruna Hotel, so I stopped to sit and rest at a tea shop. To justify using the teashop I had a coffee then two vegetarian samosas and some more coffee. In the teashop I felt protected from the entire bustle of the town. I looked back on the strange days I've spent around the hill and reflected on my Uncle's diaries. I had been sitting there reflecting on my time around the hill for a minute, then my thinking stopped and I found that I had automatically drifted in to a state of silence. The silence of my inner self was like the silence of light.

When I focused back on what I was doing, I realised that for half an hour I had just been staring straight ahead. I had been immersed in my inner self and my thinking had just interrupted me out of this state of just being. But what seems strange is that I had a conversation with a man who came and sat opposite me. I didn't know who he was but he knew of me. He was coming from the same place as the Australian Swami. I remember he said, "You who suffer the most have a greater capacity for happiness. The darkness you see is balanced by seeing more light then others can experience. You may not see it but you are special." Something about him made me now want to question him but what he said had shocked me and I wasn't sure if he had been there or not. But then I had the pleasant sense that it didn't matter anymore if he had been there or not. I had got the message that I could be happy. It was like a gift. The inner silence was more bright. It is as bright now.

+++CHAPTER 34.

Robby heard a slight crackling sound and predicted the public address system was going to burst into action. After more crackling and some feedback a woman's voice announced, first in Tamil then in English, that the flight from Chennai to London would be boarding from gate seven in fifteen minutes. Robby got his notebook out of his pocket and began to write.

Robby: Pocket Notebook Entry 30. Going through therapy got me through my trauma. It gave me insight. Religious psychology showed me how I could forgive myself. I found some inner strength meeting Asheena and Khatira. Seeing how to just be has uncovered my inner self. That is what I am. I've spent enough time looking in the rear view mirror and the past is done. Of course I have memories but they are what made me what I was. The way those people around the hill were trying to solve their problems let me see the three things I needed to heal myself and become happy. I needed insight, some strength and grace.

Looking back at Afghanistan is still important, but I look at it differently because the Afghan girl had such a look of deep peace about her when she approached me. She touched me. I know what it is but I need to put it in words and write it down. At first I spotted her in the corner of my eye, and then I saw her stare. It was her stare which I can still see. That's it. It wasn't the thousand yard stare I had when I was having flashbacks. It was another stare straight ahead. It was the same stare that my aunt had in her last few hours. Now I know I was in that young girls stare… she could see me. In her own way she was showing me how to see.

I've only just come to understand fully what that stare is. It's not a look. It is the same stare I have when I am sitting just being. Sometimes I have my eyes closed but most of the time they are open, staring straight ahead. *During these moments of silence there is great peace. For the Afghan girl to have had that stare she must have already been fulfilled, just the same as Eleanor. I can never forget the stare of Eleanor or the young girl. They showed me the most difficult thing to describe in words.*

When I see them now, it reminds me of what I've become. It's awareness and understanding how the mind likes to be the number one thing, instead of 'just being.' The mind wants to dominate by thinking all the time, leaving no time to just be still. I haven't been doing much lately apart from just being still, just being with my inner self. I'm experiencing it each day. It seems a permanent sense of happiness.

Grace

I took your life which then took mine
To pay it all back to you one day at a time
You child you left me all blown to bits
Invisibly and secretly you gave me this.

I sit and stare not at the past only into the air
There's no worry or pain just peace in this stare
My mind's gone and I'm quiet today
Now that there's nothing left to repay.

I can't be distracted from my stare ahead
Now there's no fear or screams in my head.
When my time comes to go I hope I have the stare that day
The smile of a person who knows the way.

My heroine I had to stop you because you came back again
Then I found myself doing it again and again
The memory of you in me is so much alive
But you alive, fighting, beautiful right by my side.

This can't be right we didn't do wrong
We're really friends singing the same song
It's not us that's the problem but those at the top
The politics the war games have to be stopped.

Killing was just a thought until I saw your eyes
Now it's a memory not a horrific surprise
Do I feel at peace? Yes and you do as well
We both saved each other from our future hell.

When I meet you again and look at your face
I will tell you then what I first saw was grace
I know now we saved each other's lives
Only by what we saw in each other's eyes.

"Are you on the flight to London? Are you ok? Can you hear me?" The middle aged English woman asked. Robby was just staring ahead.

"Yes." Robby looked at her.

"You were miles away. So far away. Just staring. Nothing made you blink. Where on earth were you?"

"Where I have always been... I am here."

Made in the USA
Charleston, SC
04 March 2013